Been There, Done That

Been There, Done That

DARRIEN LEE

A
SBI
PUBLICATION

A STREBOR BOOKS INTERNATIONAL LLC PUBLICATION
DISTRIBUTED BY SIMON & SCHUSTER, INC.

Published by

Strebor Books International LLC
P.O. Box 1370
Bowie, MD 20718
http://www.streborbooks.com

ISBN 1-59309-001-3
LCCN 2003100028

Distributed by Simon & Schuster, Inc.
1230 Avenue of the Americas
New York, NY 10020
1-800-223-2336

Cover Illustration: André Harris

First Printing June 2003
Manufactured and Printed in the United States

10 9 8 7 6 5 4 3

THIS NOVEL IS DEDICATED TO my husband, Wayne
and daughters, Alyvia and Marisa.

Your love and encouragement is invaluable.
I love you!

ACKNOWLEDGMENTS

The past year and a half has been unbelievable for me and I would like to take a moment to thank those people who have made this journey possible.

As always, I give thanks to God whom has bestowed some wonderful blessings upon me.

To my family, you have once again been in my corner offering support in countless ways. Wayne, my husband, I love you and I know you're proud of me. Thanks for being there whenever I needed you. Daughters, Alyvia and Marisa, you are the light of my life. I love you so much! To my Mother, Ines, I want to thank you for supporting me and for being a wonderful grandmother to my girls. When I'm on the road doing my "thang," I know they are in good hands. To my sister, Phylishia, thanks for sharing the duties of entertaining your nieces. You are definitely their second "Mother" and for reasons unknown, your home is like Disneyland to them. To my brother, Edward Jr., your support is irreplaceable. Thanks for all the "Hot-lanta" connections and for a place to lay my head when I'm in the area. To my sister, Emily, you're only a stone's throw away and I'm glad to know I have somewhere to hang out when I need to clear my head. I appreciate all your advice as well as those delicious Oreo cookies.

Sincere appreciation also goes out to all my friends who keep me focused. Just to name a few, Tracy Dandridge, Brenda Thomas, Monica

Baker, Reneé Settles, Catricia Baxter, Don Williams, Tiffany Lee, and Jackie English. To my favorite cousin, Vanessa Harris Maston, thanks for the prayers and encouragement. You have a unique vision that I value and trust. Hopefully one day you'll stop teasing me about the "green raincoat."

Fellow Authors, V. Anthony Rivers, Shonell Bacon, J. Daniels and Miguel Wilder. Thanks for the virtual hugs, kisses and knowledge.

Women of Color Bookclub members, you have stood by me and accepted me with open arms. I have nothing but love for you. China and Bianca, you are two very special fans. Thanks for spreading the word!

Artist, Andre' Harris, once again you have exploded with another great book cover. Your talent is unbelievable and I appreciate the fact that you can get inside my head and see what I see. You are awesome!

Lastly I want to thank you, Zane, and the Strebor Family for helping me live out my dream. Without you, none of this would've been possible. I hope to continue to make you proud.

Chapter One

Japan seemed like it was a million miles away. Sitting behind his desk staring at his computer, Craig Bennett was engrossed in his work as usual. It only took him five years to build Bennett and Fletcher into the success it was today. He had wealth and success, but he still felt empty. Traveling between his Philadelphia and Japan offices left him little time for a serious relationship, not that he was looking for one anyway.

It had been seven long years. However, he still felt the sting of losing the only woman he would ever love to another man. The name fell from his lips for the first time in almost seven years: "Venice." Hearing her name in his own voice startled him. He tried his best to forget her by dating other women, but was unsuccessful. She had chosen Jarvis, her childhood sweetheart whom she had married once due to an unplanned pregnancy. They lost their baby during the pregnancy so their parents pressured them into a divorce. Their love was still strong when they left for separate colleges. That's when Craig met her. She was the sister of his best friend and they unexpectedly fell madly in love. Needless to say, after a few stressful months, their relationship came to a sad end. Venice remarried her childhood sweetheart for the only reason it should ever be…true love. Witnessing her wedding was pure hell and he made a vow to remove himself completely from her life. He could never be *just a friend* like she wanted. Especially after their passionate but brief love affair in college. Since then, Craig tried not to let bitterness enter his heart, but it had. Not directly at her, but at love period. Hell, it was over-rated anyway. Angry with himself for thinking about her, he pounded his fist on the desk and put his hands over his face.

A voice came over his intercom. "Mr. Bennett?"

"Yes."

"Your Philadelphia office is on line one."

"Thanks, Virginia."

The days for Venice were starting to run together. Her job as team doctor for the Michigan State University football team only left her with a few hours of quality time with Jarvis and their five-year-old son, Brandon. Being a good mother and wife had always been important to her and she hated the fact that she had lost control of her life. It wasn't the money, because the success of Jarvis in the NFL had made them very wealthy. The fact was she had become burnt out. By both of them being on the road so much, it kept them away from Brandon and she was fed up and needed a break.

They had been married since the tender age of nineteen and were blessed with Brandon two years later. After getting drafted into the NFL, Jarvis was able to fulfill one of his dreams. The other was marrying Venice, his childhood sweetheart.

On this spring morning, Venice and Jarvis were awakened by the pouncing of Brandon on their king-sized sleigh bed.

"Momma! Daddy! Only five more months and I will be in kindergarten!"

Struggling to keep her eyes open, she pulled him down lovingly into her arms. "That's right, Lil' Man, but I wish you would stay my baby just a little longer."

"Daddy! Wake up! I'm hungry!"

Jarvis removed the comforter from over his head and smiled, seeing the two most important people in his life in a warm embrace.

"Brandon, you're always hungry. You get it from your momma."

Venice grabbed her pillow and playfully hit Jarvis. Within seconds the room erupted in a full-blown pillow fight, until they heard the sound of Brandon's sitter calling for him.

Ms. Camille had been a godsend and was recommended by the minister of their church. She was approximately sixty and lived alone—except for the times she spent the night to care for Brandon. She was widowed years earlier and never had children of her own. The children she cared for always became her babies.

"Brandon! Where are you?"

Jarvis slid back under the covers as Venice put on her robe and met Ms. Camille at the bedroom door.

"Good morning, Venice."

"Good morning, Ms. Camille."

"Good morning, sleepyhead."

Jarvis threw up his hand to acknowledge her greeting, then turned over and pulled the covers back over his head. It was only six-thirty on a Saturday morning and the first day in a long time that Jarvis and Venice didn't have to work.

Ms. Camille took Brandon by the hand. "Come on, young man, so I can make you breakfast. Let your momma and daddy sleep in this morning. Okay?"

"Okay. Will you fix me some blueberry pancakes like you did yesterday?"

"Only if you help me. Venice, lie down and get some rest. I'll take care of Brandon."

Venice hugged her. "Thank you. I'll be up in a couple of hours."

"There's no need, child. We'll be just fine. Now go to bed."

Smiling, Venice watched her close the door and listened as their voices faded in the distance.

Venice looked over at Jarvis sleeping and decided she would tell him she later wanted to take a leave of absence. For now, she needed a few more hours of sleep.

Removing her robe, she crawled back into bed. Watching him sleep had always been something she enjoyed. He was absolutely gorgeous and he was hers. His skin was the color of Hershey's chocolate, which covered a broad chest, trim waist and powerful thighs.

Venice had to get used to the large groups of women who flocked around the locker room trying to give out their numbers and anything else they thought he would take. Jarvis was grounded and dismissed their nonsense, leaving Venice no reason to worry about his fidelity. He was happily married and always made a point to acknowledge his love for her and their son when he was being interviewed.

Reaching over to stroke his cheek, Jarvis startled her by pulling her warm body against his and planted a soul-stirring kiss on her lips. She parted her lips and savored the taste of him as they moaned in unison. His hands roamed over her smooth skin, lifting her lingerie over her head. His mouth seared her body as he kissed the curve of her neck, then lower. She immediately felt the hardening of his body as they lay flesh against flesh.

"Jarvis!"

"Yes, Mrs. Anderson."

"I love you."

Staring into each other's eyes reaffirmed all the love and passion they felt for one another over the years.

"I love you, too, Niecy. Always and forever. Don't you every forget that. Okay?"

Cupping his face with her hands, she whispered, "Always and forever, Babe."

The kiss was heated and urgent as their lips joined as well as their bodies. Venice circled her arms around his neck as he continued to torture her with his kisses. Jarvis smoothed back the hair from her face so he could look into her eyes, darkened with love. Locking her legs around his tight body, she held him where she wanted and needed him to be.

Moments later, wave after wave rocked them as they gave into the release they sought. Perspiration glistened on their skin as they lay in each other's arms trying to regain normal breathing rhythm.

He smiled. "You're amazing, Niecy."

She kissed him on the cheek. "You give me too much credit, Babe."

"I don't think so and I'm not just talking about your loving. You're the best friend I could've ever dreamed of. That's important to me. You're not just my wife and the mother of my son. You are my best friend."

Venice was speechless as she hugged him. "I feel the same way and, by the way, I have something for you."

"What?"

Venice reached into the night stand and pulled out a velvet case, then handed it to him.

He sat up in bed and asked, "What's the occasion, Niecy?"

Smiling, she anxiously waited for him to open it. "It's for Loving You Always Day."

Jarvis opened the case with a grin and froze. Inside was a beautiful gold cross necklace. He had been shopping for one but hadn't been able to find one that really stood out to him. Venice found the necklace in New York when she went on a business trip with her brother, Bryan. He was a sports agent, so he invited her along for a medical evaluation of a prospective client.

Jarvis pulled the necklace out of the case. "Baby, this is da bomb! Where did you find it?"

She took the necklace and placed it around his neck. "In the Big Apple."

He got up and stared at it in the mirror for several seconds in silence. He finally turned around with a serious look on his face.

"I'll never take it off, Niecy…never. Thank you."

"I knew it was the one as soon as I saw it. Now come back over here and thank me properly."

Jarvis climbed back into bed. Venice wiggled, trying to snuggle even closer, which caused Jarvis' body to respond once again. Running his hand down the length of her backside, he said, "I told you, you are amazing."

She looked into his beautiful soul. "Amazingly in love with you."

After another heated session of making love, they came up for air again.

"Mercy!"

"I don't believe in giving you any mercy, Jarvis Anderson. You're all I've ever wanted. So rest up, big boy."

Laughing, he kissed her tenderly on her swollen lips. Within minutes, they were in a deep, well-deserved sleep.

Chapter Two

C raig received yet another message from Melanie while he was in his meeting. She was starting to get on his nerves. He told her when he left the States that he would call her if he got a chance. Now, she was starting to get on his assistant's nerves as well. He'd recently met her at a charity function and found her to be quite interesting. She was a wonderful attorney with a great future. One of her faults was the fact that she couldn't leave her aggressive behavior in the courtroom.

"Craig! Would you pl-e-e-ASE call that woman back! She's calling every hour on the hour. Maybe something's wrong."

Craig wrinkled his forehead. "I'm sorry, Virginia, and I know for a fact that nothing's wrong. I've received a couple of emails from her also. Do me a favor. Call her and tell her I said not to call back unless it's an emergency. Also tell her I received her messages and emails and when I get a chance, I will contact her."

Virginia pointed her finger at him. "You owe me big time!"

"I know and I apologize for her."

"Don't worry about it, but a day off would be nice."

He smiled as he entered his office.

Once inside, he called and ordered a dozen peach roses for Virginia as a token of appreciation. Melanie was a beautiful, sexy woman, but she was just a companion for him. Unfortunately, she wanted more than he could offer her. She wanted love and commitment...the fairy tale. He only wanted sexual gratification from her. Love would have to sneak up on him and knock him senseless. That's the way Venice had come to him and left him. Those kinds of emotions were too hard on the heart. He shook his head, gathered some blueprints for his next meeting, and exited his office.

Back in Philly, Brandon did not want to get out of the pool, even though he had been swimming most of the day. Venice taught him to swim in one of those baby classes when he was only months old. It was time for dinner and he needed to get his bath.

"Brandon! Come on out of the pool, Sweetie."

"Mom! Just a little while longer. Place!"

A husky voice followed with, "Brandon!"

"Yes, Sir?"

"Don't make your Momma have to call you again."

"Okay, Daddy. I'm getting out."

Venice glanced over at Jarvis who was relaxing in the chaise lounge reading the paper. He stared back, giving her a wink and a smile. Wrapping Brandon in a towel, she said, "Come on, Little Man, so you can get your bath. Daddy has cooked a delicious dinner for us."

"Goodie! I'm hungry, Momma."

"I know, Brandon. Let's go."

After dinner and a bedtime story beside the pool, Brandon was finally asleep. Jarvis carried his son to his room to tuck him in. After they entered the house, Venice stood up to admire the beautiful view from the hill on which their home sat. The tri-level home had six spacious bedrooms and four full bathrooms. The family room they spent most of their time in was warm and cozy with a large marble fireplace. The dining room they entertained guests in had a twelve-seat cherry table with the matching china cabinet and accessories. The lower level housed Jarvis' recreation room and weight room. This was the room in the house where he relaxed with his friends and teammates. He decorated himself by installing a large screen television, video games, bar and pool table. It allowed him to chill with the boys after a hard day at practice.

Venice's domain was a small library Jarvis designed especially for her. He knew she loved to read and no expense was spared. He wanted to make the room as comfortable and quiet as possible for her. Brandon's room was like a kid's dream come true. While not overdoing it, they made sure his room had everything a little boy should have. An adjoining room was considered his playroom where all the toys and train sets were kept. Collecting trains was something Jarvis started when he was a baby. Venice wrapped her arms around herself and thought that life couldn't get any better. She had decided that when Jarvis returned, she would tell him she wanted to take some time off.

Before leaving Brandon's room, Jarvis gave him a kiss, then turned on the monitor so they could hear him if he woke up. Returning to the deck, he hugged Venice from behind, kissing her shoulder.

"Tired?"

"Not really. Just thinking."

"What's so heavy on your mind, Niecy?"

Pulling her over to the lounging chair, he picked up the blanket to cover them from the cool night air. Snuggling her securely in his arms, he asked again, "What's up?"

Nuzzling her face into his neck, she took a deep breath. "I want to take a leave of absence from work so I can spend more time with you guys."

"Is that all? I thought something was wrong. Babe, as far as I'm concerned, you can stay home as long as you want to. I would love for you to be here. With both of us gone, it just doesn't seem fair to Brandon. I know your career is just as important to you as mine is to me, but I wanted you to take a break when you were ready for one, not because anyone asked you to."

"Thanks, Baby. I want to be the one cooking for my two men, not Ms. Camille. I want us to be able to travel with you to some of the out-of-town games. We can't do that with me on the road, too."

Kissing her forehead, he said, "Well, consider it done. You and Brandon will be with me as much as possible. Okay?"

"Okay. Now how about a real kiss."

"Yes, Ma'am."

After a series of tender kisses, they lay in each other's arms and listened to jazz until Venice drifted into a sound sleep. Holding her in his arms never felt better. He could've taken her up to bed, but decided to hold her a while longer and savor the warmth her body gave him.

Sometime later around midnight, he decided to call it a night, carried Venice inside and put her in bed. After a quick shower, he joined her, pulling her securely into his arms.

Six Months Later

Brandon was proudly in kindergarten and loving it. The NFL season had started and Venice still wasn't thinking about returning to work. Being at home had been the most relaxing time in her life. One particular morning, after taking Brandon to school, Jarvis walked into the kitchen calmly.

"Niecy, are you ready to have another baby?"

"Huh?"

Walking across the room, he embraced her. "I want another baby. Are you ready?"

Tears fell from her eyes as she tiptoed to kiss him. "You bet!"

Their kiss was sensual and tender.

"How about we get started right now, Mr. Anderson."

Smiling, he picked her up in his arms and sprinted for the stairs.

Chapter Three

Three months passed and they had been unsuccessful conceiving a baby.

"I don't get it, Jarvis. I used to get pregnant every time the wind blew and now, nothing."

"Don't worry, Babe. It'll happen in due time. Okay?"

"I guess you're right. It would be nice to tell the family when we go home for Christmas."

"I wouldn't mind if we stayed here this year. Just the three of us."

"Jarvis Tyler Anderson, you know your mother won't have it. She'll fly up here and kick our door down if she heard a rumor of us not coming home."

"You're right. What's her motto?"

In unison, they said, "Family first."

Christmas came and went as planned. Jarvis and Venice decided to celebrate New Year's Eve in Times Square before the big game. "fter an unforgettable trip filled with love and passion, Jarvis had to prepare for the Super Bowl. He was under a lot of pressure and Venice did her best to make sure he stayed focused. The game was being played in the Super Dome in New Orleans and the entire family would be in attendance. Brandon was so excited that his Daddy was playing in the Super Bowl and told all his friends to make sure they watched.

Jarvis and Venice's best friend, Joshua, was also in attendance. His pregnant wife, Cynthia, had to stay home because their baby was due soon.

In Jarvis' hotel room, Joshua said, "Well, Bro, this is it. This is what you've been waiting on."

"I know, man. I'm excited and nervous at the same time."

"You'll do fine. We'll be rooting for you."

Staring out into the skyline, Jarvis said, "Thanks."

Joshua sat back in the chair. "What's on your mind?"

"Niecy and I have been trying to have another baby. It's been four months and nothing. She's starting to get worried."

"What does she have to worry about? I'm sure after the Super Bowl, you guys will relax and you'll have her pregnant in no time."

Jarvis turned to Joshua with a serious look. "I don't think so, Joshua."

Joshua stood. "What's up, man?"

"I'm sick and it doesn't look like I'll be getting any better."

Joshua's legs gave out and he sank down in his chair. The blood left his face. "What do you mean, sick?"

Tears glistened in Jarvis' eyes as they met Joshua's. "I have a brain tumor."

For what seemed like hours, they just stared at each other, but only seconds had passed. Finally, Joshua cleared the lump in his throat.

"Does Niecy know?"

Shoving his hands in his pockets, Jarvis answered, "No and I have no plans of telling her."

Joshua made fists with his hands and asked, "How are you going to keep something like that from her?"

"I have to. I don't want her worrying about me. She has to stay focused on Brandon."

Clearly disgusted, Joshua asked, "Does anyone know?"

"Against my doctor's advice, no. You and my doctor are the only ones who know."

"Damn, Jarvis! How could you just drop something like that on me and expect to act normal around everybody?"

"You have to. I'm depending on you because I have another favor to ask and you might think I'm crazy."

Covering his face with his hands, Joshua asked, "What is it?"

"I want you to get Niecy and Craig back together."

"Now I've know you've lost your damn mind!"

Jarvis sat on the bed. "You know yourself that she was in love with him and I know for a fact that he loved her. He's the only one I trust to take care of them after I'm gone. Venice is going to be a wealthy woman and she's going to be vulnerable. I don't want her taken advantage of by men only after her money. You can understand that, can't you? I don't want her hurt, Joshua."

Choking back tears, Joshua said, "This will hurt her and it ain't right, Jarvis. You need to tell her what's going on. She's your wife and the mother of your son. She has a right to know."

Jarvis stood and walked back to the window. Without turning to face him, he said, "I've made my decision."

"Well, I think you're making a big mistake. Anyway, how do you know Craig's not married or something?"

"I've done my homework. He's single and a workaholic and hasn't dated seriously since he was with Niecy. He has a successful business in Philadelphia and Japan. He has to still be in love with her. My lawyer has drawn up my instructions and notarized everything. It's all up to you and I'm counting on you."

Not wanting to ask the question, but feeling he had to, Joshua asked, "How long, man?"

Jarvis softly answered, "Months."

Joshua snapped angrily, "Damn!"

He then stood and stormed out of the room, slamming the door behind him. Back in the confines of his hotel room, his emotions overtook him in almost a violent manner as he tore up his surroundings.

The Detroit Lions won the Super Bowl and Jarvis was the MVP. The whole family was excited and happy for him, but Venice noticed Joshua was unusually quiet.

She smiled and asked, "Hey, Josh! You okay?"

"I'm cool. Just happy Jarvis finally got that ring."

"So am I, Josh."

Later that night after hours of celebrating, Venice lay in Jarvis' arms. "Jarvis, I love you."

Tilting her chin so he could look into her eyes, he said, "'Til death do us part, sweetheart. I love you, too, and don't you ever forget it."

A single tear rolled out of her eye as he lowered his lips to hers and stole her breath with his kiss. Making love to her that night was necessary and special as he joined his body with hers.

Philadelphia was blanketed with several feet of snow. Not many people showed up for work either because of the weather or because they had one drink too many at a Super Bowl party. Craig came in, not having anything else to do. The newspaper was at the door when he arrived. He opened it to see the headline: *Detroit Lions Win the Super Bowl!* On the inside was a picture of Jarvis, holding the MVP trophy and kissing the still breathtakingly-beautiful Venice. He didn't expect to have to lay eyes on her, but it was too late now. She had already started to invade his dreams on a regular basis and it unnerved him. He used to only think of her on rare occasions, but it had increased for some odd reason. Now he'd laid eyes on her for the first time in seven years.

Throwing the paper into the trash he angrily shouted, "Damn!"

Chapter Four

Five Months Later

The month of July seemed to be an unusually wet one. This late night storm woke Venice up as it rolled through. Venice watched as the lightning lit up the room. Worried that Brandon might be afraid, she decided to check on him. Finding him sound asleep, she returned to bed and snuggled up to Jarvis. For a moment she reminisced about the intimate encounter they'd shared only hours earlier. Turning, she kissed him on the lips, but it felt strange. She stroked his face and his skin felt different, balmy.

She whispered his name to wake him to make sure he was OK. After no response, she started to shake him, first softly, then frantically.

"Jarvis! Baby, wake up!"

Still no response. Venice's heart was pounding as she reached over to turn on the light. He was still breathing but was unresponsive to her. She reached for the phone and dialed 911 as tears streamed from her eyes.

"Jarvis! Don't do this to me! Please, God!"

Luckily, Ms. Camille had spent the night. Venice ran to wake her so she could tend to Brandon. She didn't want to alarm him that something was wrong with his daddy. The paramedics were there in no time and Venice dressed hurriedly while trying to stay calm.

After reaching the hospital, Venice tried to hold it together so she could call the family. Her oldest brother, Bryan, was able to get everyone on a chartered flight. Within a couple of hours, the family was at her side. Joshua greeted her solemnly and watched her try to hold herself together.

Finally the doctor came out and explained that Jarvis had an inoperable brain tumor and had suffered a massive stroke. He was now in a coma and on life support. He went on to tell the family that Jarvis didn't want to worry the family, so he kept the news to himself. He was dying and Venice hadn't had the chance to tell him how much she loved him. It sounded like the doctor was talking in a foreign language. The doctor continued, telling the family that Jarvis had filed paperwork not to be kept on life support. Venice was in shock and for a moment she stood completely numb. Jarvis' parents and sister weren't much different. The air became thick and Venice found it hard to breathe. She started hyperventilating, then the room went dark as she fainted into her father's arms.

Hours later, Venice woke and went to Jarvis' bedside. She trembled as she watched the machines keep him alive. Crawling into his bed, she cradled his head to her chest and burst into tears.

"How could you do this to me, Jarvis? What am I going to tell Brandon? Damn you, Jarvis! I'm not going to make this easy for you! You're not going to leave us like this!"

The only response was the sound of the machine breathing for him. Tears flowed down her face as she stroked his warm cheeks with her hand. She knew she had a difficult task ahead of her. She had to tell Brandon that his daddy was sick and wasn't going to be coming home. The thought made her throat ache and nausea settled in the pit of her stomach. She barely made it to the bathroom.

The next few days were not any different and Mr. Anderson felt they were delaying the inevitable. He had read over Jarvis' notarized instructions a thousand times and the results were the same. Disconnect the life support. Mrs. Anderson brought Brandon to the hospital to say goodbye to his daddy. Venice had explained the situation to him as calmly as possible. He seemed excited to see his dad and talked to him as if he were awake. Venice knew Brandon didn't fully understand the situation.

Finally the time had come. Everyone had said their final goodbyes, which left Venice and the doctors alone in the room. Finding an inner strength, she leaned down to his ear and whispered, "Jarvis, you are the love of my life. I will never love anyone as much as I love you. You are my soul mate and I will love you forever. I guess God has something special he needs you to do. Sweetheart, I will do the best I can to raise our son to be the strong, black, loving man that you are. I'll see you soon, my love."

She leaned down and kissed his warm lips as tears clouded her vision. The doctor turned off the machine and within seconds…he was gone. Hearing Venice's screams signaled to the family that their beloved Jarvis was gone.

The next day, Venice shut down. She wasn't eating or sleeping and the family was starting to get worried. She had given up on everything and everybody, even her son. He was the spitting image of his dad and it hurt Venice to look into those familiar eyes. She was useless in making funeral arrangements. To be honest, she didn't want to have any part of it. Closed off in the bedroom was her solitude.

People were coming and going and she wasn't up to seeing anyone. The only person she would let close to her was Joshua. He, too, was worried that she was nearing a breakdown. He had to do something quick. Feeling the guilt of concealing Jarvis' secret had taken a toll on him and he needed redemption. If this meant following Jarvis' idiotic instructions, then so be it. First, he had to get Venice out of bed and back to life. She seemed to have a death wish of her own.

He approached her room and knocked on the door. As expected, he didn't receive a response. He pushed the door open to find her lying in bed in the fetal position. He walked over and softly called out to her.

"Venice, are you awake?"

"Go away, Joshua, and leave me alone."

He sat down on the edge of the bed, placing his head in his hands. He knew she was devastated, but so was he.

"Niecy, you've got to get out of this bed. You can't go on like this."

"I said leave me alone!"

He turned to look at her realizing it was going to take more than sympathy to reach her. He stood, pulled the comforter away from her body and yelled, "Niecy! I said get out of this bed and put on some clothes."

Angrily, she sat up with fire in her tearful eyes. "Joshua...Damn it! Get away from me!"

She took a swing at him, but he grabbed her wrists. He was about to lose it emotionally.

"Do you think you're the only one who loved Jarvis? I loved him, too, and I'm sure he wouldn't like seeing you neglecting Brandon like this."

"Go to hell, Joshua! I love my son!"

"Then act like it and get out of bed! You can't give up, Niecy, because Brandon needs you. We all need you."

"You don't understand! I loved him more than anything in the world! How could he keep something like that from me? How?"

She sank to the bed and covered her eyes sobbing.

Sitting next to her on the bed, he calmly said, "Because he loved you...that's how. But you have got to pick yourself up because your son needs you and he misses his dad."

She flung her arms around his neck and burst into tears. He helped her out of the bed and into the shower. Joshua was as close to her as any brother ever could be. They held no secrets from each other...until now.

Hours later, Venice was able to join the family downstairs to greet teammates, friends, and coaches who had stopped by to offer their condolences. The rest of the family had decided to go to their hotel suites to rest. This allowed her some time to be alone. One of Jarvis' teammates came by later to check in on Venice. The silence in the house was unnerving, so when the doorbell chimed, it startled her. When she opened the door, Trammel Glisten greeted her with a warm hug.

"Hello, Doc. How are you holding up?"

"I'm hanging in there, Trammel. Come on in."

Trammel followed her into the living room and sat down on the sofa. Venice curled her legs under herself.

"I was wondering when you were going to stop by. Most of the other guys came by earlier."

He played with the pillows on the sofa.

"Yeah, I didn't want to come when they were all here. You know Jarvis was my boy."

Venice wrapped her arms around herself.

"I guess you two were the closest. You spent enough time over here eating my food."

They both laughed for a moment, then once again found themselves dealing with silence. Trammel looked around at various pictures, then asked, "Where's everybody?"

Venice stood and went over to the mantle to straighten a picture. "They went back to the hotel to get some rest."

Before she could turn around, Trammel was standing behind her...close. His closeness unsettled her.

"Can I get you anything to drink or eat? There's tons of food in the kitchen."

"Nah, I'm cool."

She walked around him and toward the front door, causing him to follow.

"Trammel, I'm glad you came by but it's getting late and I'm really tired. I'll see you tomorrow at the services, Okay?"

When they reached the front door, Venice turned to hug him. He tightened his grip so she could not get away.

"Trammel! What are you doing? Turn me loose."

"Jarvis always treated you like you were better than anyone else. I want to see if he was right."

"Have you lost your mind? Get your hands off of me!"

Venice started having flashbacks of her near rape in high school.

Tears of fear and shock ran down her face as she tried her best to push him off, but she was unsuccessful. Being pinned against the front door offered no avenue for escape.

"Please, Trammel! Don't! Please!"

She could feel his hot breath as he guided his large hands under her skirt. That's when he heard a click and felt something metal pushing against the back of his head. He froze. An angry and muffled voice said, "I don't know who the hell you are, but if you move another muscle, I'm going to blow you straight to hell."

Relief swept over Venice as Joshua came to her rescue. He had a deranged look on his face as he instructed Venice to step aside. Trembling and afraid, she couldn't move. Joshua grabbed her wrist and pulled her around behind him. At that point, Joshua instructed Trammel to turn around. As he turned, he had his hands above his head and fear in his eyes.

"Don't shoot, man. Doc, I'm so sorry."

Joshua steadied the gun between Trammel's eyes. "Stand over there and don't move."

Without taking his eyes off him, he asked, "Niecy, are you okay?"

As if the air had returned to her lungs, she answered, "I'm okay."

Still angling the gun, he asked, "Who is this clown?"

Venice, with a tear-streaked face, slapped Trammel's face.

"Trammel! How could you?! Jarvis was your friend!"

He cowardly confessed, "I'm sorry. I guess I lost my head."

"So you decided to come over here and try to rape me? What would your wife and kids think? Huh? Just get out!"

"What do you want to do with him, Niecy? Do you want me to shoot him or call the police?"

Trammel's eyes opened wider in fear.

"Please, I-I won't bother you again, Doc. I promise. I'll leave."

Venice stared at him.

"Let him go. He's not worth it."

Trammel closed his eyes and let out a sigh of relief.

Joshua said, "Just one minute. I hope you realize that this woman just saved your life. You don't know how bad I want to pull this trigger. I could kill you where you stand and tell the police whatever I wanted to. I'm FBI and if you don't get some type of help, I'm going to come looking for you. You got it?"

Trammel looked over at Venice and said, "I understand, man."

Joshua opened the door and said, "Get off this property and don't come back."

As Trammel slowly backed out of the house, Joshua kept the gun aimed. Once Trammel turned to leave, Joshua shot off a round into the air. Trammel froze in his tracks before wetting his pants. Joshua slammed the door and lowered the gun.

Turning to Venice, she hugged him and said, "Thank you, Joshua."

"Go back upstairs and get you some rest, Niecy. Just be glad it was me and not Bryan or Galen. Otherwise your friend would be lying in a pool of blood right now. No one has to know what happened here tonight. I won't let anyone hurt you; you know that."

Shaken, she kissed him and said, "I love you, Joshua."

"I love you, too, Niecy."

Chapter Five

Being in Japan for the past week had drained Craig's energy. He was feeling burned out and decided he might need to take some well-deserved time off. On the plane, he picked up the *USA Today* and noticed a familiar name in the headline: *All Pro Running Back Jarvis Anderson Memorial Service Tomorrow.*

"What?"

He read on to find out that a brain tumor had caused the death of his former lover's husband days earlier. He also noticed that the memorial would be taking place the following day.

"Poor Venice...Why hadn't Bernice called?"

Craig's older sister, Bernice, had become close to Venice and her sister-in-law, Sinclair. It was odd that she hadn't called him to inform him of the terrible tragedy. He thought for a moment, then remembered that he told his dear sister that under no circumstance should she mention Venice or her family to him. He wanted that chapter of his life removed completely. It hurt him bad and the less heard about them, the better. Unfortunately, his sister had followed his instructions too well.

As soon as his plane landed in Philly, he immediately booked a flight to Detroit. For some strange reason, he felt like he needed to be there. He ached knowing the hurt Venice must have been experiencing. He wanted to console her, hold her, make the hurt go away.

Screech!!!

What am I thinking? I can't go to her. How would that look?

Widow of Jarvis Anderson being consoled by former lover...

"Ouch! Let me think for a minute. Craig, get a hold of yourself. Wait, I'll go, but I'll...Damn! "

The lady behind the ticket counter asked, "May I help you, Sir?"

"Yes, round trip to Detroit."

The memorial service was long and exhausting. Brandon clung to his mom and occasionally wept for his daddy. This didn't help Venice hold her composure, but she stayed strong for her son. Thousands turned out to say goodbye to their beloved Jarvis wearing his number twenty-eight jersey. The entire scene was over-whelming for the Anderson and Taylor families. As the families filed out of the stadium, Joshua felt a strange feeling that he was being watched. Scanning the crowd seemed useless because there were just too many people to pick out anyone in particular.

In the upper deck of the arena, a tall, sexy Craig stood watching Venice's pain consume her. It broke his heart knowing that her heart had been shattered. He wanted to wipe every tear from her cheek and let her know he was there for her. But, he couldn't. Even though he was drawn to her, he had to walk away.

"Goodbye, Venice."

The plane ride back to Philadelphia wasn't fast enough for him. Craig was experiencing a series of mixed emotions and he needed time to get them in check. He didn't understand the pain he was feeling in his heart. He heard a voice in his head.

She left you, remember?

He sat there thinking. His coworkers had told him how peaceful it was in Ocho Rios. He decided to visit Jamaica to hopefully get Venice off his mind just as soon as he could clear his calendar.

Arriving at his office that morning was a little different than any other. He found himself tired from the sleepless night and the jet lag since returning from Japan. After greeting his assistant, he sat at his desk, hoping to collect his thoughts. Who was he fooling? He wasn't able to do it last night and he sure wasn't going to be able to do it today. The images of Venice were cemented in his mind. A few seconds later, his assistant, Francine, buzzed him, saying, "Craig, you have a call on two."

"Thank you, Francine. Bennett here."

A soft silky voice responded, "Well, well, well. So you have returned and haven't even called to let me know."

Craig sighed as he closed his eyes and leaned back in his chair. "Good morning, Melanie. I got back yesterday and I'm just getting into the office."

"Then you could have called me last night. I could have made dinner for us."

Becoming frustrated, he answered, "Melanie, how many times do I have to remind you where we stand?"

There was silence for a moment, then she said, "You don't have to throw that up in my face, Craig. I just feel like you haven't given us a chance. I think we would be good for each other."

Covering his face with his hands, he said, "Melanie, we get along the way we are. There's no sense complicating matters."

"Craig, don't you think I'm tired of being your little booty call whenever you feel like it?"

He stood up and looked out over the Philadelphia skyline. "That was your call, Melanie. I told you up-front that I wasn't looking for a relationship. Don't get me wrong; I enjoy the sex, but that's as far as it will ever go."

She snapped back. "Who in the hell made you so cold?"

"I'm not looking for love, Melanie. I tried that and my reward was a kick in the ass."

She sighed. "Baby, we can take it one day at a time. I'm really feeling you now."

Craig snapped back to reality. "Like I said, Melanie, I'm not looking for love."

"Okay, okay. Well, are you still going to escort me to the African-American Attorneys Dinner tonight?"

He leaned over to check his calendar. "I told you I would, Melanie. You don't have to beat me over the head with it. Look, I have work to do. I'll pick you up at six o'clock. Goodbye."

Melanie blew him a kiss through the phone, causing him to roll his eyes. Before hanging up, she said, "That kiss is only the beginning of what I'm going to have for you tonight. See you later, Darling."

Craig didn't respond. He hung up the phone and laid his head down on his desk. He couldn't remember how and why he allowed himself to date Melanie as long as he had. Here he was, six months later, and he realized there was no way he could continue this way with her. He'd been meaning to tell her several times before, but changed his mind. It was like she sensed he was going to break up with her and she went into a crying fit. This time, he wouldn't change his mind. If his mother were still alive, she would be very upset with him for using Melanie and all the other women he had bedded this way. She always taught him to respect women and not to sleep around for recreational purposes. He decided he was going to end their relationship after the dinner. God knows his mind was consumed with only one woman…Venice, and the fact that he was having these strange pains in his chest.

Craig picked up the newspaper and read that Venice and her family had one more service to endure. Jarvis was going to be buried in their hometown, so he knew that trip was going to be especially difficult. All of their former classmates and friends were going to be the hardest hit. Somehow, he knew Venice would be most affected there. He felt sorry for her because he knew the degree of love she carried for Jarvis. He also remembered the depth of love he'd shared with her, but lost.

Chapter Six

It had been five months and Venice hadn't given the family any indication that she wanted to return to her home in Michigan. Jarvis' mom saw unnerving signs in Venice's behavior and felt that it was best that she not be left alone. It wasn't that she was suicidal. It was that she seemed to be mentally and physically exhausted. Mr. Anderson asked the Taylors if they thought it would be best if Venice had a change of scenery. Mrs. Taylor answered, "I don't think sending her away would be best for her. I think she needs as many of us around her as possible right now."

Mrs. Anderson agreed with her. "Brandon still hasn't adjusted to the fact that his dad is gone and he may be traumatized if Venice left him right now."

As they continued to discuss the situation, Bryan butted in. "Has anyone asked Venice what she wants? Ya'll are discussing her like she can't think for herself. She's not an invalid. She just lost her husband and she's devastated. I'm not saying a vacation wouldn't do her justice. I'm just saying ask her what she'd like to do. It's obvious she doesn't want to set foot back in her house. We need to sit down with her and find out what she wants to do with the house and Jarvis' things. She hasn't contacted the lawyer about Jarvis' will or anything. The last thing I want to see her do is have a nervous breakdown or something. Don't treat her like a child. Just talk to her."

Silence engulfed the room and the parents agreed they would talk to Venice the following day.

Later that night, Venice had cried all the tears left in her body. She lay in Jarvis' bed in the basement of his parents' home. She turned to see a sleeping Brandon resting peacefully beside her looking just like his dad. She kissed his cheek and stared at the most important person in her life. She had heard her parents and in-laws discussing her mental state earlier and they couldn't be more wrong. Yes, she was hurt and depressed, but leaving Brandon was the last thing she wanted to do. He was all she had left and she wasn't about to abandon him. He needed her and she needed him. Turning back to look at the clock, the time was two forty-five a.m. One last tear rolled out of her eyes. She was comforted by a telephone call earlier from her best friend, Chanelle. She, along with Joshua and Jarvis, all grew up together. Chanelle was very upset because she was unable to attend the service. She ached for her friend.

Working as a surgical resident in a Baton Rouge hospital, plus the fact that she was seven months' pregnant prevented her travels. Chanelle and Craig's friend, Spoonie, had been married for about three years. Spoonie was working as a professor at Southern University in the field of Computer Technology. After a brief conversation, the two vowed to get together as soon as possible before hanging up. Venice lay there in the dark with a heavy heart and uncertain future. Before sleep overtook her, she whispered, "I miss you, Jarvis."

Last night was a disaster. When Craig told Melanie that he didn't want to continue their dead end relationship, it shocked her. She obviously didn't see it coming or better yet, she didn't want to recognize it. Craig was known to turn many female heads when they were out together and being seen was one of Melanie's hobbies. This was a life Craig didn't want any part of. He didn't want to be any woman's trophy.

When he arrived at his office, surprisingly, Melanie was waiting on him.

When he saw her, he asked, "What are you doing here, Melanie? I said all I'm going to say to you last night."

"Darling, I wanted to give you time to sleep on it. You can't mean those things you said. We've been together for six months. Doesn't that account for something?"

Craig opened the door to his office and motioned for her to enter. The last thing he wanted was for Melanie to throw a tantrum in front of his staff. He sat his briefcase down and said, "Look, Melanie, we don't want the same things. About the only thing we have in common happens to take place in the bedroom. It hasn't been all bad. I'm just dealing with some things in my life right now that I have to work out."

She folded her arms. "Does it have to do with another woman?"

He looked up seriously and said, "Melanie, don't even go there. You know you haven't been the only woman I've dated over the past months. Why are you trippin'?"

She walked over, wrapped her arms around his waist, and said, "Because I know I mean more to you than the others and I love you, Craig."

He hugged her. "I care about you, Melanie, but that's as far as it will ever go. We had a good time so let's end it like that, as friends, okay? I'm sure Mr. Right is out there for you, but it's not me. Try to understand where I'm coming from. I told you, I'm not looking for love."

She stared into his sensual eyes, then leaned up and placed a tender kiss on his lips. Releasing him, she turned to leave his office. "Craig, you'll come to realize that you're making a mistake. I'm the best woman for you. You'll be back."

He shoved his hands in his pockets. "Goodbye, Melanie."

The next morning, Venice called the family together. She reluctantly announced that she wanted to take Jarvis' fifteen-year-old sister, Portia, and Brandon on vacation. Portia was still deeply hurt by the loss of her brother, who at times had been like a father to her. They were closer than close and she had withdrawn from the family. In the den of her parents, her father asked, "Baby, where are you going?"

"I don't know, Daddy. I'm going to check around and see what I can get on short notice."

"How soon are you planning on leaving?" her mother asked.

"Tomorrow can't come too soon for me, Momma. I have to get away from here. Too many memories, too much hurt."

Jarvis' dad walked over and hugged her. "Venice, I think it might do you some good to get away somewhere quiet so you can think. There's a lot of business that has to be taken care of, but it can wait until you feel up to it. Okay?"

"Thanks, Pops. I can tell you that I don't want to live in that house anymore. I just can't bear it."

Tears filled her eyes and she met Mrs. Anderson's worried gaze.

"Mom, I'm okay…really. Don't worry."

Mrs. Anderson bolted from her chair and held Venice tightly to her bosom and whispered, "Venice, don't be afraid to give love a second try. Your life didn't end when my son died. You have been a strong black woman to overcome all the difficulties thrown your way and in time, this too shall pass. Just remember the love you shared together and keep it in your heart always. Then, my sweet daughter, allow yourself to love again. Only then will you be able to put this pain behind you. Okay?"

Venice was speechless as she realized Mrs. Anderson had lost her only son and was hurting just as much, if not worse than she was. Venice held her hands. "Mom, I'll think about what you said. I just need to get away. I hope it's OK if I take Portia out of school for a while."

Wiping her eyes, she said, "Baby, she needs this just as much as you and Brandon. Don't worry about us. God will strengthen all of us."

Nodding, Venice said, "Well, I have some calls to make. Thank you all for being here for me.".

With that statement, she left the room and immediately went upstairs to call Joshua.

Joshua had been Venice's motivator as usual, so when she called him for suggestions, he jumped on the unexpected opportunity to suggest Jamaica. How lucky could he get? He prodded Venice the previous day, suggesting a secluded getaway to somewhere tropical. He also went as far as to suggest the accommodations, knowing his contact had informed him exactly where Craig Bennett was staying

In Ocho Rios. His contact had also told him that Craig was traveling alone and was staying just two cottages down from where Venice would be staying. A quiet cottage on the beach would work best for Venice and the kids, giving them complete privacy and hopefully something else…a second chance.

Four days later, the families gathered at the airport to see them off. Tears filled all eyes except Brandon's and Portia's. They couldn't wait to hit the sandy beaches and turquoise blue waves. Hugs and kisses all around made getting on the plane hard, but necessary. Mrs. Taylor asked, "Venice, how long are you planning on staying?"

"Don't know. I'll call when we get settled. Love you all."

Bryan came up and hugged her particularly long. "Stay strong, baby girl. You call if you need anything. I mean it."

"Thanks, Bryan."

Joshua was last as he approached with his hands in his pockets.

"You'd better hug me, Josh!"

"Still bossy, I see."

Releasing the embrace was especially hard. He had no idea what the results would be of this idiotic scheme Jarvis had him put into play. Venice was his best friend and he didn't want to do anything to turn her against him. Her emotional well-being was on the line and he had to protect her at all costs. Sending his contact to Jamaica to observe Venice would have to do for now. He instructed him to call with daily updates and to report any problems.

"I'm going to miss you, Josh."

"I'm going to miss you, too. "re you sure this is what you want to do?"

"I think so…it'll probably do me some good. Portia and Brandon also. Thanks for suggesting it. I just can't deal with going back into that house seeing his things. Josh, I swear I can still smell him, feel him. Am I nuts?"

Stroking a lone tear from her cheek, he said, "You're not nuts, Niecy. Take your time. Okay? Go get your life back."

"Thanks. Well, we'd better go. Tell Cynthia goodbye."

"I will. Have fun and you call me if you need me and I don't care what time. Call, do you understand me?"

Leaning to plant a tender kiss on his lips, she answered, "Yes, Sir! I love you, Josh."

"Love you, too. Be careful."

Chapter Seven

Since arriving on the island days earlier, Craig still had not been able to relax. He was constantly approached by beautiful women offering him a night of pleasure. Others just slipped their phone numbers into his hands. He didn't expect this kind of attention. He just came to relax in peace. " casual sexual fling was definitely not what he was looking for. But, maybe that was exactly what he needed to help erase the images of Venice from his dreams and the pain in his chest. His doctor couldn't find anything wrong with him physically, so he concluded Craig was having anxiety attacks due to stress. He was tired of waking up dripping with perspiration and hearing himself call her name and he could not, for the sake of him, get her image out of his mind.

She looked so sad and so lost at the services. She no longer wore her thick mane straight. Instead she wore it long and wavy, giving her a sophisticated look.

After five months, he wondered how she was doing. It had taken him exactly that much time to clear his calendar and brief his offices on upcoming projects. Lamar Fletcher was running the office in his absence. They had met in graduate school and he had been a trustworthy partner ever since. Craig gave Fletcher all his confidence in keeping things running smoothly while he would be away. He was going to enjoy a break from one of his designers, Katrina Simmons. She was a bright, attractive woman but didn't know how to take no for an answer. On several occasions, she had asked him out. Craig just wasn't interested, especially with an employee. For some reason the flirtations continued and when confronted, she acted as if he took her comments out of context. Coming short of letting her go, he gave her one last warning, then transferred her to Lamar's design team. She wasn't happy about it, but she had no choice in the matter.

Craig was beginning to look forward to his vacation. This would be the first in a couple of years and just what he needed.

On this bright sunny afternoon, he decided to walk down the beach to a nearby restaurant for lunch. He put on some khaki shorts, which clearly exposed long, muscular legs. The white shirt, which fit to perfection, left nothing to the imagination except that he kept his body in tip-top condition. His skin had darkened slightly from the normal caramel to a shade deeper. He spent his mornings jogging and evenings swimming in the warm blue water outside his cottage. Sometimes he felt himself propelled to check in at his office, but his assistant refused to oblige him. Craig remembered he had given his trusted partner his blessings in handling things, but he was now beginning to get bored. It had only been four days and he was seriously considering cutting the vacation short. After double-checking his appearance in the mirror, he stuffed his keys in his pockets and headed down the beach.

Reaching the cottage after an hour's drive from the airport, an exhausted Venice and entourage had arrived. Their cottage was just as the travel agent described: secluded with a feel of home. Portia and Brandon immediately ran to claim their rooms.

Portia asked excitedly, "Can we go swimming?"

Venice answered, "Don't you want to rest for a while first?"

In unison they responded, "No! We want to go to the beach."

"Give me a minute to unpack and take a shower and we'll all go."

"Cool!"

Brandon, imitating his aunt, said, "Cool!"

Entering the confines of her room, Venice sank to her bed and let out a loud sigh. Lying back to stare at the ceiling, she said, "Jarvis, Babe, I…"

"Momma! Hurry up!"

Startled by the interruption, she pulled herself up and reached for the phone to call her parents and in-laws to let them know they had arrived safely. After several minutes of unpacking, she finally stepped into the hot relaxing water of the shower. She just stood there until anxiety almost overtook her. She closed her eyes and prayed…hard. Finally the tears came, then she began sobbing. Not wanting to upset Portia and Brandon, she found an inner strength to get control of her emotions so they wouldn't hear her. After several moments, she was able to calm herself and put on her bathing suit. It was one Jarvis had bought her earlier in the year and the lavender two-piece matched her skin perfectly. It was quite revealing, but she had no reason to concern herself with such nonsense. Portia and Brandon sprinted for the beach with Venice trailing carrying a book to read. She was happy to have the privacy of the cottage so she wouldn't have to socialize with other vacationers. This area was less populated and perfect for relaxation.

Once again, Craig played with his dinner, not necessarily hungry. The island love music playing softly in the background was enough for him. He asked the waitress to arrange for a carry-out container and he headed back to his cottage. The sun was starting to set and Craig loved this time of day most of all. It was when the world seemingly came to a halt and exhaled. Sadly, he had no one to share it with. There was one woman who had interested him the previous day, but it all flew out the window when she fondled him under the table. That type of aggressiveness was a turn-off. Or could it be that he had been so out of touch with women and this was what they did to gain a man's interest? If it was the truth, he was lost. Her touch didn't do anything but make him hurriedly pay the ticket and excuse himself. The walk back would hopefully help ease his mind. Once back in his cottage, he would decide if he should give this so-called vacation a few more days. Walking along the beach had a calming effect on him until he saw lovers strolling arm-in-arm, which unnerved him. He could see his cottage ahead of him and couldn't wait to retreat to his deck to watch the sun set on the cool blue waters.

Spending the evening on the beach did feel good. Now hunger had settled in their stomachs.

"Tomorrow, kids, we'll go to the market to get groceries. Tonight, we'll walk down to a restaurant for dinner. Okay?"

"Okay, Venice. I'll help Brandon with his bath while you get ready. Oh, Venice?"

"Yes?"

"Put on something cute."

"Cute?"

"Cute."

Returning to her room, Venice was confused with Portia's request. She had already laid out a long, lime green sheer skirt with a matching halter top. Moments later, they locked up and headed down the beach for dinner.

The sun's rays danced brightly in Craig's face. It was then he realized that he had fallen asleep on the sofa. He never made it to the deck as planned. Waking up with a crook in his neck wasn't on the agenda. At least he didn't dream about her last night. Staggering into the kitchen, he turned on the coffee maker, which showed five thirty a.m. He yawned and headed to the shower. Today, he was going to make himself have fun if it killed him.

Down the beach, Venice laced up her tennis shoes, put on her hat and sunglasses and pulled her long black hair into a ponytail. She kissed Portia and Brandon on the cheek, then left Portia a note so she would know where she was. They all had ended up sleeping in Venice's bed, which became cramped after midnight. Hopefully a morning jog would help. It had been weeks since she felt like jogging, but for some reason, with the crashing of the waves, it seemed right. She hadn't really slept.

Her heart still ached, but she was trying to cope. The sun was coming up, which reflected off the red spandex short set that was molded to her obvious curves. After a series of stretches, she clipped her cell phone to her hip and headed south down the beach.

Craig stepped out of the shower and wrapped a towel around his lean body. He headed to the kitchen for his coffee. After adding a small amount of cream, he stepped out onto his deck at the precise time Venice ran past his cottage. He stood stunned and breathless. What a sight! He hadn't seen anyone and anything as beautiful since...*her.* He couldn't take his eyes off of this woman who ran past his cottage without so much as a glance his way. *Beautiful!* All sorts of thoughts ran through his head before he shook himself back to reality. Maybe he was imagining the whole thing, but she was real. This woman reminded him so much of Venice...too much. He felt it would have to be a blessing to find someone resembling her.

He mumbled, "I have got to find out who that woman is. This may be a good vacation after all."

He hurriedly dressed, then waited out on the deck for the brown beauty to make a return trip down the beach. He waited for two hours, but she never returned. Finally he realized that the direction she was running must have been her return route. *Stupid!!*

Venice returned to the cottage before Portia and Brandon woke up. This allowed her time to take a relaxing bubble bath and prepare breakfast. After her jog, she decided to go shop for groceries. Luckily, there was a shuttle to bring her back to the cottage so she wouldn't have to walk with all her bags. She chose a pair of white shorts and a thin blue tank top. Her white sandals topped off her ensemble. The jog felt good and she was determined to run every morning on the sandy beach.

Chapter Eight

It had been three days and a tour was the plan of the day. Portia and Brandon anxiously waited for Venice to get dressed. She chose form-fitting denim shorts and a yellow crop top. She slid her feet into some comfortable sneakers and grabbed her purse. The tour lasted approximately two hours and when they returned to town, Venice decided that night would be the last to eat out for a while.

They enjoyed their meal, trying not to become sad when they reminisced about fun times with Jarvis.

Craig sat at his usual table in the casual Jamaican-style restaurant. As he scanned the menu, he felt familiar hands touch his shoulder from behind.

"Melanie! What are you doing here?"

Melanie leaned down and kissed him on the cheek. Her teal and yellow dress accented her flawless skin tone. She sat opposite him and covered his hand with hers.

"Darling, I just couldn't leave things as they were. I guess you could call this my last stand."

Craig put his hands over his face. "Melanie, please...I can't do this anymore. Why are you making this so hard? Why can't you understand that I don't want the same things you want?"

He stared at her in amazement. The waiter approached and handed her a menu.

She smiled. "Sweetheart, let's just enjoy our meal. We can talk about that later."

He shook his head. "Melanie, you're headed back to Philly in the morning. I mean it."

"We'll see, but we do have tonight, Darling. I just hope that I can change your mind."

After dinner, Melanie excused herself to the restroom. Craig sat wondering how his life had taken this awkward turn. He came to Ocho Rios to get his head together and relax. Drama with Melanie was the last thing he expected or wanted. What he didn't know was that he hadn't seen drama yet. While waiting for Melanie to return to the table, he heard a sound he thought he would never hear again.

It couldn't be.

Craig's head turned again to the familiar sound of laughter.

What is happening to me? That silky laughter can only belong to one person... But she wouldn't be in Ocho Rios. If I could only see this woman's face.

The restaurant was full and Portia and Brandon were finishing up their dessert when Portia noticed him.

"Venice, there is a fine brotha over there and he keeps staring over here."

"Portia, don't start."

"No, for real! He is staring. Turn around and look."

"I will not and stop staring. It's not polite."

"Venice, you have got to take a look at this one. He's banging. Oh…and he's headed this way."

Heat engulfed her face as a husky and familiar voice said, "I just knew I had to be dreaming."

Venice looked up into the face of Craig Bennett and met his seductive gaze.

"Craig?"

"Venice!"

Portia watched the penetrating gaze they gave each other and asked, "You two know each other?"

They were both silent.

Since she didn't get a response, she said, "Hello! Did anybody hear me?"

Venice turned toward Portia. "Yes, we went to college together."

Craig was unable to tear his eyes away from her. She was still as beautiful, if not even more beautiful, than he remembered. He couldn't imagine her becoming more stunning…but she was.

Shoving his hands into his pockets, he said, "Venice…I-I huh…"

"Nice to see you again, Craig. It's been a long time."

"That it has."

Silence again surrounded them as he continued to stare. Venice lowered her eyes to her lap.

"Venice, aren't you going to introduce us?"

"Oh…I-I'm sorry. Craig, this is my sister-in-law, Portia, and…"

Extending his hand to Brandon, he said, "Young man, I can see who you are. You have got to be Venice and Jarvis' son."

Smiling, Brandon said, "Yes, Sir. My name is Brandon."

"You look just like your dad."

"My daddy's in heaven."

Venice tensed, hearing those words, and turned away to absorb the comment, hoping she would not become emotional. The shock of seeing Craig was enough to make any woman emotional. He stood tall and possessed that strong sex appeal she remembered. Wearing a black shirt with a pair of wheat-colored pants, he looked confident and in control as he stood just close enough to make her uncomfortable. Her skin became hot as his intense gaze burned into her body and his scent hypnotized her.

Portia started smiling, noticing the obvious attraction and said, "Brandon, let me take you to the restroom before we leave."

"I'll be right back, Momma."

"All right, sweetheart. Portia, you two make sure you come right back. We have to go."

Craig followed with, "See you guys in a minute."

As Portia and Brandon slid out of the booth, Craig sat directly across from her and took her hands into his.

"Venice, I don't know what to say. I'm so sorry about Jarvis."

The moment he touched her, he felt it. The spark traveled through his body causing goose bumps to appear on his skin. She jerked her hands away from him, but she still couldn't look into his sensual eyes. Softly, he said, "Sweetheart, I wish I could've been there for you."

Talk about the calm before the storm; it came with a fury. Her head snapped up to meet his sultry eyes.

"But you weren't! Were you, Craig? I haven't so much as heard or seen you in seven years and you think you can just walk up to me and act like everything's cool? Why didn't you return any of my calls, my letters? Huh? What happened to 'Venice I will always be there for you, no matter what?' Answer that, Craig Bennett!!"

In his defense, he answered, "I couldn't, Venice. I didn't want to cause…"

Putting her hand up, she said, "Save it! Don't you say another word! As far as I'm concerned, you don't exist. I didn't exist for you, so you don't exist for me. Let's just keep it that way!"

"Venice, please let me explain."

She stood up from the booth, seeing Portia and Brandon returning. She was not going to let him get to her. She was not going to cry, but she wanted to. He stood and she leaned in as close as possible so their lips were inches apart.

"Stay away from me, Bennett! You got that?!"

Craig grabbed her wrists and yelled, "You think you're the only one who's hurting? I've been hurting for seven long years and I'm still hurt, Venice!!"

"Take your hands off me!"

"Oh, it's going to be like that? Well, that's fine with me! You stay out of my way and I'll stay out of yours. I think this island is big enough for the two of us. Don't you?"

Silence engulfed them as they stared at each other, breathing hot air through their nostrils. He slowly released her and ran his hand over his head and across his chest.

"Venice, I'm sorry I grabbed you like that..."

Still again, she lashed out saying, "Forget it, Bennett!"

About that time, Melanie approached and asked, "Craig, Sweetheart, are you ready to go? Oh! Hello."

Stunned, Venice looked at Melanie, then back at Craig.

Melanie asked, "Darling, aren't you going to introduce me to your friend?"

Craig couldn't tear his eyes away from Venice. He didn't even hear what Melanie had asked. Venice's heart began to beat hard against her chest. Her face became hot as she realized Craig was there on the island with another woman and was trying to get all up in her personal space.

Venice looked at Craig. "Yes, Craig, why don't you introduce us?"

Still staring, he mumbled, "Melanie, this is Venice. Venice...Melanie."

Melanie outstretched her professionally-manicured hand.

"Nice to meet you, Venice. Have you and Craig met before?"

Venice quickly shook her hand and nervously said, "We used to know each other a few years ago."

Craig laughed sarcastically.

"Used to know each other...funny, Venice. That's very mature."

Melanie eyed the two and asked, "Is there a problem here?"

Venice said, "No problem at all. I was just leaving. I hope you two have a nice evening. Goodnight."

Portia approached and saw the stress on Venice's and Craig's faces. She also noticed another woman standing with them.

"What's wrong? Venice, are you okay?"

Fumbling with her purse, Venice said, "I'm fine, Portia. You and Brandon tell Mr. Bennett and his friend goodnight."

Craig extended his hand to Portia and Brandon and introduced them to Melanie.

Venice turned her back to him and proceeded to leave the tip. Oddly, she felt hurt and jealous, but she had no right. She knew she had hurt

Craig terribly when she married Jarvis and hearing those words yelled at her stung. Any woman would kill to have a man in their life as wonderful and loving as Craig.

She tried to hide her obvious jealousy from Craig.

"Let's go, kids. I have a headache."

Craig came over to her and stood close, so much that she could feel the heat from his body.

He whispered, "Venice, look, we need to talk, but…"

Gritting her teeth, she answered, "I said, forget it, Bennett!"

Feeling at the end of his rope, he pulled her to the side and looked directly into her eyes.

"Woman, I allowed you to walk away from me once and I'll be damned if I let you do it again. I've been there, done that. Do you understand?"

Venice pointed her finger at him. "No! You understand this! You don't tell me what I can or cannot do! Goodbye!"

Taking Brandon by the hand, she practically ran out the door. Portia looked at a defeated Craig and said, "Goodnight, Mr. Craig. I hope we get to see you again. Goodnight, Miss Melanie."

Solemnly, he answered, "So do I, Portia. Goodnight."

Craig sank back into the booth and dropped his head. Melanie sat opposite him.

"What was that all about? Who is that woman?"

He snapped at her angrily, "Look, Melanie! It's none of your business! I came to Ocho Rios to relax. Drama from you or anyone else is not what I signed up for…understand? Now, I'm going to make sure you get back to your hotel and then I would appreciate it if you would please take the next plane back to Philly. It's over, Melanie. I can't put it any clearer than that!"

Melanie took a deep breath. "Wow! Craig, you really mean it, don't you?"

Feeling exhausted, he took her hands into his. "Yes, Melanie, I do and I'm sorry for going off on you. I'm just tired, Okay? Thank you for being a great friend, but please let's leave it this way. Okay?"

She smiled, leaned over the table, and kissed his lips tenderly.

"Okay, Craig, you win. Look, I don't know why your friend is so upset with you, but whatever it is, I hope it doesn't mess up your friendship."

He looked at her knowing he could never reveal to Melanie the depth of his past relationship with Venice. If he did, she just might try to hang around to make things more complicated after all. At that same moment, he realized that Venice was the woman he saw jogging on the beach. He also realized that he was still very much in love with her and it made him sick to his stomach. A sharp pain radiated through his chest. He grimaced for a few seconds, then took a sip of water.

"Thanks, Melanie."

"Are you okay, Craig?"

"I'm fine."

"Now, Mr. Bennett, would you be so kind as to walk me to my hotel?"

"Sure. Let's go."

He took a moment to decipher what had happened, then they rose and quietly left the restaurant.

Venice's heart took a justified kick. She returned to the restaurant to retrieve her sunglasses at the very moment Melanie passionately kissed Craig. She decided to let the sunglasses stay in the restaurant.

I should be happy that Craig found someone else to love. I guess I deserved this. Goodbye, Craig.

In another part of the restaurant, a gentleman pulled out his cell phone and placed a call.

"Yeah…it's me. They finally ran into each other and it was ugly. She was upset, but I think it was just the shock of seeing him. Also, there was a woman who showed up unexpected at Bennett's table. He apparently knew her. I'll check her out and get back to you."

After hanging up, he folded his newspaper under his arm and walked out into the cool Jamaican air.

Chapter Nine

Venice was almost dragging Brandon down the beach.

Portia yelled, "Venice, you're going to pull Brandon's arm off!"

She stopped in her tracks and fell to her knees so she could be eye-level to him.

"Brandon, Momma's sorry. I didn't mean to walk so fast. Is your arm OK?"

"I'm fine, Momma, but why where you so mad at Mr. Craig?"

Portia joined in. "Yeah, what's up and who was that woman with Mr. Craig?"

Venice stood, brushed the sand from her skirt, and answered, "I don't know who she was. I guess she was his girlfriend. Look, I don't want to talk about him, okay?"

"Why, because you like him?"

"Portia, chill with that. Okay?"

"It was obvious he liked you. He couldn't stop staring at you. He wasn't even paying that woman any attention."

Venice sighed.

"It was a long time ago, Portia. Unfortunately, I hurt him very bad, so can we please not talk about him anymore? I have a headache. I'm surprised you're pushing for me to hook up with somebody, anyway."

"Why, because of my brother? Venice, are you saying you will never marry again?"

Feeling exhausted, she said, "Portia, I don't know what I'm saying. All I know is I'm still in love with Jarvis."

"He loved you, too, but he's gone, Venice."

"Don't you think I know that, Portia? I don't need people reminding me all the time. Look! Craig hates me…okay? Also, there was a woman hanging all over him, if you didn't notice."

Portia looked at her seriously and said, "The way he was staring at you, I believe he's in love with you, not that woman."

Folding her arms, Venice said, "Right, words of wisdom from a fifteen-year-old."

Portia's feelings were hurt by Venice's comment, but she knew she was dealing with a lot of emotions. She lowered her head. "I'm sorry, Venice, I didn't mean to push you. I just thought it would be nice to see you smile again. I just thought Craig might be the one to put a smile on your face."

Venice hugged her tightly and apologized. "I'm sorry, Portia. I didn't mean to hurt you. I know you're only looking out for me. I confess…I fell in love with Craig when we were in college, but I had always been in love with your brother so I chose Jarvis. And Portia, I don't regret it one bit."

"So you were in love with him?"

"Yes."

"Did Jarvis know about him?"

Venice sighed and answered, "Yes."

Tears glistened in both of their eyes. Portia kissed her sister-in-law on the cheek.

"Venice? I think there's still something there between you two."

Venice burst out laughing nervously.

"Sure, Portia. You could tell by the way we were yelling at each other."

Portia reached for Brandon's hand. "That's what I'm talking about. If it's not love, it's clear you still have some type of feelings for each other. Look, we don't have to talk about him anymore. Okay?"

"Thanks, Portia."

They continued their walk, hand-in-hand, back to the cottage.

Craig took the long way back after walking Melanie to the hotel. How in the world did he end up on an island with the only woman he had ever loved? Her fiery temper ignited his and now he didn't know what to do. Their argument was not what he expected, nor was his own outburst. He was curious to find out if she still loved him. She once told him she would always love him, no matter what. Then he remembered his promise. *Venice, I will always be there for you.* He had failed on his promise; now he needed to find out if she kept hers. He was scared to risk his heart again, especially with her. He didn't want to let love take another punch at his heart, but you only live once. It had been five months since Jarvis died, but he wondered if it was too soon to push her?

Craig walked around the shops of the village for hours. He was in no hurry to return because he knew his dreams would be consumed with visions of *her.*

When he did finally return to the cottage, he decided to call his childhood friend, Skeeter who was a prominent attorney in Dallas. In a few months, he would be moving to Philadelphia to join a prestigious law firm.

"Hey, Man."

"Hey, Craig, what's up with you? Why are you sounding so down?"

Craig sighed. "You're not going to believe this, but guess who's here on the island with me?"

Skeeter yawned while sitting in his home office.

"Don't tell me Melanie has trailed you down there."

"How did you know?"

Skeeter shook his head. "I'm a lawyer. I get paid to get into people's heads. Besides, Melanie's not the type of woman to go down without a fight."

Craig let out a big sigh and said, "I guess, but she finally got the picture and agreed to stop trying."

Skeeter laughed. "Good! I hope she sticks to it."

"Me too, man. Anyway, Melanie wasn't who I was talking about."

Skeeter sat some paperwork aside. "Damn, man, just how many women do you have?"

Craig sighed again and rubbed his chest in silence. "Don't start, Skeeter."

Skeeter sat up in his chair. "You okay, Craig?"

"Skeeter, Venice is here. I ran into Venice today."

"What!"

"Exactly! Man, I freaked out. I approached her, we chatted for a moment, and then all hell broke loose. She went off on me about not contacting her after all these years and I tried to explain, but she wasn't hearing it. That's when I snapped."

Skeeter chuckled. "Damn, Craig, what did you do?"

"I grabbed her wrists and told her she wasn't the only one who had been hurt. I mean I know she lost her husband, but damn!"

Skeeter laughed again. "Wait a minute! You grabbed her?"

Craig rubbed his hand over his head. "Yeah, I guess I did. I wasn't thinking, Skeeter. I haven't seen her in seven years and...I...I..."

Skeeter interrupted. "Damn, Craig! Venice took your ass through the mud and you're still in love with her. Aren't you?"

Rubbing his chest, he said, "I don't know what I'm feeling, man. All I know is I'm having all kinds of emotions right now. We were at a restaurant and Melanie got all curious, but she thinks we're just friends."

Skeeter said, "Man, women have radar on stuff like that. Melanie knows there's more going on there. You're just not going to argue in public like that with just a friend. Where is Melanie?"

"I walked her back to her hotel. She's flying back to Philly in the morning." Craig took some bottled water out of the refrigerator and said, "I came here to get Venice off my mind and damn it if I didn't run into her. What are the chances?"

Skeeter jotted some information into his Palm Pilot and asked, "Whatcha gonna do, dog?"

Craig smiled. "I hope you don't talk like that in court, Skeeter."

"I don't. I pull out all my charm and charisma for the ladies in court."

They laughed together, then Skeeter asked, "Seriously, Craig. What are you going to do? It's obvious you're still into the woman. Otherwise you wouldn't be so worked up about it. Can you get past all that bitterness she left you with? I mean you've been bumping and grinding with women for several years trying to find her clone. Now, unexpectedly she's available. Are you really going to put your heart out there again?"

Craig stood and walked out onto the deck. He leaned over the rail, taking in the scent of the salty waves.

"I don't know, man. She was pretty fired up. She told me to stay away from her, but I don't know if I can. Especially after looking into those brown eyes, you know? I have to find out what's up."

Skeeter closed his briefcase and said, "Well, whatever, man. You're a good one 'cause I couldn't do it. I hope everything works out for you. Keep me posted. Sorry I couldn't get away to hang out with you down there. Hell, I'd love to have a ring-side seat for this. For real, Craig, be careful. Don't let Venice dog you again. Aight?"

Craig walked back inside, leaned against the kitchen counter, and sighed.

"I hear you, Skeeter. How's the move coming?"

"It's coming along. I'm tying up my cases here and should be in Philly by February."

"You know you're welcome to stay with me if you don't find a place in time."

Skeeter laughed. "Thanks, man, but my real estate agent sent me the picture of a good prospect."

"That's great! If you want me to, I'll do a drive by and check it out for you."

Skeeter stretched and laughed again, saying, "You already have your hands full, my man. Anyway, I'm flying up this weekend to check it out. I'll let you know what happens."

Craig folded his arms across his chest. "Well, if you want to stay at the house while I'm down here, make yourself at home."

"Thanks, Bro. I think I'll take you up on your offer."

"Skeeter?"

"Yeah, man."

"No strange women in my house."

Skeeter grinned. "I'm going to be too tired to chase the women of Philly on this trip, partner."

"Good. I'm sure you could use the R & R, and Skeeter? Thanks for listening. I'll call you in a couple of days."

"You'd better call. Look, I'm headed to bed. Be safe and relax. Just let things happen, Craig. Don't force it. Okay?"

"Yeah, man. Thanks. I'm out."

"Peace!"

Craig hung up. Glancing at his watch, he realized it was two thirty-five a.m. He mumbled, "Another sleepless night."

Venice stared at the clock and it read two thirty five a.m. She had been trying to fall asleep for hours, but she couldn't. Her heart was still racing and she was unexpectedly sweating. It was a warm night, but not unbearable. She refused to admit the source of her problem…Craig Bennett. Where had he been all those years? Why was he there? Who was that woman? So many questions eluded her. She never could forget those eyes, so dark and readable. The desire he carried for her was still there. She saw it and it scared her. Unable to sleep she rose and walked out onto the deck. The night air blowing in from the ocean did little to cool the heat her body now radiated. Leaning over the railing she closed her eyes and inhaled the sweet scent of the tropical flowers. Immediately a vision of Craig invaded her thoughts.

Stop this! Forget him! Damn! Who am I fooling? The look, the touch was still there. This isn't right. God help me. Jarvis, why did you have to leave me? Joshua, I'll call Joshua. He'll help me.

Venice returned to her bedroom and called, knowing it was an ungodly hour to call. Joshua and his wife, Cynthia, always told her to call anytime. That time was now.

A sleepy voice answered, "Hello?"

"Josh?"

"Venice?"

"Yeah, it's me."

"Is everything okay? What time is it?"

"I know it's late, but I had to talk to you."

"What's up, Niecy?"

"I have a problem."

In the background she heard Cynthia's voice ask if everything was okay. Joshua assured her Venice was fine and just wanted to talk. Cynthia took the phone from him because she needed to know for herself.

Cynthia asked, "Venice, is everything really Okay?"

"It will be, Cynthia. Sorry for disturbing you guys."

"Don't worry about it. I'll be sleep again in no time. Love you and I'll talk to you soon. Here's Josh."

Cynthia was somewhat reassured as she handed the phone back over to Joshua. Rising out of bed, he went into the kitchen so his wife could go back to sleep. Joshua asked, "Okay, now what is the honor of this late night call? I haven't heard a wink out of you in days. What's wrong?"

Venice sighed. "Joshua, he-he's here."

"Who?"

"Craig."

Joshua couldn't let her know he knew exactly what she was talking about.

"You mean Bennett?"

"Yes, Joshua, in the flesh. I freaked out, he freaked out, and we ended up yelling at each other. Seeing him again after all these years really shook me up."

"What did he say?"

"Before the yelling, he told me he was sorry to hear about Jarvis. I confronted him about not returning my letters and he tried to explain, but I didn't want to hear his lies. That's when we started arguing."

Joshua asked, "What else?"

"He told me we needed to talk but I told him to stay away from me."

"Do you really mean that, Niecy?"

She let out a deep breath and said, "He was with a woman, Joshua."

Joshua spoke calmly, saying, "Can't be serious if he was all up on you like that."

"Craig Bennett is history."

"Is he? What would it hurt to hear the man out? Aren't you curious to know what's been going on with him?"

"I thought you would understand, Josh."

"I understand that you were in love with him once."

I never stopped loving him, Joshua..

"What am I going to do, Joshua?"

Joshua poured himself a glass of milk. "I think the man deserves a chance to explain. What do you have to lose?

"I can't disrespect Jarvis like that."

Joshua searched the cabinet for cookies. "You think talking to the man will disrespect Jarvis? Girl, you're trippin'."

Sitting in the recliner on the deck, she sighed and said, "I have nothing to say to or hear from Craig Bennett."

"Venice Taylor Anderson! You have got to get your life together. Let me ask you something. When are you going back to Michigan? You haven't set foot in your house since Jarvis died. You act like you have a death wish yourself sometimes. We all miss Jarvis, but we still have to live. So do you. Do you honestly think that Jarvis wouldn't expect or want you to meet someone and possibly remarry? You're twenty-six, for God's sake. Have you forgotten that you damn near didn't marry Jarvis because you were in love with Craig? You know I love you more than anything and I'm going to tell you the raw truth. Just hear the man out. Okay?"

Joshua heard one sniff, then another among their silence.

"Joshua, I'll call you later."

"Niecy?"

"I love you, Josh."

"I love you, too, Niecy. Goodnight."

Joshua hung up the phone, then wondered if he might have pushed her too far. It was too late to worry about that now. He just hoped she would at least give Craig a chance to explain. He was also curious about the woman Craig was with. He would get his partner to check into it.

Venice didn't know what time she finally went to sleep. She did know Joshua said some things to her she didn't want to hear because they were all true.

Chapter Ten

Craig really needed the morning jog. He'd taken Melanie to the airport earlier and now he was ready to get back to his vacation. He really never went to sleep, but he was determined to keep his spirits high. He dressed in his jogging attire and laced up his Air Jordans. The moment he stepped out onto the beach he felt the calm and relaxation of the island, which would become his refuge. After stretching a little, he started north toward town. After about thirty minutes, he caught a familiar figure headed his way. His heart started fluttering as she got closer and closer. She was in her own little world. Craig tensed with anticipation. As they passed, he said, "Morning, Venice."

"Craig."

Neither broke stride but he couldn't help but turn around and look at her. She looked so beautiful, even early in the morning. He was a little hurt that she never turned around to glance at him. It was then that a pain shot through his chest. He immediately stopped and grabbed it. He bent over and rubbed the area. Breathing was becoming difficult as he dropped to his knees.

Down the beach, Venice was finally able to swallow the lump in her throat. Craig was the last person she expected to run into on the beach. She had hoped to get her jog in earlier than normal, just in case. She stopped to check her watch and turned to look over her shoulder in his direction. What she saw caught her immediate attention. Craig was hurt. She sprinted back to his side where she found a man trying to help him.

Frightened, she asked, "Craig are you okay?"

The stranger asked, "Ma'am, you know this gentleman?"

"Yes, I do. Craig, what's wrong? Did you hurt yourself?"

Craig sat down on the sand.

"I'm fine. Just give me a minute. It's just anxiety."

The stranger asked, "Ma'am, do you want me to call a doctor?"

"That won't be necessary. I'm a doctor."

Venice dropped to her knees in front of him and started examining him. Her touch was nothing short of magical. Craig couldn't believe the effect this woman had on him. His body tingled just from the contact they were sharing. She checked his pulse and eyes and found nothing visually wrong.

"You've had this problem before?"

"Yes. I'll be fine so if you move, I can get up."

Venice removed her hands from his arm so he could stand. They stared at each other for a moment, then Craig turned and thanked the stranger for his assistance.

As the gentleman went on his way, he turned and said, "Thank you."

"I didn't do anything."

"You came to help me and I appreciate it."

Venice folded her arms and asked, "Can you make it back to your place okay?"

"I'm sure I can."

Venice stared down at the sand. "Look, I'd feel better if you let me walk you back. Okay?"

"Thanks, but I'd rather you didn't."

Heat started to rise from her neck to her face. She sighed. "At least let me call your girlfriend so she can come pick you up."

Craig was silent as he stared at her. He then replied, "I can make the call myself if I need to, thank you."

"Fine! Goodbye!"

She turned and started walking back down the beach, obviously pissed.

Craig stood watching her departure.

This was your idea, Sweetheart, not mine.

Hearing Portia and Brandon arguing over the remote control brought her out of her sleep. She didn't sleep very well, because she worried about Craig all night. Even though she wanted him to stay away from her, she was still concerned. There's no way that woman he was with cared about anyone but herself. She couldn't possibly take care of Craig properly. A soft knock on her door and a tiny voice calling for her made her sit up in bed.

"Momma?"

Fingering her wavy hair into place, she answered, "Come in, Brandon."

Jumping onto the bed, he hugged her neck and gave her a big kiss on the cheek.

"Good morning, Momma!"

"Good morning, Lil' Man."

While Brandon brushed her long strands of dark hair from her eyes, she asked, "What do you want to do today?"

"Portia and I want to go down to the beach. She said she would help me build a sand castle. You're coming, aren't you?"

"I wouldn't miss it, but let's eat breakfast first."

"Portia already fixed breakfast for me, Momma."

"She did? Well, you have a great aunt, don't you?"

Brandon hugged her again.

"The best! Now can we go down to the beach? We already have our swimming clothes on."

"So I see. Let me get a shower first and I'll go with you. Okay?"

"Okay, Momma, but hurry."

After a quick shower, Venice dressed in a bright yellow bikini. Eyeing herself in the mirror, she noticed that having Brandon had enhanced her curves instead of destroyed them. To complete her ensemble, she wrapped a matching sarong around her hips and joined the others for a day of fun.

About an hour or so had passed since they started swimming and playing on the beach. Venice decided to rest for a while and let the kids play. As she walked back to their towels, several men turned to stare. Unlike them, she showed no interest in their wandering eyes. Her conversation with Joshua played over and over in her head and she found it hard to concentrate. She told the kids she was going to be reading and for them to stay close to the beach. Venice adjusted the umbrella over her seat and pulled out her book, occasionally glancing up to make sure the kids were safe.

Down the beach, Craig gripped the binoculars tightly as he watched the men drool over Venice. She looked sinful and forbidden in her swimsuit. His body hardened at the thought of touching her soft brown skin. He mumbled to himself, then grabbed his towel and headed for the beach.

"Mr. Craig!"

"Hello, Brandon...Portia."

Venice's head snapped up from her book. Their eyes met and held for a moment.

Smiling down at her, he said, "Hello, Venice."

"Craig."

What the hell is he doing here? Shouldn't he be playing house with his runway model?

Not wanting to make a scene, Venice decided to ignore him and continued reading her book. But, she couldn't. Seeing him in those black swimming briefs caused a fluttering in her stomach. The silky hair on his chest beckoned for her touch. Heat swept over her immediately and it angered her. Portia and Brandon were enjoying his company as he helped them build the sand castle. Craig decided it was best that he kept his distance from Venice for a while. His emotions were too explosive to chance another confrontation. Besides, he's the one who should've been pissed off, not her.

Later, as he swam with the kids, Brandon yelled, "Momma! Come swim with us!"

She yelled back, "Not right now, Brandon. Maybe later."

Craig saw an opening to tease, hoping to break the ice. He asked Portia and Brandon if they wanted him to get her. They both agreed. Venice didn't even hear him approach until he had swept her up into his arms and headed for the water.

Angry, she yelled, "Put me down, Bennett!"

Holding her close to his body, he said, "The kids want you to swim with them. Quit being a spoiled sport."

Before she could say another word, he threw her into a wave. He knew she was going to come up fighting, but what the hell? He'd held her in his arms and it would be worth the fight. Portia and Brandon applauded after Craig tossed her into the water. When she came up for air, she swam directly over to him and tried to push him down in the water. Instead, he wrapped his strong arms around her, pinning hers down to her sides. Feeling her soft, wet body pressed against him aroused him instantly.

"Let me go, Bennett!"

"Only if you behave and if you don't, I will dunk you right here and now."

"You wouldn't! Why won't you leave us alone and go play with your little Barbie doll."

She's jealous!

Craig smiled.

"Sweetheart, I *will* dunk you unless you agree to sit down and talk to me. As far as Melanie is concerned, that's none of your business."

Anger choked her as she tried unsuccessfully to free herself from his grasp. She gave up.

"We have nothing to talk about, so I guess I'd rather be dunked."

She didn't think he would really do it.

Craig kissed her on the cheek. "Suit yourself, Sweetheart." He fell back into the water with Venice still in his arms, pulling her under with him. A perfect dunk. Coming up for air and swimming away from him, she said, "You'll pay for that!"

Smiling he thought, *I'm counting on it, Sweetheart.*

Portia was on the towel laughing when Venice returned to the beach fuming.

"O-o-o-o, Venice, you two have got it so bad for each other."

She was furious as she toweled off vigorously.

"What are you talking about, Portia?"

Adjusting her sunglasses, she said, "Don't mind me, I'm only fifteen, but I like him. He's handsome, nice and has a banging body."

"And he has a woman unless you've forgotten!"

Portia sighed. "Whatever, Venice. Look, I love you, but I'm going out there with them to have some fun. I wish you would come, too."

Venice finished drying off and glanced out over the cool blue water where she watched Brandon casually playing in the water with Craig. It was clear he had won both Portia's and Brandon's affection in such a short time. She didn't know what he was up to, but had to keep Craig Bennett at arm's length. He was just too sexy and dangerous.

Why won't he go away? Why isn't he with that woman?

"Portia, you can forget about Craig. I'm going inside to take a shower and start dinner. Keep an eye on Brandon and don't leave this area of the beach. Okay?"

"Okay…Chicken."

"I'm going to act like I didn't hear that."

Portia laughed and went to join Craig and Brandon in the waves.

After her shower, Venice changed into a pair of khaki shorts and a red halter. Dinner would consist of baked chicken, rice and green beans. As she set the table, she shivered, still feeling the places on her body his hands had touched. That strange fluttering in her stomach had also returned. Venice gleamed at the beautiful table setting. A few more minutes and dinner would be ready.

Portia was right about one thing. She was too chicken to stay out on the beach with Craig. She tried to convince herself that her body's reaction to his pressed against hers was unwelcome. The truth was, it felt wonderful.

"Momma! Momma!"

Venice's heart leapt into her throat as she heard the serious tone in Brandon's voice. She ran to the deck to meet Brandon and Craig with Portia in his arms.

"What happened to Portia?"

Seeing the fear in Venice's eyes, Craig spoke softly.

"She just stepped on a jellyfish, but she'll be okay."

"Momma, you should have seen it!"

Dismissing Brandon, she went to Portia as Craig laid her on the sofa. Tears glistened in her eyes.

"We should call a doctor!"

He gave her an intense gaze.

"There's no need, Venice. Plus, if my memory serves me correct, you are a doctor."

Her angry eyes met his calm ones as she yelled, "Don't you patronize me!"

Craig firmly said, "Venice, calm down before you scare her."

"You can't tell me what to do, Craig!"

Craig looked at the woman, who was filled with fire.

"She'll be okay, Venice. Just sore for a day or two."

Portia intervened saying, "Hey, you guys! Stop it! I'm okay...really."

Venice grabbed her hand. "I'm sorry, Portia. I didn't mean to scare you."

"It doesn't hurt that much."

Craig stood tall over Venice. "If you don't mind, look in your kitchen and see if you have some vinegar."

"Vinegar?"

Craig smiled. "I guess they didn't cover that in med school, huh? You're supposed to put it on the wound."

Venice looked him square in the eye.

"That's low. Even for you, Craig."

Before he could tell her that he was just joking, she turned and disappeared into the kitchen. She returned with the vinegar and applied it to Portia's foot in silence. A lone tear rolled down her cheek as she spread some antibiotic ointment on her foot. Craig wanted to pull her to him and tell her he was sorry, but he couldn't...not now. Venice finally noticed Craig dripping on the carpet and sent Brandon to get him a towel.

After helping Portia to her room, into some dry clothes and then bed, she returned to the living room to find out that Craig had fixed Brandon's plate for him. She didn't realize she had been in the room with Portia for nearly an hour and completely forgot Craig was there. Approaching the table, Venice calmly said, "Look, Bennett, thanks for helping with Portia and Brandon. I don't think I would have been able to deal with it by myself. I'm sure your friend is probably wondering where you are and I'm sorry you had to hang around so long, but I appreciate it."

He came to her. She lowered her gaze, not able to look into those eyes. He raised her chin to look at him.

"Venice, I'm sorry I yelled at you in the restaurant. If I could take it back, I would. But remember, you hurt me."

His eyes were magnetic and they drew her to him. She couldn't speak or admit that he was right. He was absolutely gorgeous. He removed his hand, backed away.

"Portia will be fine. Give her something for the pain and she should sleep fine."

"Look…Craig, I'm sorry also for being so…"

"Don't apologize for acting out your feelings. I guess I was acting out my feelings, too. I hadn't allowed myself to let go emotionally after you left me. I guess seeing you again brought all that emotion back."

Silence filled the room as they stared into each other's eyes. Venice broke the silence.

"I'm sorry I hurt you, Craig, and I hope you'll be able to forgive me."

"I already have."

"Well, if you didn't have company, I would invite you to stay for dinner."

Grabbing the towel, he said, "Maybe some other time. I need to get out of these wet clothes."

A memory of him out of his clothes popped into her head and she closed her eyes and let out a breath.

"Walk me to the door and give me your number so I can check on you guys later, or do you still want me to stay away from you?"

Those eyes, so intense, so revealing. Venice wiped her sweaty palms on the sides of her shorts, then wrote out the phone number and handed it to him.

"Bennett, I don't want to cause any problems between you and Melanie. I have to admit that I did overreact. I mean…I really haven't been myself since…well, since you know. Plus, I guess I was shocked to run into you after all these years."

He winked at her. "I understand, Venice. Well…I'd better go. See you later, Brandon."

"Bye, Mr. Craig."

As they walked out onto the deck, he took her hand into his. He stroked the back of it with his thumb. Her knees became unbalanced as he leaned in to kiss her on the cheek. Her flowered scent sent chills over his body.

"Goodnight, Venice."

"Goodnight."

Walking away, he said, "Tell Portia goodnight also."

"I will."

She stood, unable to move for a moment. He was doing it for a second time, sweeping her off her feet. When he got to the bottom of the steps, he slowly turned. "Venice?"

"Yes?"

"I just want you to know that I stayed away not because I wanted to, but because I had to. I don't want to stay away from you anymore and just for the record, my relationship with Melanie has been over for a while now. We're just friends. Goodnight."

Before she could respond, he was only a silhouette and she stood paralyzed. Her mouth was opened, but nothing came out.

A stranger standing nearby tucked his binoculars away and pulled out his cell phone to place a call back to the States.

"Hello?"

"Things are looking up."

"What happened?"

"The girl was stung by a jellyfish, but she's okay. He took her inside the house and as he was leaving, she allowed him to hold her hand and kiss her on the cheek."

Joshua said, "What about the woman?"

"I found out she was his ex-lover. He put her on a plane back to Philadelphia this morning."

Joshua closed his eyes with relief.

"Much better. Keep me posted. She placed a call to me last night. I may be visiting soon to check the progress, up close and personal. Good work, Manley. Stay with them and don't let Venice out of your sight."

"You're the boss."

Chapter Eleven

Back in his cottage, Craig went directly into the shower to wash the scent of the ocean from his body. Being in Venice's presence rocked him once again. Pain shot through his chest and he braced himself against the tile walls. It took a moment, but the pain finally subsided. After dressing, he strolled into the kitchen and took some antacid. He was at a crossroad now and he didn't know what to do. This woman was causing his mind and body to go crazy. Was he a fool to even think about setting his heart up for another failure? Venice left him devastated emotionally.

I can't go through it again. I just can't.

He took some time to call his sister, Bernice, because he needed some guidance. He told her everything that had happened so far. Over an hour later, he hung up the phone feeling better, but still confused. His sister was always able to be objective in helping him with solutions of the heart. He still didn't know what he was going to do about Venice. Leaning back against the sofa he decided that he would just have to take one day at a time and see what happened.

Craig called as he promised to check on them. Brandon and Portia were tucked safely away in their warm beds. Venice looked in on Portia every hour, unable to sleep. This man was shaking up her foundation. Jealousy swept over her for a moment before she curled up beside Brandon. She did see Craig kissing that woman in the restaurant. Could she trust he was telling the truth? Was his relationship with Melanie really over? Did she even care?

Over the next two days, there was no sight or sound from Craig. Venice was now wondering if she had successfully pushed Craig away. Brandon and Portia asked if she had seen him, which she hadn't. While he was asking for her number, she didn't think to ask him for his. For emergencies only, of course. Venice didn't want to admit to herself that she did indeed miss him showing up.

Portia had recovered from her jellyfish sting and there was a carnival in town. Brandon couldn't wait to get on the different rides and neither could Portia. They made their way around the different carnival games and food booths.

While standing near some candy apples, she heard a familiar voice.

"Would the pretty lady please buy a hungry man a candy apple?"

She turned to gaze into Craig's dark, hungry eyes. "Hello, Bennett."

Reaching up to remove strands of hair from her eyes, he responded, "Hello, yourself. Where are the kids?"

She pointed upwards as they whizzed by on a carnival ride.

Craig smiled and confessed, "I've missed you guys."

"They've missed you."

Coming closer, he asked, "What about you?"

Dropping her head, he cupped her chin so he could look into her eyes. Taking a chance, he asked, "Well, have you?"

She sighed, answering, "I guess I did and if I can take back all the pain I caused you..."

Placing his finger over her lips, he silenced her.

"Have dinner with me tonight so we can talk."

"I can't."

"Ouch!"

She pulled away and smiled. "It's not that. I don't have anyone to look after the kids. Besides, your friend doesn't seem like the kind of person who would want me intruding on your vacation."

Craig laughed. "First of all, I'm talking about having all of you over for dinner. Secondly, I told you that my relationship with Melanie is over. We're strictly friends and she's in Philly." Leaning in even closer, he whispered, "Lastly, I hope to have dinner alone with you a little later."

His devilish grin gave away promises flickering in his eyes.

"Mr. Craig!"

Brandon ran toward them and leapt into Craig's arms. Tears filled Venice's eyes as she listened to Brandon quiz Craig on why he had disappeared for two days.

He laughed and explained, "I had to fly out on business. I guess I should've called, huh?"

"Momma always tell Daddy. If you're going to be late or have to go out, call or leave a note."

Venice realized Brandon was still talking about his dad in the present tense and it saddened her.

Craig noticed also and said, "I'm sorry, Brandon. I guess I didn't think I would be missed." He looked directly at Venice, knowing the wall of ice built around their hearts was slowly melting. It didn't help that the urge to kiss her was growing stronger and he didn't know how much longer he could stand it. The main question was if she would even let him kiss her.

Portia said, "Come on, Craig. Let me show you how to win a big teddy bear."

"You're on."

Before the evening was over, Craig and Portia were even with two giant stuffed animals apiece. On the way home, they enjoyed ice cream cones for dessert. He ached slowly as he watched Venice lick the ice cream from her cone. One day soon, he hoped to use some to pleasure them both. His thoughts made his body respond. It took a few minutes of serious concentration to get his body under control.

Later that evening they shared a nice dinner prepared solely by Craig. The kids were impressed, but Venice had always known Craig was an excellent cook. Later, Portia and Brandon enjoyed a swim in Craig's pool while Venice helped him clean up the kitchen. Watching him reach and bend was making the simple task of washing dishes difficult. His denim shorts revealed long muscular legs and powerful thighs. A body she was very familiar with. The red T-shirt molded his trim waist and broad chest. She swallowed and found the strength to speak.

"Craig, thanks again for dinner."

Smiling, he said, "It was my pleasure."

After placing the last plate in the cabinet, Venice started for the deck. Craig reached for her arm and pulled her to him. He looked down into her shy eyes and drank in her beauty. He felt her body shivering against his as he ran a finger down her cheek.

"You look beautiful tonight."

"Thank you. You don't look so bad yourself."

Venice could feel the hardening of her nipples through the thin dress covering her skin. Playing with the spaghetti straps on her dress, he said, "You know, even though my heart was crushed like hell, I never stopped loving you. I hope you never lost the feelings we had between us 'cause they're too strong, Sweetheart, and I know you feel them, too. I don't blame you for telling me to stay away from you."

Feeling confused, she said, "Craig, I-I...shouldn't have said that. I'm the one who should apologize to you for causing you pain and for..."

He lowered his head and gently pressed his lips to hers. She was unable to finish her sentence. Reluctant at first, she finally gave into the intoxicating effect of his kiss. He pulled her tighter against his hard physique and she arched her body into his as he deepened the kiss. Venice moaned as his tongue danced with hers. Fighting for control, he also let out a moan, then broke off the kiss. Still holding her, he fought to regain normal breathing rhythm. Venice was dazed and felt like she was having an out-of-body experience. Like in the past, his kiss seared her lips. Embarrassed at her response, she lowered her head and backed out of his embrace. She folded her arms and tried to rub the goose bumps from them.

He smiled. "Venice, I don't regret kissing you and I hope you don't either."

"I don't, but it's late. We need to get back to our cottage."

Stepping around him, making sure she didn't make eye contact, she called for Portia and Brandon to get dressed. Leaving him alone in the kitchen with his thoughts, he knew he had made progress.

He'd taken a chance with his heart for a second time. She'd actually kissed him back, which told him she wanted it just as much as he did. But, what did he really want? Did he really want to risk it all again? He'd tasted her sweet lips and there was no turning back now. He decided, on that very spot, that he would risk his heart in the name of love—one more time.

Chapter Twelve

The next few days flew by as the second week of their vacation came to an end. Venice was still shaken by her response to Craig. The words spoken to her by her mother-in-law often replayed in her head.

Don't be afraid to love again.

Venice wanted to love again, but she wasn't able to let go, not yet. She didn't even know if she would ever be able to let go. Losing Jarvis was sudden and devastating. His memory was too important to her and she wasn't about to do anything to damage it.

Running into Craig had conjured up all kinds of emotions. There were questions she needed answered and the only person who could answer them was turning her life upside-down.

The following day, while she was relaxing in her room, Venice heard the doorbell. She wasn't expecting anyone. Portia and Brandon were playing cards in the living room when Venice rose to answer the door.

"What's happening, Mon?"

Venice put her hands on her hips and asked, "Joshua! What are you doing here?"

Portia and Brandon sprang from their seats and ran to greet Joshua. Brandon jumped into his arms and hugged him tightly around the neck. He came in and sat his bags inside the door.

Venice asked again, "Joshua, what are you doing here?"

Grinning, he said, "I was worried about you. I haven't heard from you since our conversation last week, so I decided to come check on you guys."

Venice put her arms around his neck, kissed him on the cheek, and said, "Thanks for coming."

"Uncle Josh, will you go swimming with me?"

"Of course, I will. Portia, you guys go get ready."

An excited Portia said, "Cool, Josh. Come on, Brandon, I'll race you."

Before they took off, Venice told Portia and Brandon to take Joshua's bags into the spare bedroom. Venice looped her arm inside his and walked him out onto the deck.

"Ah-h, man, this view is unbelievable, Niecy."

"Joshua, I'm so glad you're here. How long are you staying? A couple of days. You should have brought Cynthia and the baby."

Leaning against the rail, he said, "Maybe next time. So…what's up with you?"

"Not much."

"Oh, really? So, why do you have that glow?"

"I do not!"

"Yes, you do. Now tell me."

Venice turned, looked him in his eyes, and whispered, "I kissed him."

Folding his arms across his chest, he smiled. "Well?"

"Well, what?"

"Don't play with me, Niecy."

"Okay, okay. It was nice…real nice."

Joshua raised his eyebrows. "Did you tell him you loved him?"

"No!"

"Why not? It's true, isn't it, Niecy? Are you going to stand there and tell me you don't love him?"

Venice looked out over the blue waters in silence. She turned to him with tears in her eyes. "I can't do this, Joshua. It wouldn't be right. Anyway, he reminded me how much I hurt him."

"Niecy, love is love no matter what. Few people have the opportunity of finding love twice in a lifetime, Niecy. You're one of those few. Don't throw away your chance to be happy again."

"I hurt him pretty bad."

She concealed the fact that Craig had confessed that he still loved her. She wasn't ready to share that with him.

Joshua laughed and said, "Niecy, the kiss was a clue of his feelings. Where was the mystery woman when all of this was going on?"

Venice closed her eyes.

"He told me she was his ex and that they were just friends now. She's gone to Philadelphia."

Looking at her seriously, he asked, "Is that where he lives?"

"I guess."

Pulling her into his embrace, he said, "Don't you think love has to still be in his heart? Just talk to him, Okay?"

The tears rolled down her cheeks and Joshua wiped them away before embracing her. Brandon ran up to them.

"I'm ready, Uncle Josh."

Picking Brandon up, Joshua said, "Okay, my man. Let me go change and we'll hit the beach." Before leaving, he turned and said, "Just think about what I said, Niecy."

Venice was happy Joshua was there to keep Brandon and Portia company while she tried to sort out her feelings. She was afraid. Actually, she was scared to death. Losing Jarvis had caused her to shut down. Little did she know, Craig had also given up on love…until now.

S tanding under the hot steam of the shower, Craig mumbled, "These sleepless nights are starting to get old." He had tossed and turn yet another night. He still had no idea how he was going to approach the situation. However, kissing her was a start. Her response surprised even him. He really didn't expect her to let herself go like she did and could still feel the sensation of her body pressed against his. The memory caused a weakening in his knees. In the past, Venice had always been in his system. This time was no different. Bracing himself against the shower wall, he turned off the water and stepped out of the shower. He was going to do what Skeeter suggested: Just let things happen.

Joshua had taken Portia and Brandon fishing, giving Venice the day to herself. She hadn't heard from Craig and felt uncomfortable calling him. She had decided it would be best if they just remained friends. Her marriage to Jarvis was very public since he was a sports celebrity. For her to be in a new relationship so soon wouldn't look good. Her only choice was to tell him face-to-face why they shouldn't let things go any further. She would also rationalize the fact that things were moving too fast for her. Walking over to her closet, she quickly dressed in a lavender tank top with a matching mini-skirt. She adjusted the straps of her sandals, then checked her makeup. She left Joshua a note and headed for Craig's cottage feeling confident and in control.

When Craig opened the door, all her control and confidence flew out the window. She was speechless as her eyes scanned him from head to toe. He stood glistening with water and a towel wrapped around his waist. No matter how hard she tried to swallow, her throat was as dry as the desert.

"Craig, I-I'm sorry, I should have called."

Smiling, he said, "Hello, beautiful. Come on in."

Embarrassed, she stuttered, "This is a bad time for you. I'll come back later."

As she turned to walk away, he said, "Venice, if you leave, I promise I will dunk you every chance I get."

She couldn't help but giggle as he stepped back so she could enter. Venice tugged on her purse strap as she stood right inside the door. She could smell the manly scent of the soap he had just showered with. Nervousness overtook her as he approached and took her hand, leading her into the living room.

"Venice, make yourself at home. I'll be right out. If you want anything, help yourself."

She watched him retreat to his bedroom, then closed her eyes remembering every inch of muscle. Her stomach fluttered at the sensual memory of his well-defined physique pressed against her skin. It was hard to breathe, knowing he was naked in the next room. Walking into the kitchen, she opened some bottled water to remove the dryness from her throat. Within minutes, he was back dressed in a pair of shorts and T-shirt.

Damn!

Those eyes were burning into her like hot coals. He entered the kitchen and also pulled bottled water from the refrigerator. Venice leaned against the sink as he came and stood directly in front of her.

Damn! This woman is driving me crazy.

He took a sip of his water and said, "You look luscious in that outfit and you smell wonderful. To what pleasure do I owe this nice visit? I hope you're here to finally accept my dinner invitation?"

"Craig, I-I..."

Hold it together, Venice, you can do this. Tell him.

"Where are the kids?"

"They're with Joshua."

"Joshua's here? Good! You have no excuse for not having dinner with me tonight."

"Craig, I can't. Too much has happened between us."

Coming closer, he revealed, "I'm willing to risk my heart again with you, Venice. Can't you also chance loving again?"

She looked up into his serious eyes. "What I can't do is risk losing someone I love again. The timing is not right, Craig. Besides, this wouldn't be right."

Removing the bottled water from her hand, he pinned her between his body and the counter. She felt his sweet, warm breath against her cheek. Venice shivered as he lowered his face and planted a provocative kiss on the curve of her neck, then her cheek. He noticed her immediate response. Smiling, he continued his exploration on the other side of her neck and cheek. Venice's breathing became erratic as his sweet torture overpowered her.

With her palms pressed against his chest, she begged, "Craig, please."
His own breathing was becoming short and erratic.

"I'm trying, too, Sweetheart. I've missed you so much."

"Craig, didn't you hear a word I said?"

"No."

Seconds later, his lips descended upon her, covering hers greedily. Her arms reluctantly went around his neck as she pressed her body closer to his. She whimpered as he pulled her hips firmly against his desire. He reached up and covered her breast, stroking her swollen nipple with his thumb. Venice laid her head against his chest in silence. He ran his hand softly up and down her back as he tried to regain control.

"Venice? Venice? Sweetheart, are you okay?"

"I don't know what's happening to me."

"I feel the same way."

He took her by the hand and said, "Come...we need to talk."

Finally able to move, he led her back into the living room and sat on his large leather sofa. Not wanting to release her from his embrace, he continued to hold her close.

"Venice, I know you're afraid to open up, but so am I. When you married Jarvis, I was hurt and my world stopped revolving. You wanted to be friends, but there was no way I could be just a friend to you. I was too much in love with you and I still am. Sweetheart, if I had the opportunity to be around you while you were married to Jarvis, I don't think I could have been able to keep my hands off you. I didn't need that kind of temptation. I was raised to respect marriage, but I freaked when I lost you. I figured the best thing for me to do was stay away from any and all contact with you, so I decided to try and move on with my life.

"Venice, when Jarvis died, I wanted to be there for you, but I didn't want the media starting a scandal about your ex-lover consoling you. I couldn't take that kind of chance. I came to Detroit for the memorial service..."

A startled Venice asked, "You did?"

"Yes, and I ached because I couldn't take your pain away. I had to stay away. That's why I came here. After seeing you in so much pain, I needed seclusion to try and clear my head because I was in pain myself."

She asked softly, "Craig? Why haven't you gotten married?"

Without hesitation, he answered, "You weren't available."

Dropping her gaze, she asked, "But what about Melanie and I'm sure there were others?"

He cupped her face with his hands. "Melanie wasn't for me. Actually, I haven't met anyone I would consider spending my life with. I guess you can say I wasn't willing to put my heart out on a silver platter again. Look, Venice, you have been the only woman I have ever loved."

She raised up, looking into his sincere eyes. "Thank you. I thought you hated me and that's the reason you stayed away."

Stroking her cheek, he said, "That would never happen. I was definitely hurt and very bitter. Recently, I've been remembering how we were together. It was strong then and it's strong now."

She looked away holding back her tears.

"Craig?"

"Yes, Darling?"

"I have to admit, I felt pain and jealousy like I never felt before when I saw Melanie kiss you in the restaurant. My reaction surprised me and I didn't know how to handle it."

He smiled. "You saw that? Well, that kiss was our goodbye kiss. Seriously, we're only friends now, Venice. I had dated Melanie for a long time, but I knew nothing would ever come out of our relationship except a friendship."

She touched his hand. "I'm sorry, Craig."

"I'm not. I knew God had something better in store for me."

In a whisper, she said, "That's beautiful, Craig."

He turned her to face him. "I really am sorry about Jarvis. The short time I knew him, I admired him for his love and dedication to you. I realized that the day we had lunch together when Joshua was in the hospital. He was a good man."

The tears she had tried to hold back flowed from her eyes as he snuggled her closer.

"I can't be in a relationship with anyone, Craig. It's too soon."

"Have dinner with me tonight so we can talk about it. I know you're overwhelmed with seeing me again and I don't mean to come on so strong. You've been to hell and back and I want to be here for you and Brandon. What you've experienced, no one should have to deal with so young. I know death is inevitable for all of us, but to have a young child involved is making it harder to deal with, I'm sure."

Smiling, she looked up and leaned in to kiss him on the cheek.

"It does and Craig, everything you said is true. I'm overwhelmed and I have my moments of depression. I'm still trying to work through this void in my life and it's very hard. So hard that it makes me ill at times. I'm not ready to put that on anyone else right now. I need time and I don't know how much time it'll take for me to get better."

"I know it's going to be a long time before you feel like yourself again, but I want you to know that I'm here for you. Okay?"

"Thank you, Craig. Look, it's Joshua's first night here and I want to cook him a nice dinner. How about we have dinner tomorrow?"

"Tomorrow it is."

Standing, she asked, "Why don't you join us tonight?"

"Maybe another night. I don't want to intrude on Joshua's first night here."

"Okay, if you change your mind, come on over."

He walked her to the door. "I'll keep that in mind. Would you like me to walk you back to the cottage?"

"No, I'll be fine, thanks."

"See you tomorrow and tell everyone hello."

He took her hand into his and kissed the back of it, then watched her walk back down the beach. After closing the door, his phone rang.

"Hello?"

"Mr. Bennett, this is Katrina."

"Hello, Katrina. Is everything okay at the office?"

"Yes and I'm sorry to bother you, but there is a problem with the Garrett Design. Lamar is in Japan so he told me to contact you."

"What's wrong?"

"Lamar has booked me on a flight to bring the changes to you. I'm arriving in the morning on flight 178 at nine."

Sighing, he answered, "I'll pick you up and tell Lamar to call me ASAP."

"Will do, Mr. Bennett, and again, I'm sorry to disturb you."

"No problem, Katrina. I'll see you in the morning."

Hanging up the phone, Craig hoped that business would not interfere with his pleasure. Everything had to go smoothly with Venice.

Chapter Thirteen

Venice had no idea what to wear to dinner with Craig. She was nervous and excited all rolled up into one. After trying on several outfits, she settled on a long snug-fitting white chiffon skirt with a matching midriff. When she arrived at Craig's house for dinner she froze when a gorgeous, long-legged Amazon answered the door dressed in denim shorts and a purple tank top. She swung her honey-blonde microbraids back to reveal sea-green eyes.

"May I help you?"

Feeling awkward, Venice asked, "Is Craig in?"

Smiling devilishly, she answered, "Oh, he's in the shower, but he'll be right out. And you are?"

"The woman who owns my heart," Craig acknowledged as he crossed the room and kissed Venice proudly. Relief swept over her, but confusion still lingered. Who was this woman acting so comfortable with Craig?

"Venice, this is one of my designers, Katrina Simmons. Katrina, this is Venice Anderson."

Shaking hands, Katrina said, "Nice to meet you, Venice. You look familiar. Have we met before?"

"Not to my knowledge, but it is a small world."

"Indeed it is."

Venice was still somewhat shaken but was able to hold her ground and extend her hand to the woman. Craig was relaxed, standing in the center of them wearing black dress slacks and a white shirt. Wrapping his arm around Venice's small waist, he offered her a seat.

"Venice, Katrina had to fly down to discuss business. Unfortunately, we didn't finish until a few minutes ago. She won't be able to fly out until the morning so I hope you don't mind going out for dinner instead."

"No, I don't mind."

Venice could see the woman sizing her up as the competition. She'd seen that look in women's eyes before and Katrina wanted Craig.

He grabbed his keys and said, "Katrina, I'll be back later. Call Lamar and let him know everything's settled and that you will have the changes back in the office by tomorrow afternoon. Goodnight."

"Goodnight, Mr. Bennett. Nice meeting you, Venice."

"Likewise."

The walk down the boardwalk was quiet. The silence was finally broken when Venice asked, "Is Katrina staying in the cottage with you tonight?"

Smiling and wrapping his arm around her waist, he said, "She works for me…period."

Lowering her head, she said, "You didn't see what I saw."

He stopped and turned her to face him. "What did you see?"

"She wants you."

Smiling, he said, "Venice if I didn't see it with my own eyes, I would say you're jealous."

Venice looked away, too proud to admit her jealousy.

"I'm sorry, I have no right to pry."

Absorbing her comment, he realized she was serious.

"Venice, if Katrina has any ideas, she's wasting her time. I'm only interested in being with one woman…you." Pulling her closer, he said, "Before I say another word, I need to tell you that you look absolutely beautiful, and tomorrow morning Katrina will be out of our way."

Resting her head against his chest, she said, "I'm more worried about tonight." Pulling away, she stared him directly in the eyes. "Have you ever slept with her?"

Craig pulled her back into the confines of his arms. He needed her undivided attention. He couldn't believe she was worried about him being alone with Katrina. The worry and sincerity was there in her dark brown eyes.

"No, Venice, I have never and will never lay a hand on her. Okay?"

Wrapping her arms around his neck, she nuzzled her face into his neck. He held her securely and realized he couldn't risk messing things up, especially after covering so much territory with her.

"I'm so scared, Craig."

"Of what?"

"All these emotions that I'm feeling."

Running his hand up the length of her back, he said, "It's Okay, Sweetheart, and I understand. I'm scared, too. I'll get Katrina a hotel room for tonight. I couldn't bear the thought of you not trusting me."

She snuggled closer. "It's not you I distrust. Look, I'm sorry. I have no right to interfere, especially after telling you I can't have a relationship with you."

"Well, I hope I can change your mind about that and you have every right to express your concerns. She's out of there. When we get to the restaurant, I'll call and book her a hotel room for the night."

Back at the cottage, Katrina was furious. She knew it was Venice who had thrown a wrench in her plans to seduce Craig. Moments earlier, he called to let her know he had booked her a room at a nearby hotel and was sending a car to transport her there. As she threw her personal items into her suitcase, she screamed, "Where the hell did you come from?! Okay, if you want to play dirty, I can play dirty. It's on now, you bitch!"

Katrina continued to throw clothes into her suitcase. She was in deep thought because she was sure she had seen Venice somewhere before. Talking to herself, she said, "I might have my work cut out for me, but I'm not about to let you come here and take Craig away from me. Craig Bennett will be mine."

Returning back to Craig's cottage after dinner made Venice feel uneasy. Her womanly instincts told her Katrina wasn't too happy about getting kicked out of Craig's cottage. After calling Joshua to check on the kids, she took off her sandals and stood on the deck, looking out over the dark beach. Craig offered her a glass of wine and began to massage her tense shoulders. The minute his large hands came in contact with her bare shoulders, she felt her body react.

"Why are you so tense?"

"You make me tense."

"I was hoping you would be able to relax around me by now. It's not like we don't know each other."

"You make it hard, Bennett."

Taking a sip of wine, he said, "That's an understatement, Sweetheart."

Turning to face him, she studied his face. He was so calm, so relaxed.

"How can you be so relaxed when I feel like I'm falling apart?"

"Because I know who and what I want even though I'm scared as hell. Venice, you're stronger than you give yourself credit for and I know you're still in pain."

He sat the glass down and came closer.

"Venice, I've always been curious about something and I hope asking you will not upset you."

She turned to him. "What is it?"

Craig hesitated for a moment, then picked up his glass, taking a sip of wine.

"What was it about Jarvis that you loved so much?"

Venice hugged herself and looked out over the beach.

"Craig, a lot of people didn't understand Jarvis like I did. Some saw him as possessive, bossy and aggressive. They just didn't know him and I mean really know him. He was a beautiful and loving man. Since I lost him, I've been remembering the very reasons why I loved him so much. I loved Jarvis because he was in my blood. That may sound strange to some people, but that's how we affected each other."

Craig stood and listened to her in silence. She walked over to Craig and looked him straight in the eyes.

"Craig, Jarvis moved me intellectually, every time we debated an issue.

He moved me emotionally, every time he entered the room. He moved me spiritually the first time I heard him pray. He moved me physically, simply by running his hand across my cheek. Like I said, he was in my blood."

Craig now understood how Venice could love Jarvis the way she did. He had similar reasons for loving her. Her demeanor had suddenly changed. Her thick lashes hid her eyes as she dropped her head.

"Venice, are you okay? I didn't mean to upset you."

She looked up. "I'm not upset." Then in almost a whisper, she asked, "What do you want from me, Bennett?"

He ran his hands down her arms. "I've already told you."

Looking into his passionate brown eyes, she said, "Tell me again."

"I'd rather show you, Venice."

The kiss came urgently and her arms looped around his neck as he pulled her hard against his body. He groaned as her tongue darted against his. He grabbed her full hips and pulled her even tighter against the yearning of his body. She wiggled closer to fit her body to his which matched perfectly.

Breaking the kiss only for air, he unexpectedly whispered, "Marry me, Venice."

Stunned and speechless, she froze. Lifting her into his arms, he carried her into his bedroom and laid her upon his soft mattress. She closed her eyes as she savored the feel of his mouth on her lips, neck and roundness of her breasts. He looked into her eyes as he slowly removed the midriff to reveal cinnamon-peaked nipples. Slowing his movements, he covered one, then the other with his mouth, sucking and teasing each one with his tongue. She writhed beneath him wanting and needing more, so much more. She'd longed to feel this way again, but she had no idea it would be with him.

"Craig…"

"Yes, Sweetheart?"

"I-I…"

She couldn't speak. What he was doing felt so familiar, so right and yet so forbidden. Slowly, he trailed his kisses down her flat stomach, then lower as he removed her skirt. All that were left were scant, white-lace bikini panties, which were quickly discarded.

"My God, Venice."

She blushed and wondered what she had got herself into. It had been about six months since she had made love, and fear was starting to drift in on the moment. Removing his clothes, he covered her body with his, and said, "I love you so much, Venice."

"Craig...wait! Stop! I can't do this. I'm so sorry."

His dark gaze met hers, then Venice shyly turned away. He decided to give her some needed space as he rolled onto his side and faced her. Tears filled in her eyes as she tried to form words that would not come.

With his voice barely above a whisper, he said, "Baby, it's okay. Maybe this wasn't such a good idea. I shouldn't have pressured you."

She opened her eyes as he stroked his cheek lovingly with the palm of her hand.

"You didn't pressure me, Bennett, and it's not your fault. But, for some reason it feels like I'm cheating on Jarvis."

Kissing her palm, he said, "You don't have to explain anything to me. I should have been more sensitive to the situation." At last, they hugged tightly and lay in each other's arms. They stayed this way in silence for over an hour until they both fell asleep.

CHAPTER Fourteen

The sound of the crashing waves roused Venice from sleep. She opened her eyes to find Craig still asleep with his arms wrapped securely around her. For some reason, she felt different… relaxed. As she reached up to touch his face, his eyelids slowly opened as her hand was retreating. They stared at each other as their hearts pounded with desire. It was almost unbearable to hold her warm nude body against his without wanting to bury himself deep inside her. For now, he would have to chill.

He pushed auburn strands of hair from her warm eyes, and said, "Well, Sweetheart, I guess I'd better get you home."

Nuzzling her face into his neck, she pressed her body closer, not really wanting to leave. She leaned up and kissed his earlobe. Before he knew it, he sucked in a sharp breath. His body couldn't deny what his heart was feeling. He always had a hard time controlling himself anytime he was near her. Tonight was no different.

"Venice?"

"Yes?"

"I think you'd better stop that. I'm a weak man right now. It's taking all my strength to keep from making love to you."

"Sorry."

He searched her eyes to tell him what she wanted…what to do. She smiled and raised her head to kiss him. He met her halfway and covered her lips fully with his. The familiar sounds coming from her told him all he needed to know. She did love him and he would never let her go again. He tenderly kissed the corners of her mouth before mating his tongue to hers once more. His body once again became rigid against the softness of hers.

"Mercy, woman!"

"I'm sorry. We'd better go."

"Sweetheart, don't apologize for the way you make me respond."

She lowered her eyelids and blushed as she gently touched him there. She felt him shudder against her hand and softly said, "I'm not teasing you, Craig. I'm just remembering how we were together and how you felt. I'm still so scared. I want to make love to you. I just can't. I'm still so mixed up."

He covered her hand with his. "I understand. We'll just have to take it one day at a time because you're not going to get rid of me."

They laughed as she slowly removed her hand.

He faced her and whispered, "Spend the night with me."

She looked into his passionate eyes. "I don't want Brandon to wake up and worry because I'm not there. He won't understand."

Craig raised up on his elbow. "Even though I need a cold shower, I'll make you a deal. Come try out this Jacuzzi with me and I promise to have you home before Brandon wakes up."

"You've got yourself a deal, Bennett."

Pulling her from the tangled sheets of his bed, he led her to his large tub and began to fill it with warm soothing water. Settling between his legs, she lay back against his chest and said, "This reminds me of your Jacuzzi at your house. I used to love getting into that tub. You really did spoil me."

He ran his hands through her thick mane. "I hope I get the chance to spoil you again."

She turned her head and kissed him on his neck. "Thanks for understanding, Craig."

"Venice?"

"Yes."

"Close your eyes."

"Why?"

"Just close your eyes, woman."

She shut them and could tell he had leaned over.

"You can open them now."

She screamed in shock. In front of her was a huge platinum diamond ring.

"I take it you like it?"

The tears ran down her face like a small river as she took the small velvet box in her hands in awe.

Solemnly, he said, "You know I'm weak to your tears."

"Craig…this…is…so…"

He massaged her shoulders. "Since I asked you to marry me, I wanted to make it official."

"When did you get this? It's beautiful!"

He kissed her on the cheek. "About seven years ago."

Venice's body froze and she turned to face him.

"Seven years ago?"

He wrapped his arms around her. "Do you remember our last night together when I was packing for Japan?"

Lowering her eyes, she answered, "Yes."

"Remember the cufflinks you sat on that were sitting on my bed after we made love?"

Venice thought for a moment, then said, "How could I forget? You're not saying this is what I sat on."

"That's exactly what I'm saying. I had planned to ask you to marry me on New Year's Eve, but Jarvis beat me to you. That night when you came over, I had it out to put in my safety deposit box. I almost passed out when you sat on it. I was afraid you were going to open it."

Venice turned, straddling his body. "Why me?"

"What do you mean?"

She met his tender gaze. "How did you know I was the one for you?"

He smiled. "It's kind of like how you felt about Jarvis. Somehow I knew the precise moment I laid eyes on you. You affected me like no other woman had in the past. It was kind of scary and there were times it made me physically sick just thinking about it."

She punched him on the shoulder. "Thanks a lot, Bennett. "

He laughed. "I'm not saying you made me sick, Sweetheart. I'm saying you entered my soul. No one had ever done that before you, or has since you."

Caressing her thighs, he said, "That night when you came over to break up with me, I freaked. I'm sure you remember I was kind of crazed. I thought about showing you the ring but that would've been playing dirty and I don't play dirty. I just couldn't stand the thought of you walking out on what we had. I never got over it either. Nanna had told me a while back that my soul mate would come to me in an usual way. I figured they were making a lot of noise and, at the time, I wasn't listening to anybody. I guess I should have had a little more faith. I would've never wanted you to come back to me this way. A lot of people are hurt because of it and it's hard for me to be happy about it. You know?"

She touched his cheek. "You don't have any reason to feel guilty. This is all so strange for me. You know, us meeting again like we did, but I guess it's not for us to second-guess."

Craig didn't answer or look at her. It was obvious at this moment he was feeling the guilt. She studied his face and said, "Bennett?"

"Yes?"

"I don't know where we're headed, but I do know that I don't want to hurt you again. That's why I don't think a relationship would be in our best interest right now."

"I appreciate your concern. That really means a lot to me but I'm really nervous about us."

She leaned down and kissed him on the cheek. "You don't act nervous to me."

He smiled. "I've become pretty good at hiding my fears and pain over the years."

She settled back between his legs and leaned against his chest. "So you've been holding on to this ring all these years? Why?"

In almost a whisper, he said, "I just couldn't part with it. I take it everywhere I go. I didn't have the heart to return it. I guess I was holding onto a part of you."

Venice looked down at her left hand where the wedding rings Jarvis gave her rested. Craig sensed her sadness and said, "Venice, I just hope that somewhere in the very near future you will be able to let me make you and Brandon happy again. I love you. Only you."

She dropped her head. "Craig, I want to be able to move on with my life, but it still hurts."

He pulled her against his chest. "Take it with you and hopefully I'll get to slide it on your finger one day. Okay?"

She closed her eyes. "Everything about you feels so right, but I have to consider Brandon and my in-laws and how this will affect them."

He kissed the top of her head.

"I understand Venice and just so you'll know, I'm not going anywhere. Understood?"

"I understand and thank you."

She kissed the lips of the man she knew in her heart at that moment loved her mind, body and soul. She also accepted the fact that she still loved him, too.

The soak in the Jacuzzi did wonders for her tense muscles. They finally dressed and headed out the door to beat the rising sun. When Venice entered the house, Joshua was in the kitchen making coffee.

"What are you doing up so early, Joshua?"

"I guess my body's still on the baby's clock."

Craig grinned. "Good to see you, Joshua."

Joshua extended his hand to shake Craig's, then pulled him into a brotherly embrace. Teasing, Joshua asked, "Craig, what the hell you doing bringing my girl home so late?"

Laughing, Craig said, "I tried to keep her longer, but she wanted to get home before Brandon woke up."

Joshua poured three cups of coffee and admitted, "Brandon and Portia haven't long gone to bed."

Venice looked at him. "Joshua! What have you three been doing all night?"

He leaned over the bar, grinning. "I should be asking you two the same question."

Craig shoved his hands in his pocket and smiled with guilt. Venice blushed and said, "You don't ask people questions like that. You are so nosey, Joshua."

"So is either one of you going to tell me?"

Craig took a sip of his coffee. When he lowered the cup, he answered, "I plead the fifth. But, if you really want to know, we…"

Venice punched him in the arm, saying, "Craig!"

Joshua looked Venice in the eyes. "I'm happy for you two."

Venice said, "All you need to know is we had a good time."

He rinsed out his cup. "I bet you did. Well, I'm going to try and turn in again. Craig, it's good seeing you and I hope to see a lot more of you. Maybe we can go deep-sea fishing before I leave."

"It's good seeing you again, too, Joshua. I'm sorry I've been away so long, but it couldn't be helped."

Joshua came over to him and embraced him again.

"Let the past stay in the past. I'll hook up with you later. Goodnight or good morning, however you want to look at it. See you in a few hours, Niecy."

"Goodnight, Josh, and thanks for watching the kids."

Closing the door to his bedroom, Joshua dropped to his knees.

"Thank you, Jesus!"

Craig finished his coffee, then said, "I'd better get home."

Venice went to him and wrapped her arms around his waist. He returned the embrace and they just held each other for a moment in silence. The rhythm of their hearts beating against each other filled in the words. Venice finally stared up into his eyes.

"I wish you could stay longer."

"So do I, but you need to get some rest."

Venice ran her hands up his chest until her arms were around his neck. He smiled down at the woman he cherished. He embraced her and placed a series of passionate kisses upon her lips.

"Craig?"

"Yes."

"I'm about to start making noise."

He smiled and said, "Well, you better get me out that door fast because in a minute, we're gonna wake up this whole house and I'm not going to care."

They laughed together.

"Will you come back later and hang out with us?"

"You bet."

Venice looped her arm in his and walked him to the door. After one last kiss, she said, "Call when you get back to the cottage."

"I will. Sweet dreams and I love you."

As he walked out to his car, Venice said, "Craig?"

"Yes?"

"I never stopped loving you either and I'm going to talk to Brandon and my in-laws and see how they would feel about us being together."

He strolled back up to her, embraced her, then asked, "Are you saying 'yes' to my proposal?"

"I'm saying maybe."

His heart leapt in his chest as he swung her up in his arms.

"Thank you, Venice. Just knowing you love me makes me the happiest man on earth."

Skeeter looked at the clock, then answered the phone angrily.

"Yeah!"

"Could I speak to Winston Carter III?"

Skeeter yelled, "What the hell do you want, Craig? And why are you using my real name?"

Craig yelled back, "Wake up, Dog!"

"Man! Do you know what time it is? What the hell is wrong with you calling me this time of morning?"

Craig laughed. "I got my woman back, Skeeter!"

"Who?"

"Quit playing, Skeeter. You know I'm talking about Venice."

Skeeter grumbled. "I know. That's great, Craig, I'm happy for you. Now can I please go back to sleep? I have to be in court in a couple of hours."

Laughing, Craig apologized, saying, "Sorry, man, I just wanted you to be the first to know. I'll call you later."

Skeeter rubbed his eyes. "Craig...seriously...I'm really happy for you. Hit me back later."

"Thanks, Winston. Goodbye."

"I'm gonna whip your ass when I see you, Craig. Goodbye."

Craig hung up, feeling like he was on cloud nine.

Chapter Fifteen

Back in Philly, Katrina fumbled through her day, still upset that Venice ruined her plan of seduction. Francine, her friend and Craig's assistant, asked, "What's got you all wound up?"

Pulling on a braid, she said, "Don't repeat this, but our dear boss has got himself a real girlfriend."

Francine checked her makeup and said, "You have got to be mistaken. I mean, Craig dated several women, but the only woman he's ever spent time with was that Melanie woman and he got rid of her, thank God."

Katrina, dressed in a designer green suit to accent her eyes, leaned back in her chair. "Exactly! I knew Melanie was no threat. It was obvious he didn't really care for her. So where did this one come from? They acted like they've been dating for a long time, too. He said she was the woman who owned his heart and he was kissing on her and everything. I swear I've seen her somewhere before. I just hope I can remember where. It's only a matter of time, then look out."

Francine turned back to her computer. "Girl, you need to give it up. From what you're describing, it's serious between him and whomever she is and don't forget, he's warned you before about coming on to him."

Katrina turned Francine's chair around. "The games have just begun, Girlfriend. You'll see."

Francine, a single mother of a seven-year-old daughter, said, "Okay, Kat, your ass is going to be out of a job and you know you can't afford to get fired with your expensive taste."

"Getting Craig Bennett is worth losing a job over. He's fine as hell and let's not forget, he has a fat bank account. Anyway, after I get him, I won't have to worry about working anymore."

Francine got up and poured a cup a coffee.

"You'd bet not let Lamar hear you talking that foolishness. You know they're boys."

Spinning around in her chair, Katrina said, "I'm not worried about Lamar. Craig will be mine just as soon as I get Ms. Thang out of the picture."

"Whatever, Kat. I'm going to lunch. You coming?"

"Yeah, I'm right behind you."

The last week of vacation was coming to a close. Joshua volunteered to accompany Brandon and Portia back home. They had missed a few weeks of school and needed to get back. This allowed Venice and Craig some time alone. Their departure was bittersweet for Venice. She hadn't been separated from Brandon since Jarvis had passed away and was a little worried about his response.

"Brandon, Momma will be home in a few days, so you make sure you mind your Uncle Josh and your grandparents. Okay?"

Hugging her, he said, "I will, Momma, and don't forget to call me every night."

"I will, Lil' Man."

"Okay, Momma. Bye, Mr. Craig. I had fun playing with you. I hope we get to play again real soon."

He squatted down eye-level with Brandon and gave him a heartfelt hug.

"Me, too, Brandon. Portia, it's been a pleasure getting to know you. You're going to break some hearts in a few years."

Blushing, she said, "Thanks, Mr. Craig."

They hugged and he gave her a tender kiss on the cheek.

Brandon tugged on Craig's shirt and motioned for him to lean down so he could whisper in his ear.

"Mr. Craig, take care of my Momma while I'm gone. Okay?"

Craig smiled. "I'll take real good care of her, Brandon. I promise."

Venice asked, "What are you two whispering about?"

"Nothing, Momma."

Joshua said, "Okay, troops, let's get on this plane before they take off without us."

He pulled Venice into a tight embrace and whispered, "Follow your heart, Niecy. Don't fight it. It had to be a higher power to bring you two together after all these years. Don't let love slip away, okay? I love you, Girl."

She looked into his eyes.

"I'll try not to disappoint you, Joshua. As usual, I don't know what I would do without you. You have come to my rescue so many times. Thank you and I love you so much."

Smiling, he kissed her and said, "I know. Now let me get on this plane before it leaves me. I'll call the minute we get to the house. Have fun."

"I'll try."

He went over and hugged Craig. "Take care of my precious cargo. She's irreplaceable."

Embracing her from behind, Craig answered, "I will, Joshua, and thanks for everything."

"No problem. See you later."

They stayed until the plane took off, then walked hand-in-hand in silence to Craig's waiting car.

The next three days, they pretty much stayed in seclusion bringing each other up-to-date on their lives. Venice confided in Craig that she hadn't stepped foot back into her home in Michigan since the tragedy. He offered to accompany her there, but she declined. She told him she needed to do it alone. There would be so many memories and emotions to deal with. Not wanting to hurt his feelings, she offered to fly to Philly for a visit after she took care of her personal business. He was excited because he had planned to offer just that to her. Jarvis' father and her dad, along with Bryan and Joshua, were going to be with her when she went to the house to remove Jarvis' personal items. She explained that handling his clothes was going to be the hardest of all. Stroking her cheek, he told her he wished he could help remove her pain. Holding his hand to her cheek, she thanked him for his compassion.

"Are you planning on keeping the house?"

Lying in his arms, she said, "I don't think I want to. It'll be too difficult to live there after what happened. It's the only home Brandon knows, but he can adjust to a new house."

Kissing her forehead, he said, "Everything will work out, Sweetheart."

"I guess. We have a will, but I haven't had the heart or nerve to meet with the lawyer. My father-in-law told me Jarvis had his revised so I have no idea what's in it. I really don't care. I'm not going to be able to look at his car or anything else. It still hurts so much. I do plan to keep the Mercedes he gave me for my birthday. I couldn't bear to part with it."

Venice grew quiet for a moment.

Craig broke the silence by telling Venice about his offices in Philly and Japan and about commuting back and forth. He described his home in Philly, which seemed warm and cozy and kid-friendly. He talked about his sister and her husband, J.T., and their children. Venice remembered Bernice was very nice to her when she was dating Craig years ago. She asked about his grandmother who was still a shop-a-holic.

On one or more occasion, his grandmother told him that things would work out for him when he was mourning over his breakup with Venice. Craig thought she was crazy, but after running into Venice, he now believed in his dear grandmother. He didn't know if she had strong faith or if she was psychic or something. Venice asked about his handsome and womanizing friend, Skeeter. He told her that Skeeter was an attorney and still running a harem of women. Laughing, he admitted that Skeeter would eventually meet his match and Venice agreed.

Before they knew it, their vacation together had come to a close and it was time for them to go their separate ways. They had shared and given a lot to each over the last few days and it was hard to say goodbye. Craig had to leave for Japan in two days and, as expected, he asked Venice to join him, but she couldn't. As they stood in the airport, he hugged her and told her that he was going to miss her. She put her arms around his neck, closed her eyes and kissed his lips. First it was tender, but as he held her to him, it became obvious they didn't plan on breaking the kiss anytime soon. Neither cared that they were in a crowded airport as finally they came up for air.

Venice asked, "Do you mind if I wear your ring on my right hand for now?"

"I don't care where you wear it, Sweetheart. Just remember I'm the only one who will put it on your left hand. Got it?"

Smiling and lying her head against his chest, she said, "Yes, Sir!"

She reached inside her purse, pulled out the velvet box, and slid the diamond on her right hand.

"What do you think?"

"It would look a lot better on the other hand but that'll have to do for now."

Smiling, Venice received her boarding call.

"I'll call you when I get home."

Kissing her forehead, he said, "If you don't, I'll hunt you down and dunk you."

She laughed. Giving him one last passionate kiss, she said, "I do love you, Bennett."

"I know. I love you, too, and Venice, for the record, I'll understand if you turn my proposal down. You've been through a lot and I don't want to make things worse for you and your family."

"Craig, you're amazing. Whatever I decide, I'm happy to have you in my life again. It's a blessing and I'll cherish you always. Well, I'd better get on the plane. I'll talk to you later. Goodbye."

"Thanks. Goodbye and have a safe flight."

"You, too."

He watched her walk down the long hallway, drinking in the sight of her shapely figure. She had gained a few pounds since he'd last seen her, but it was all in the right places. The short red dress hugged her curves lovingly. He growled as two other male passengers followed, discussing her sexy figure with one another.

Chapter Sixteen

Twenty-four hours back in Philly, he was unable to concentrate. Hearing Venice's voice over the phone made it seem like she was thousands of miles away. She had called the night before to let him know she'd made it home safely. In a couple of days, she would be thousands of miles away from him. Japan was going to be lonelier than ever this trip. Venice was back in his life.

About that time, Lamar burst into his office, "Look what the cat drug in!"

Smiling, Craig responded with, "Hello, Lamar."

"You look like you're well-rested and what is that on your face?"

Craig went to the mirror on the wall, searching for something on his face. "What are you talking about, Lamar? I don't see anything."

Lamar crossed the room and put his arm on his friend and partner's shoulders. "The smile, my friend. Who put that smile on your face?"

Craig shoved him. "Go 'head on, man. You play too much."

Sitting back down in the leather chair opposite Craig's desk, he asked again, "Who is she? You know you're going to eventually tell me anyway, so you might at well tell me now. Only a woman can put that kind of smile on your face and I know it wasn't Melanie."

Craig picked up some mail on his desk. "Don't you have some work to do?"

Rising from the chair, Lamar headed for the door.

"I know when I'm getting thrown out. I'll be in my office when you're ready to tell me who she is."

"Get out of here, Lamar."

Before he closed the door, Craig said, "Lamar."

"Yeah?"

"Thanks for covering for me. I really appreciate it."

"No problem, partner. See you later."

Lamar smiled and closed the door.

Craig shoved his hands in his pockets and turned to look out over the Philadelphia skyline. At that very moment, the love of his life was in Michigan sifting through what was left of the life she had with Jarvis. He knew the pain she would endure could be a setback for them, but he prayed the love she had for him would outweigh her pain.

It only took about an hour for Jarvis' lawyer to go over the details of his will. Her dad, her father-in-law, her oldest brothers and Joshua were there as Venice sat numb to the words she had just heard. Jarvis had planned everything out in detail. He left the decision up to Venice whether to keep or sell the house and cars. He requested two full scholarships be set up at their high school for underprivileged students with high grade-point averages. He left substantial monetary gifts to his family and closest friends and particular charities. He requested Venice fund a youth and educational center in the inner-city of their hometown. The bulk of the estate was left to Venice and Brandon. Being well taken care of financially was an understatement. When the last sentence was read, the lawyer informed the family that Jarvis had made a video tape for Venice's eyes only. She looked up in shock, not knowing if she would be able to handle looking at his face one more time.

"Daddy, I can't do it."

"Yes, you can, baby. Hopefully you can go on with your life after hearing what he has to say. We'll be right outside."

As the men filed out the room, each gave her a hug and kiss for strength.

She stared into the eyes of the strong men as they left her behind the closed door.

After the lawyer set up the tape, he gave Venice the privacy she needed. It seemed like hours went by before the tape began to play and Jarvis' image appeared on the screen.

Hey, Babe,

I am so sorry I had to hide my illness from you. Please don't be angry with me. I loved you and our family too much to burden you with my pain. My main concern was to make sure we lived our lives as normal as possible, even to the end. When I was diagnosed, I couldn't bear seeing you hurt and stressed out because of it. That's why I didn't tell you. I spent my last days loving you and Brandon without any distractions. I wanted so much to grow old with you, but I guess God had a different plan for me. I don't want you to lose your faith, causing you to question God's motive. Accept and go on with your life and cherish the many years of sweet memories we had together. I know by now you have shed many tears and experienced some heartache. I'm going to need you to be strong for our son. He's going to need you because he may not understand what has happened. Don't be afraid to open your heart and love again. I mean that with all my heart. We'll see each other again one day, but for now I need you to be strong for our son and, most importantly, for you. I'll love you always, Niecy. You will always be the light in my life. Goodbye, Sweetheart.

When the tape finished, Venice sat there feeling a slight burden lifted, but emotionally drained. Somehow this tape had helped give her some closure to her magical life with Jarvis. Her blouse was wet with tears she wasn't even aware had fallen until she felt the moisture on her face. She took a moment to compose herself. She clutched the tape to her heart, and joined her family in the reception area.

Over the next few days, Venice worked with her family to finalize the last details so she could try to move on with her life. Several times, she wanted to call Craig to see how things were going with him, but declined. She really did miss his smile. He had given her his number in Japan, but she decided not to disturb him. She realized he probably had a lot of work to catch up on after returning from vacation. In a few days, he would be back in the States, and she would stay true to her word and pay him a visit.

Venice was unsure what to do next in her life. The movers had arrived to pick up the furniture for transport back to her hometown for storage. Brandon didn't seem to let the move depress him. Being at home with his cousins kept him preoccupied, plus he loved the school there. Bryan and Sinclair had their hands full with Brandon and their five-year-old, Bryan Jr. Sinclair swore it seemed as if ten grown men were playing in the house when it was only the two. Crimson and Portia hung out together in the mall and at school activities. They had always been close and both were beginning to get interested in boys. Bryan almost lost his mind when he caught fifteen-year-old Crimson kissing a boy in his rec room one night. He blew his temper, then threw the boy out, threatening his life. It was a week before Crimson would speak to him. Bryan said he was getting too old for this. He had been through this fire with Venice in her teen days. However, Crimson and Venice were like night and day. Venice, being his sister, was open and confided in him about boys, etc… His daughter, Crimson, was different. She was sneaky…too sneaky. He knew he would have to be harder on Crimson.

Back in her hometown, Venice and her entourage were greeted warmly by her family and Jarvis' family. Venice, for some reason, had always been partial to the men in the family. Her mom never felt left out because she kept a separate and special relationship with her. Mrs. Taylor was very outspoken and always told you what was on her mind. Venice got her strength and courage from the men; love and understanding from the women. When they arrived at Bryan's house, Brandon ran out and jumped into his mother's arms.

"Momma! You're home!"

"I sure am and look what I brought you."

"Wow!"

Venice handed her son a new train to add to his collection. She also made sure she had plenty of gifts for the other kids. Her mom said, "I know you all are hungry. Dinner is ready so come on and eat."

The men followed Mrs. Taylor and the rest of the family into the dining room. Venice sat on the plush sofa in the living room in silence. Mrs. Anderson asked, "Honey, are you okay?"

"I will be, Mom. Thanks for asking."

She sat down next to Venice. "I know what you had to do was difficult, baby, but things will get better. You'll see."

Venice closed her eyes and prayed that she was right. As Mrs. Anderson rose to go into the dining room, Venice reached for her hand and said, "Mom, can I talk to you for a minute?"

She sat back down next to Venice. "Sure, baby. What is it?"

Tears stung Venice's eyes as she swallowed, trying to form words. Mrs. Anderson asked again, "Venice, what's wrong? Whatever it is, it can't be that bad. Is it about Brandon?"

"No, Ma'am. I don't know how to say it."

"Venice, just say it."

Venice raised her right hand. "Have you noticed this ring on my finger?"

She reached for Venice's hand and studied the ring closer. "No, but it's a beautiful ring. Does what you want to tell me have to do with this ring?"

The tears rolled down her cheeks and Venice rested her hands in her lap in silence. Her voice, sounding barely above a whisper, said, "Mom, I ran into an old friend in Ocho Rios. He's the one who gave me this ring. The engagement ring he was planning on giving me seven years ago."

Mrs. Anderson now understood where the conversation was headed.

"Venice, how do you feel about this young man?"

"I don't know, Mom. It just doesn't seem right. I don't want to disrespect Jarvis."

Reaching over to hold Venice's hand, she asked, "Is this the young man you were dating in college?"

A stunned Venice said, "You knew about that?"

Smiling, she said, "Jarvis came to me looking like a sick puppy one day and told me all about him. I think in a strange way, he admired him. Jarvis had gotten so comfortable with your relationship that he didn't think anyone could shake it up. Men take us for granted sometimes so they need something to shake them up every now and then. I have to shake his dad up sometimes, even now. Anyway, Jarvis was so worried he was going to lose you. He even pointed the young man out to me at the wedding. What I'm trying to say, Venice, is we never doubted your love for our son. I just wished we had left you two alone when you first married. Anyway, that's water under the bridge now. What I'm trying to say is, you and Brandon were the best things that could have happened to him. People should quit trying to figure out love and just accept it. If you love this man, and you know he loves you, then quit worrying about appearances. If you're worried about us, don't. You are a beautiful, young woman and after what you've been through, you deserve some happiness in your life. If that young man can give you happiness and wants to marry you, then you have our blessings. Portia told us all about him. She said he was very nice and that he really cared for you and Brandon. Venice, Jarvis would want you to be happy. You have to believe that, Sweetheart. Okay?"

Venice couldn't believe Jarvis told his mom about Craig. She was beginning to feel a little relieved.

"I don't know what to do, Mom. I mean, I don't know how Brandon will take another man in our lives."

"Venice, you're not trying to replace Jarvis. You've loved this man once and, for some reason, you two have found each other again. That has to speak for itself, doesn't it?"

Still holding hands, Venice said, "He wants me to marry him, but I think it's too soon. Jarvis hasn't been gone long and I don't want the media causing a scandal and hurting Brandon or embarrassing the family."

Mrs. Anderson leaned over and kissed Venice on the cheek.

"Quit worrying about all that stuff. There's no law on how long you have to wait before you can fall in love again after losing someone to death. Life is too short to waste on such trivial things. By the way, what's this young man's name?"

"Craig Bennett."

"Well, from what I've heard from Portia, he sounds right for you. We would love to meet him."

"Mom?"

"Yes."

"Thank you."

"You're welcome, Venice. Now come get some dinner."

Seventeen

Craig seemed preoccupied as he walked through the construction site. As he unrolled the building plans, his cell phone rang.

"Hello?"

"Mr. Bennett, I have your grandmother on the line."

"Thanks, Virginia. Put her through."

He waited and heard singing on the line. He smiled and said, "Nanna?"

"Oh, Craig! How are you, Son?"

"I'm fine. Is anything wrong?"

Laughing, she said, "Lawd, no, Child! I was just checking in with you to see how things are going and when you're coming home."

"Uh-huh. Well, Nanna, I should be home in a couple of days."

"Good."

Nanna then said, "So, when are you going to get a life, boy?"

"What do you mean, Nanna?"

"You know what I mean…settle down, have a family. You're not getting any younger, you know."

Craig smiled. "Don't worry about me, Nanna. I'll be okay."

"Craig, I just want you to be happy. I hate you're up there in that big house all by yourself. It's time you settled down."

He smiled again. "Thanks for being concerned about my love life, Nanna, but I'm doing just fine."

"You can't be if you're all alone."

"I won't be alone. Skeeter's moving to Philly, remember?"

"I'm not talking about Skeeter and you know it."

Craig turned to see his foreman motioning for him to come over. He laughed. "Nanna, I love you, but I have to get back to work. I'll call you when I get back to Philly. Tell everyone hello."

"I will and have a safe flight. Son…I love you, too. Goodbye."

Craig hung up and shook his head. Nanna had tried, on more than one occasion, to fix him up with different women. Needless to say, none of them ever touched him the way one particular woman had. He couldn't wait to see the expression on her face when he told her about Venice.

It had been a long day. Craig was happy to get back to his home away from home. It was a large penthouse in an affluent part of the city. He leased it for himself and Lamar to use when they traveled there on business. After eating dinner at a nearby restaurant, he retired to his bedroom and thought about calling Venice. The time difference made it difficult, so he decided to wait until he got back to the States to call. As he turned on the TV, his telephone rang.

"Hello, Craig."

Craig sighed. "Hello, Melanie. What can I do for you?"

"You don't have to be so punchy. I was just calling to see if you've had a change of heart."

Craig rubbed his head. "Melanie, I meant what I said. Look, I'm tired and it's been a long day. I'm sure we'll run into each other around Philly, but as far as us being anything except friends…forget it. Okay?"

Melanie sighed. "Oh, well, you can't hate a girl for trying. Have a safe trip back."

"Thanks, Melanie. I'll talk to you later."

The next few days went by like all the others. Venice kept Sierra for Joshua and Cynthia so they could have some quality time alone. One day, while she was hanging out with Joshua in the park, she said, "Josh, I need to get back to work. I'm getting restless."

"Nobody's stopping you but you. It's been six months."

"I don't have anywhere to live. I need to look for a house."

"Here?"

"Why not?"

He just stared at her.

"What's going on with you and Craig?"

She turned away. "He's in Japan right now."

"Didn't you say something about going to visit him when you got your business taken care of?"

"He hasn't called."

He reached over and turned her around.

"Don't you think the man is trying to give you some space? He knew what you had to do in Michigan. I'm sure he was trying not to crowd you, Niecy. Call the man and go visit him like you said you were. He's probably worried about you. It would help if you reassured him a little. You do love him, right?"

Throwing a piece of bread to the ducks, she sighed.

"Very much, but he wants to get married."

"And the problem is?"

"I'm scared and I think it's too soon. I had a nice talk with Mom the other day about Craig. I showed her the ring and told her everything. You know I had no idea Jarvis had confided in her about Craig. She said I had their blessings if I wanted to marry him."

"Then why aren't you on a plane to Philly?"

"I don't know, Joshua."

He threw some more bread at the ducks. "It's about time you listened to someone. You wouldn't listen to me. If you love the man, Niecy, then you should be with him. Everybody seems to be okay with it except you."

"I have one more person to clear it with…Brandon."

"Good luck, Sis."

"I'll need it. Thanks."

Later that night after bath time with Brandon, they cuddled in the bed together. Venice felt like this time was better than any to talk to him about Craig.

"Momma, will you read me a story?"

Smiling, she said, "I sure will, Lil' Man, but say your prayers first."

Brandon got down on his knees and began his prayers. It always took a while because he had to bless each and every member of their family... Joshua included. He always ended asking God to take care of his dad and to let him know that he and his momma loved and missed him very much. The prayer was tender, sincere, and from the heart. Venice was so happy Jarvis gave her a son and would do anything to protect him.

As he climbed into bed, Venice asked, "Brandon, what do you think about Mr. Craig?"

Brandon's face lit up. "He's fun and nice, just like my daddy. I had fun when we were on the beach and he took me fishing, remember?"

Venice ran her hand over his short wavy hair.

"Yes, Sweetie, I remember."

She watched him as he thumbed through books, trying to decide which story he wanted her to read. Venice felt chills running through her body as she watched him. He looked so much like Jarvis it shook her emotionally just to look him in the eyes.

Handing her the story he had selected, he said, "This one, Momma."

"Good choice."

Brandon scooted over closer to her, getting ready for his story. When she didn't start reading, he said, "I'm ready, Momma."

"I'm sorry, Baby. I've got something on my mind that I want to talk to you about."

Come on, Venice. You can do this. Take a deep breath and just say it. Go!

She turned to him. "Brandon, how would you feel if Momma and Mr. Craig got married?"

There, I did it.

She held her breath as Brandon searched her eyes seriously.

"Will he be my daddy?"

"Sweetie, Craig is not trying to replace your daddy. Jarvis will always be your dad, no matter what. But, if you ever need anything or want to talk, he will be there for you just like your daddy was."

"He likes you, Momma."

Surprised, she asked, "How do you know that?"

"He told me when we went fishing. He said he loved you and he told me that I was just as special."

Venice's heart began to ache. How could she not see the instant affection between Brandon and Craig? Every time he came around, Brandon practically dived into his arms.

Venice was finally able to form words and said, "He's right, Lil' Man. You are as special as they come. He cares a lot about you. So what do you think?"

Brandon hugged his momma. "Yeah, Momma!"

"Are you sure?"

Brandon grabbed his book, settling under the covers. "I'm sure. You smile when he's around. When you smile, Momma, I know you're happy. You haven't smiled much since Daddy went to heaven."

Venice embraced him tightly. "I love you, Lil' Man. I'm so glad you're my son."

"Me, too, Momma. Now can you *pleeease* read me a story?"

She kissed him and said, "You bet."

Craig threw his luggage on the floor and immediately checked his messages. It took several minutes of listening to Lamar, his grandmother, and Bernice before he got to the important message.

Craig, I hope you had a safe flight. It's about 6:30 p.m. on Wednesday evening and I wanted to see if it was still ok if I came for a visit. Just let me know. Bryan's friend, Larry said he would fly me up. I'll be at Bryan's house at 555-0608. I miss you. Hope to hear from you soon. Goodbye.

Craig was so excited that he failed to jot down the number so he had to play the message again. He looked at his watch and realized it was about eleven thirty p.m. her time. Taking the chance she would be awake, he dialed the number.

A deep, masculine voice answered, "Hello?"

"Bryan?"

"This is Bryan. Who's calling?"

"Craig…Craig Bennett."

"What's up, Craig?! It's good to hear your voice. It's been a long time."

"Yeah, too long. Look, I'm sorry I…"

"Don't worry about it, man. Venice explained everything to me. I can't say I blame you. I know how much you care about her."

Craig ran his hand over his hair.

"Well, Bryan, care is not a strong enough word to describe how I feel about your sister."

Bryan lay back on his sofa, smiled, and said, "Somehow I knew that. Do you want to talk to her?"

"Is she up?"

"Yep, she still has a hard time sleeping. She's been up with me reviewing recruits almost every night. She went upstairs to check on the kids. Hold on a second. Venice! Telephone!"

Venice was pouring some soda in the kitchen when she picked up the extension and hollered, "I got it! Hello?"

"Good evening."

Grinning, she answered, "Good evening to you, Bennett. I take it you got my message."

"I sure did. How fast can you get here or do I need to come get you?"

Giggling like a schoolgirl, she said, "I can be there tomorrow afternoon, if that would be convenient."

"You mean you can't come tonight?"

Laughing, she said, "What am I going to do with you, Bennett?"

In a devilish whisper, he said, "I'm sure I can help you come up with a few things."

A tingle ran from her head to her toes when he hinted at sensual promises.

"Venice?"

"Uh-huh?"

"Did everything go okay? I mean are you all right?"

Solemnly, she played with the telephone cord. "It was bittersweet. I felt like my heart was ripped out all over again, but having the guys there with me helped a lot. Things are going to be so different. I still feel so lost."

Craig pushed his hands into fists, feeling useless because he wasn't there to console her.

"I understand, but we still have each other. Remember? Get some rest, we'll talk tomorrow. It's supposed to snow so bring plenty of warm clothes and call me in the morning and let me know what time you'll arrive. I want to have dinner waiting for you when you get here."

Feeling a little mischievous, she asked, "Bennett, are you planning on cooking for me?"

"Sweetheart, I plan to do all sorts of delicious things for you."

Her legs turned to jelly remembering how Craig Bennett could back up every word he said.

"Well, I guess I'd better pack and get some rest."

Fighting for strength, he said, "Yes, Darling. Make sure you get plenty of rest because we're going to be very busy once you get here. I've missed you."

"I missed you, too, Bennett. I'll see you tomorrow. Goodnight."

Craig put the phone back on the cradle, feeling his heart swell with love. He also noticed that it had been weeks since he'd had chest pains. The anxiety he was feeling had subsided since he and Venice had gotten back together.

The next morning, Venice called and gave Craig her flight information. He went into his office to take care of a few details before cutting his day short. His employees noticed his cheerful attitude but had no idea what was the source of it. However, they definitely wanted to know. Craig glanced at his watch and called for his assistant to come into his office.

"Francine, reschedule my meeting with Greg Baxter until next week. That should clear my book until Monday."

She recorded the notes in her planner, then asked, "Craig, is everything okay? You seem preoccupied."

He twirled around in his chair. "Couldn't be better, but thanks for your concern."

Francine sat down in the soft leather chair and said, "Okay, Craig, don't forget the Architects Banquet next month."

"I won't forget. Black tie, correct?"

She closed her appointment book. "Yes, and hopefully this year I will be ordering tickets for you and a date."

Smiling, he said, "Francine, you worry too much about my love life. I'll be just fine."

"You have to get out more, Craig. I'm starting to worry about you. All work and no play will make Craig a dull boy."

Laughing, he said, "I do date, Francine."

She put her hands on her hips. "If you're talking about that Melanie woman, that was a waste of your time."

He stood, smiling. "I take it you don't like her very much."

"Let's just say I don't think she's the one for you. She's so superficial and fake."

Craig walked around to Francine, kissed her on the cheek, and said, "I appreciate your honesty and I'm taking the rest of the day off."

She turned with a stunned look on her face. "Is everything okay?"

He grabbed his coat and briefcase. "Just fine, Francine. I won't be in tomorrow either. I've already spoken with Lamar so, unless it's an emergency, I don't want to be disturbed. Okay?"

With a grin on her face, she said, "Okay, Craig, and have a nice day off."

Putting on his jacket, he said, "I plan to. See you Monday."

"Goodbye, Craig."

CHAPTER Eighteen

A few hours later, Francine and Katrina sat in a restaurant a few blocks from the office.

"Francine, why is he taking the day off tomorrow?"

"Kat, he didn't tell me and I didn't ask. The man's my boss. I wasn't going to ask him about his personal life."

"Well, did he mention anything about going out of town?"

"I said he didn't tell me but he was smiling when I asked him if I will be ordering two tickets for the banquet this year."

Katrina sat back in her seat.

"Something's up and I know that woman is involved. He's been a different person. He's not focused on business as much as he was before he took that vacation. Yeah, something's up."

Francine took a sip of tea.

"Katrina, if the man wanted you he would have made some type of move by now. You need to face the fact that he's not interested in an affair with you."

Katrina took a bite of her lunch.

"I bet he's going somewhere to be with her. I might just have to pay Craig Bennett a surprise visit to his house tomorrow to see for myself."

Francine dropped her fork.

"You're not going to stop, are you, Kat? You're going to make that man have you arrested for stalking or, better yet, fire you."

"Whatever! I have got to find out if he's meeting up with that...that woman!"

Craig stood at the door waiting for Venice to step off the plane. Seeing her again made him excited and nervous. He still had to make sure he didn't push herBespecially since she'd just gotten back from leaving her life with Jarvis behind her. She entered the doorway and smiled. Craig's heart skipped a beat as he watched her walk down the steps. He scanned her body from head to toe. The faded jeans she wore hugged every delicious curve she owned, and the tangerine-colored sweater didn't hide the fullness of her breasts either. His mouth became dry and his groin hardened from the mere sight of her. He starved to hold her in his arms and kiss every inch of her soft brown skin.

He mumbled, "Mercy."

As they approached, Craig extended his hand to Larry, thanking him for flying Venice to Philly. Venice stood next to Larry, waiting to greet her man...*her man.* She liked the sound of it, but was marrying Craig still the right thing to do? Larry kissed Venice on the cheek and told her he would pick her up when she was ready. Craig offered to pay for Larry's hotel room for the night, but he declined, saying he had a good friend in Philly he was staying with. After Larry left, Venice walked up and lay her head against his chest and closed her eyes. He immediately embraced her.

"Let's go home before the snow gets any worst."

Looking up into his loving eyes, she said, "Sounds good to me, but may I have a kiss first?"

He smiled and lowered his head. Pulling him in closer, she let the warmth of his body ignite hers. She moaned and he groaned, then he broke away in order to breathe.

"Let's go, Sweetheart."

Venice gasped when she laid eyes upon Craig's beautiful two-story home. It was lovelier than she could have imagined.

Pulling into the long driveway, he asked, "So, what do you think?"

"I think it's gorgeous! Did you do the landscaping yourself?"

Proudly, Craig said, "Yeah, but J.T. and Skeeter helped. Wait until you see the backyard. My niece and nephew love it. I made sure I had plenty of yard for them to play in."

He pulled his SUV into the garage next to a champagne-colored Lexus. Venice asked, "Is this yours, too?"

"Yes, but I don't drive it much. You're welcome to it anytime you want."

About that time, Katrina, who had been slouched down in her car for about an hour, raised up.

"Just what I suspected. That wench is in town. We'll see about this."

Upset that Venice was with Craig, she drove off spinning her wheels in the snow.

Venice opened her door and climbed out before he could come around the truck.

He said, "I see you're still an independent woman. I was going to open the door for you."

Grinning, she answered, "I'm sorry. Do you want me to get back in?"

"You're a comedian, too."

Turning away, she grabbed one of her bags and proceeded to the kitchen door. He shook his head and followed so he could unlock it. Before dinner, Craig gave her the full tour of his home. Each room was decorated in different themes from Japanese and African art to a New Orleans jazz/ Mardi Gras theme. Her favorite was his family room, where a baby-grand piano rested in the corner. A large marble fireplace was the centerpiece. Large, soft leather furniture in an ivory color gave the room a warm feeling. As she stood there enjoying the fire, she remembered that Craig had a beautiful voice. So good that, at one time, she suggested for him to pursue a singing career. Hopefully, she would get to hear his angelic voice before she left next week. Upstairs, he showed her each of his four bedrooms. One was definitely a child's room. He had mentioned his niece and nephew visited often. The last room was his master bedroom and it was breathtaking. The large poster bed was decorated in gold and ivory. The carpet was plush ivory with a beautiful gold area rug on top. At the foot of his bed was a padded cedar chest. As she walked around admiring the room, she noticed he had a fireplace also.

"Well, Venice, do you think you'll be comfortable here?"

She turned to him.

"Craig, this is absolutely beautiful. These colors go wonderful together. I see you still have your African statues. This black, ivory and gold is definitely you."

He folded his arms and leaned against the doorway.

"I'm glad you approve."

She turned. "Without a doubt. Will you build a fire tonight?"

Coming to stand beside her, he said, "Whatever you want. I want you to be as comfortable as possible. The bathroom's over here."

He took her hand and as they walked inside, just the size of it over-whelmed her. The decor of the bathroom matched the bedroom as well. She couldn't wait to get into that huge garden tub. She noticed Craig still loved having candles and greenery around it.

"Bennett, you are such a romantic. Don't ever change."

He embraced her from behind, resting his chin on her head, and said, "As long as I have you, Sweetheart, I plan on staying a romantic."

She turned with tears in her eyes, wrapping her arms around his neck. "Thank you."

He held her tightly to his chest. "No, thank you for letting me back into your heart. I will love you forever."

He kissed her with all the passion in his soul, causing her to feel his inflamed love. She pulled him closer as his warm lips danced over hers, giving her the very essence of him. No man could kiss a woman like this and not love her with all his soul. At that moment, she knew she could no longer deny what everyone had been telling her. This love…their love was destined to be.

After releasing for a short breath, she said, "Craig Alexander Bennett, I do love you."

His eyes became misty.

"It seems I've waited a lifetime to hear you say those words."

Resting her head against his chest, she whispered, "Would tomorrow be too soon to get married?"

Caressing her back, he said, "Sweetheart, please don't joke about that."

She raised her eyes to meet his gaze as she removed the ring from her right hand and handed it to him.

"You're serious, aren't you?"

"I love you, Craig, and if you don't hurry up and put that ring on my left hand, I'm going to dunk you."

His trembling hand slid the ring onto her left hand.

"I love you, Venice, and if you want a wedding tomorrow, we'll have a wedding tomorrow."

Picking her up into his arms, she wrapped her legs around his waist.

"That's what I want, but can we start the honeymoon now?"

He moaned and carried her to his large bed and covered her body while he buried his face into her neck. His warm breath was sweet as he planted kisses upon her lips and neck, then lower as he unbuttoned her sweater. Removing it and her lacy bra was no task for his eager hands. He couldn't wait to caress the softness of his woman's body, who by tomorrow would be his wife. She saw the desire in his eyes as he unsnapped her jeans and slid them over her shapely hips. He gasped when he looked upon the skimpy undergarments covering her womanhood. He didn't know how much more he could take as she wiggled her hips when he removed them. Drinking in the sight of her was like looking at a mirage.

Unbelievable.

She raised upon her knees and pulled his shirt over his head, then dipped her head to run her tongue over his chest. His body jerked as she played in the silky hair covering his chest. Her hands inched lower until she found what she sought. Squeezing ever so gently, he groaned in her ear. Moments later, he stood before her fully aroused. She pulled him to her and kissed him fully on the lips, moaning his name.

"Craig, make love to me."

Brushing her hair away from her eyes, he said, "I'll be right back."

She wrapped her legs around his waist. "You don't have to protect me, Sweetheart. Nothing would make me happier than having your baby. Brandon has been talking about having a brother or sister and by tomorrow, I will be your wife anyway. Right?"

"Sweetheart, you having my baby would be the answer to all my prayers, but when our baby is conceived, you will be my wife. I hope you understand."

She smiled. "I understand, Babe, and you're right."

"So are you ready to get this party started?"

Giggling, she said, "Cross my heart."

He responded by kissing her lips and the curve of her neck greedily. She arched into his strength as his hands explored her starving body.

He caressed one breast while attending to the other, then inching lower. She gripped the sheets as his warm lips found her moist heat and he tasted her.

She screamed, "Bennett!"

The rest was incoherent moans and groans as he feasted on her woman-hood. His assault was taking her to heights she never felt possible. Yielding to him completely left her begging him to fill her very essence. After several moments of pleasuring her, he applied protection, then entered her body, inflaming them into an inferno far beyond any passion they'd shared before. Never in his life had he given, taken, and shared like he did with her. His thrusts were demanding and needy, as he united their bodies in a fiery passion. Her nails dug into his back, but he felt only pleasure. He filled her tight space, stretching her to accommodate the length of him. She also felt nothing but sheer pleasure as he devoured her mouth, drowning out her whimpers of passion when he quickened his pace. The emotions overtook them both as he moved in and out of her body first slow, then urgently. Arching to meet his demand was overwhelming as he whispered his love into her ears.

She moaned louder as he pushed his body deeper and confessed breath-lessly, "I love you, Venice." Another thrust and he said, "This is what you do to me." One last thrust and he moaned, "Venice! Oh, God, help me!"

She screamed out a variation of emotions in Spanish as she shuddered beneath him. Their coming together came sudden and hard. Unable to control his body any longer, he willed his body to finally give in to her explosive passion.

Silence engulfed the room moments later as she massaged his back.

"Craig, I can't wait for tomorrow."

Kissing her flat stomach, he said, "Me, either, and after dinner, I plan to love you all night long."

Still exhausted, he rolled over, pulling her atop his body. Feeling his strong hands caressing her body, she said, "In that case, I'm starving. Let's hurry up and eat."

"Don't move, Venice. Dinner is coming to you. I don't want you to leave my bed."

She smiled and watched him dress in some sweat pants and a T-shirt. "Whatever you say." He bent down and kissed her. "I'll be right back."

He did as he said and brought the entire dinner to the bedroom. They enjoyed the meal he had prepared before getting back to their loving.

As they finished their dinner, his telephone rang. He leaned over and asked, "Who could this be? Hello?"

"Craig Alexander Bennett! Why didn't you tell me you and Venice were back together? I can't believe you would keep something like that from me. If it wasn't for your sister, I wouldn't know what was going on. You let me go on and on about you settling down when I called you in Japan. You could have told me then. You know how much I love that girl. How is she? Where is she? Is she okay? It's so sad about her husband. Well, don't just sit there…say something!"

Craig put his hand over the mouthpiece. "It's Nanna and we're busted. Bernice told her about us."

Venice smiled.

"You should have already told her, Bennett. She's gonna whip your butt when she sees you."

He could hear Nanna calling his name. He finally said, "Nanna, I'm here. I was going to tell you as soon as I had a chance."

"Well, what were you waiting on? Where is she? "ll Bernice told me was that you ran into each other and were seeing each other again."

Craig ran his hand up Venice's thigh caressing it lovingly.

"Nanna, Venice is here with me now so I'll fill you in on everything later."

"Let me at least say hello to the child for one second."

"I love you, Nanna, but your seconds are more like hours. Venice just got here today so you two can talk tomorrow. Okay?"

Nanna paused. "Well…okay, but I want to know everything. Tell her I'll call back tomorrow, and Son?"

"Yes, Nanna?"

"She's the one. I love you. Goodbye."

"I love you, too, Nanna. Goodbye."

He smiled at Venice and hung up the phone.

"Are you in trouble?"

He pulled her into his lap. "Never when you're concerned. She said she will call you tomorrow."

Hours later, Craig lay awake and listened to the clock strike three. He and Venice had spent countless hours making love and christening his garden tub. Not able to stay awake any longer, Venice succumbed to sleep snuggled securely in Craig's arms. However, he was too wound up to sleep. Tomorrow he would finally make her his wife and become a father to her son. His prayers had been answered in more ways than one. He decided he would announce his marriage to employees later. He hoped Venice would agree to a nice reception for their families and friends in the future. For now, he hoped to enjoy their bliss in private. He kissed her forehead and closed his eyes, finally drifting into a deep, satisfying sleep.

CHAPTER Nineteen

The phone ringing at six was unwelcome since he had just fallen asleep a few hours earlier. Venice was still sleeping comfortably against the warmth of his body. Craig growled at the thought of someone at his office disobeying his request to be left alone. Then he thought it might be a call from either of their families.

The phone was already on the third ring when he found the strength to pick up the receiver. In a groggy voice, he answered, "Hello?"

"Man, I'm sorry to call you at home, but…"

Craig whispered firmly, "No, Lamar! Whatever it is, no!"

Lamar pleaded, "You know I wouldn't disturb you if it wasn't important."

Craig sighed and put his hand over his face. "What is it, Lamar?"

Lamar went on to explain the crisis. Craig, half-listening, leaned down and kissed Venice's cheek. She stirred slightly, inching closer against his body reminding him that he was all male. He was brought back to reality when he heard the words, "fly out today."

"What did you say, Lamar?"

"Were you listening to me at all? I said Garrett wants us in Chicago by noon. He said the designs are still missing some detail."

Craig sat up angrily in the bed and whispered, "Forget it, Lamar. I have plans today that I cannot break. You can handle Garrett."

"He wants us both or he's going with someone else. You know we can't let Garrett get away from us. This project alone is worth one-point-two million. Whatever you have planned, I'm sure you can reschedule."

Craig closed his eyes and slowly got out of the bed, careful not to wake Venice. He strolled into the bathroom and continued to listen to Lamar run their accounts down for him. Craig sat at the vanity.

"Man, you just don't know what you're asking me to give up."

"Well, a woman must be involved. Is she worth it, man?"

Feeling a headache coming on, he rubbed his temples.

"She's priceless compared to that million-dollar deal. I would never put my company or anything else ahead of her."

"Damn! I have to meet the woman who has reeled in Craig Bennett."

Craig sighed. "Between you and me…we're getting married today. So flying out to Chicago is out."

"Married!"

"I mean it, Lamar! No one is to know about us yet."

Laughing, Lamar asked, "Where did you find a fiancée? 1-900-get-a-wife?"

"You're real funny, Lamar. She's the only woman I have ever loved. We lost track of each other and now we're together again and I'm not going to mess this up."

Sensing Craig's annoyance, he asked, "You're for real, aren't you? I'm sorry, man. Congratulations! But, I'm sure she'll understand if you explain it to her. Anyway, we should be back by tonight. Enjoy each other over the weekend and get married on Monday."

Craig stood up. "I'll call you later, Lamar."

Lamar responded, "I'll pick you up at eight thirty. Our plane leaves at nine thirty and Craig, I'm really happy for you. I can't wait to kiss the bride."

"Goodbye, Lamar."

Craig turned and saw Venice standing in the doorway wearing only his T-shirt. With her arms resting provocatively on her hips, his body instantly responded.

Smiling, he said, "See what you do to me?"

Coming over to him, she sat in his lap. "So I noticed. You affect me the same way, but Bennett, I know you're not about to blow off a million-dollar deal because of little ol' me?"

He caressed her thigh. "How much did you hear?"

Taking his hand in hers, she said, ""ll the important stuff. Now go ahead and take your shower so I can get you dressed."

He didn't want to move. Sadly, he said, "Venice, I would never put off marrying you."

"You will today and I'm going to help you. We've waited years, so what's a few more days? Now get in the shower. Time is wasting. I'll be here when you get back."

He pulled her against him.

"That's why I love you. You're everything I've ever wanted. Now, the only way I'm getting in that shower is if you come with me."

She embraced him and said, "I'll follow you anywhere, Bennett."

They entered the shower and steamed up more than just the mirrors.

Katrina sat in her doctor's office waiting for her name to be called. Getting bored, she picked up several magazines and thumbed through them. She had skimmed through about all of them when another patient returned one to the table.

"Sports…oh well, it's better than nothing."

Turning the pages, her eyes froze as she came across a picture and article. The article was on the MVP of the previous Super Bowl and titled: "Triumph and Tragedy of a Superstar." In the picture was a joyous Jarvis and Venice holding Brandon on the field after the Super Bowl. She gasped and hollered, "So that's where I know you from! I knew I had seen you somewhere before." She read the article taking in all the details of their storybook romance and the unexpected illness that claimed his life. Finishing the article, she smiled and put the magazine in her purse.

"Well, well, well. Poor little Venice. I'm going to have to pay you a little visit. You're not about to get your hands on Craig Bennett."

Moments later, Katrina's name was called to enter the doctor's office. Smiling, she rose and said, "It's going to be a great day after all."

Straightening Craig's tie, Venice said, "Be still, Bennett. Your ride will be here any minute."

He grabbed her around the waist.

"We should be headed downtown to get married."

She finished straightening his tie and said, "You just hurry up and get back tonight."

He grazed his mouth against hers, teasing and biting her lips gently. She pulled him to her and deepened the kiss, which sent a wave of heat over her.

"Whew! On second thought, Bennett, blow off that meeting!"

He looked startled.

"Just kidding, but I am tempted to hold you hostage."

Kissing her lips again, he said, "You're tempting and I love you."

Running her hands up his chest, she lay against him and closed her eyes just as the doorbell rang.

Craig gritted his teeth and said, "Damn! Lamar's here!"

Pulling him by the hand, they headed downstairs.

She said, "Quit pouting, Craig. The sooner you leave, the sooner you'll get back."

"I guess. Come on so I can introduce you to Lamar."

He scanned her body up and down. "I wish you would've chosen a different outfit."

"What's wrong with this outfit? I'm just getting ready to workout."

He scanned her again, taking in the sight of her in the spandex feeling possessive. He didn't want Lamar or any man to see her body. He kissed her on the forehead.

"You look beautiful, Sweetheart. Don't mind me. I'm just being over-protective."

Moments later, Craig opened the door and invited Lamar inside. He introduced them.

"Nice to meet you. I've heard great things about you."

Craig saw Lamar staring at Venice. "Lamar, close your mouth."

Lamar complied, still stunned by the beauty standing in front of him.

"Thank you and I'm sorry for staring. Craig didn't tell me you were gorgeous."

Smiling she said, "Thank you."

Craig rolled his eyes. "Cut it out, Lamar."

Lamar hugged and kissed Venice.

"Congratulations and I can see my man has great taste. You are as charming as you are beautiful."

Blushing, she said, "I feel like I'm the lucky one. He's one of a kind."

Lamar grinned.

"That he is. Well, I guess we'd better get going and I'm sorry to interrupt your plans."

Venice shook his hand again. "I've waited a long time for this, man. A few more days won't hurt."

Lamar said, "You are special. Watch your back, Craig."

"I told you, Lamar, you play too much. Now get away from her."

Venice playfully slapped Craig on the hand. "Craig, be nice."

Lamar shoved his hands into his pockets.

"Craig, I'll meet you in the car. Nice meeting you again, Venice."

Looping her arm with Craig's, she said, "Likewise and you make sure you bring him back in one piece."

Lamar turned to respond but before he could, Craig slammed the door in his face. "That wasn't nice!"

"He'll live. That's what he gets for spoiling our wedding day."

Venice hugged him tighter. "It's not his fault, Babe. Now kiss me."

He pulled her into the safety of his arms and touched his lips to hers with heat and desire. She moaned as she pressed her body closer to the full length of his. Breaking the kiss wasn't easy as he brushed her cheek and neck with sprinkles of kisses.

Breathless, she said, "Get out of here, Bennett, before I change my mind."

Opening the door, he said, "Are you sure you're going to be okay until I get back?"

"Yes, now go!"

"Keep my bed warm until I get back."

"I will, drive safely."

Hours later, after her workout, Venice showered and curled up with a book, then the telephone rung.

"Hello?"

"This is Katrina Simmons from Mr. Bennett's office. Is this the house-keeper?"

Venice immediately remembered Katrina. She gripped the phone.

"No, Katrina, this is Venice. Craig's friend you met in Ocho Rios."

Faking her shock, she said, "Oh! Venice! How nice of you to visit our little city. Well, I called because I have some papers that Craig needs to look over before Monday. I know he's out of town with Lamar, so I thought I would drop them off on my way home, if that would be okay with you."

Venice hesitated, knowing this woman definitely wanted Craig.

"Well, if he needs them, I'm sure it will be okay. What time should I expect you?"

Grinning on the other end of the phone, she said, "I'll be there in about an hour."

"Then I guess I'll see you then. Goodbye, Katrina."

They hung up mutually. Katrina spun around in her chair.

"Let's get ready to rumble!!"

Katrina was definitely prompt. The doorbell rang and Venice was dressed in a pair of leggings and one of Craig's dress shirts. She answered the door.

"Hello, Katrina. Come in."

Katrina fingered her braids. "Thank you. It sure is cold out there."

"I'm sure it is. May I take your coat?"

"Thank you, Venice."

They stood in the foyer, taking in the sight of each other; each wondering what the other could be thinking. Katrina's short navy suit fit her to perfection. She was very attractive on the outside, but something about her disposition assured Venice that she was no challenge.

She finally asked, "Katrina, could I get you something warm to drink?"

"You know I think I could use a cup of hot chocolate. Thank you."

They retreated into the kitchen where Katrina took a seat on a bar stool.

As Venice fixed the cocoa, Katrina asked, "So how long have you known Mr. Bennett?"

Making eye contact, Venice answered, "About seven years."

Venice handed her the cup, which she immediately sat down.

"Seven years?"

Katrina looked at every detail of Venice's face. She saw her natural beauty and became jealous that Craig chose Venice instead of her.

"I met Craig in college."

Taking a sip of the cocoa, Katrina said, "I see." She almost dropped her cocoa when she noticed the huge diamond on Venice's finger. "Wow! That's a beautiful ring."

Venice's face heated knowing she had forgotten to take the ring off. She didn't want to ruin their plan of keeping their marriage a secret for a while.

"Thank you."

Venice could tell she wanted to quiz her, but she wasn't about to put their business in the street. She looked at her watch and said, "Katrina, I'm kind of busy, so if you have those papers for Craig, I would like to get back to what I was doing."

I bet you do. I know he better not have given you that ring...

Ready to push the issue, Katrina said, "You know, Venice, I knew I had seen you somewhere before. Then just the other day I picked up a sports magazine and there you were. You, your husband and son."

Venice's eyes widened, not knowing where the conversation was headed.

"What's your point, Katrina?"

She got up from the bar stool, came over and stood directly in front of Venice. Pointing her finger, she said, "Don't you think I'm going to let you walk in here and take Craig Bennett away from me. I've been working on him for three years. Now that I'm close to having him, you show up trying to ruin everything."

Venice took a step toward her.

"First of all, I don't have to take what I already have. Secondly, if it takes you years to get a man, you don't deserve one. Now get out of this house!"

Standing toe-to-toe, Katrina said, "Not so fast. I have connections and if you don't want to see your name in print as the whore you are, you'd better pack up and go back where you came from. I'm sure it wouldn't be hard to get the public to believe that you were having an affair behind your poor dying husband's back. Your sweet little boy wouldn't be able to hold his head up, now would he?"

The breath left Venice's body as she realized Katrina might be able to do what she was threatening.

Katrina yelled, "If you don't break off whatever it is you have with Craig and leave before he returns, expect your family to see you like they've never seen you before! The way technology is today, it wasn't hard to put your face on the body of another woman who happens to be in a compromising position with two men. It wouldn't be hard to convince Craig or the public that the picture was taken before your husband died. And if you tell Craig about our little conversation, the information with the picture automatically goes to print."

Venice stared at her, then grabbed her by the arm and pulled her to the front door. She opened it and yelled, "You skank bitch! If you do anything to hurt or embarrass my son, my family, or Craig, you'll regret it the rest of your life. Now get the hell out of here and don't you ever come back!"

She shoved Katrina so hard, she fell face first into the snow. After throwing her coat out to her, Katrina hollered, "I'm going to get you for this!"

"I'll be waiting, Katrina!"

Venice slammed the door closed and immediately covered her face and burst into tears. How could this woman be so mean and spiteful as to hurt a little boy? Venice was not about to let this wench turn her life upside down. What better revenge it would be than to marry Craig first thing

Monday morning. Even though she knew the tabloids would only print lies, it still could cause Brandon and the Andersons a lot of undeserved pain. She had to think this through before Craig got back tonight. A lot of people could get hurt, but she had to do what was best for the family.

Chapter Twenty

It was two a.m. when Lamar dropped Craig off. The meeting took a lot longer than he anticipated. Anxious to hold Venice in his arms, he took the stairs two at a time until he reached his bedroom. The room was dark, but as he went farther into the room, he realized she wasn't there. His heart sank with worry as he turned on a nearby lamp. On the bed was a note and on top of it was the diamond ring he had placed on her finger earlier.

Sweetheart, after you left today, I had a long time to think about what we were about to do. I came to the conclusion that things are moving too fast for me. I'm not saying I don't want to marry you. I'm saying I can't marry you right now. There are some things that I have to work out, so please trust me. For now, I don't want you to call or try to see me. I think it would be best for both of us. Please trust in our love.

I love you forever,
Venice

He twirled the ring on his finger, then crumbled the paper and threw it across the room, and yelled, "Damn it, Venice!"

Picking up the phone, he called Joshua. He didn't care about the time. All he cared about was knowing where Venice was.

A sleepy voice answered, "Hello?"

"Joshua, this is Craig. Have you seen Venice?"

"I thought she was with you."

"She was. We were supposed to get married today but I had an unexpected meeting to attend in Chicago this morning. Things were perfect when I left, but when I got back I found her engagement ring and a note telling me she couldn't marry me lying on the bed. What's going on with her?"

"I don't know, Craig. Don't worry, I'll find her."

Craig hung up the phone, not knowing what to do next.

Don't do this to me again, Venice.

Joshua called Craig Saturday afternoon and informed Craig that Venice had not returned home. He didn't want to worry her family so he didn't pry any further questioning them. He tried to comfort Craig saying, "Look Craig, Venice could be anywhere. Maybe she just needed some time alone. I'm sure she'll call to talk to Brandon. I'll get back with you later. Try not to worry and get some rest. You sound like hell so I know you look like hell."

"Yeah, Josh. That's because I'm going through hell."

Sighing, Joshua said, "I know. I'll talk to you later and try to get some sleep."

When Joshua hung up the phone, he immediately placed another call.

"Manley?"

"Yes?"

"This is Joshua. I have another job for you. Pack your bags. I need you to go to Philly. Something has happened to make Venice run away from Craig and I need to know what."

"No problem, Joshua. I'm packing as we speak. Fill me in."

Venice hadn't been able to get a good night's sleep since she'd left Craig. Her heart was aching and she needed to feel complete again.

Climbing out of bed, she smelled bacon and coffee. After a hot shower, she dressed and headed downstairs.

"Good morning, Venice."

"Good morning. How are my sweet little angels?"

Venice hugged Craig's niece, Samantha, and nephew, Thomas James. They had fallen in love with each other over the last two days. Venice told Bernice that Craig had to go out of town and she thought this would be a good opportunity for them to catch up on things. Bernice knew Craig was often called out of town, so she didn't give her visit much thought. A few days earlier, she spoke to her brother who announced that Venice was in fact there for a visit. Venice had successfully fooled Bernice and her husband, J.T., and this would be the last place Craig would think to look for her. This would give her ample time to try and find out who Katrina Simmons was and how to stop her.

Venice spent her days watching the kids while J.T. and Bernice slept. Both were still on the night shift, Bernice as a nurse; J.T. as a plant engineer at a local company. Normally, Craig's grandmother kept the kids during the day, but was thankful for a break since Venice was in town. The kids did spend their nights with their great grandmother, so that routine was not broken. Venice took them to the movies, the park and the mall. These six-year-olds were loving and energetic and it made her long to hug her own son.

The nights were long and lonely. She missed everything about Craig, his scent, his touch and his smile. Venice spent hours on the computer and the phone but to no avail. She still had not found out much information on where Katrina Simmons came from. Feeling exhausted and defeated, she sank to the floor of her room and sobbed.

Joshua. I need to talk to someone.

Picking up the phone, she called her best friend.

"Joshua?"

"Niecy, where the hell are you?! Craig is worried sick and so am I! Why would you just up and leave and not tell anyone what's wrong or where you are?"

Venice tried to form words, but it hurt too much. Finally, she said, "Joshua, I'm being blackmailed."

"By who? Why?"

Wiping her eyes, she said, "One of Craig's female employees is in love with him. She wants me out of the picture or she'll go to the tabloids and tell them I cheated on Jarvis when he was sick."

Joshua gripped the phone in anger and braced himself against the kitchen counter. He tensed, knowing someone was causing Venice serious pain. He calmed himself.

"Who's doing this, Niecy?"

"Some woman named Katrina Simmons."

"Where are you?"

Climbing up off the floor, she said, "I'm visiting Craig's sister and her family. I told them Craig had to go out of town so there's no reason for them to call him to check."

"What if he calls them? Don't you think you need to at least call and let him know you're okay?"

Running her hands through her hair, she answered, "That's a chance I'm going to have to take. I couldn't come home because that would be the first place he looked. Look, Josh, I can't talk to him right now. I hurt him again and I need to work this out and make things right. I'll be damned if I let that woman hurt my son or my family."

Solemnly, he said, "I understand, Niecy, but please think about calling Craig. He deserves to at least know you're okay."

"I don't know, Josh. I've been trying to find out any information I can so I could stop her, but I can't."

Josh stared out his window into the dark night. "Do you want me to help?"

"Not right now. I need to do this myself. Thanks anyway."

"Niecy, can I at least tell Craig you called and that you're okay? I won't tell him anything else, but that you're trying to work some things out. I really wish you would reconsider and call him."

Venice dabbed her tearful eyes with a tissue. "You can call him. I can't handle it right now."

"Okay, but think about what I said. He's a good man. Give me the number where you're staying."

"Okay."

Craig was back to his old grouchy self and the chest pains had returned. His smile was gone. So were the sounds of him whistling as he walked through the office. Francine noticed the turnaround in his behavior and was concerned. He walked past her desk without so much as a "good morning." She looked up at him and asked, "Craig, is anything wrong?"

"No, Francine, and if you don't mind, hold all my calls until further notice."

He didn't look back as he closed the door of his office. Minutes later, his telephone rang. Angrily, he picked it up and yelled, "Francine, I told you I didn't want to be disturbed!"

Francine was startled by Craig's demeanor.

"I'm sorry, Craig, but a gentleman by the name of Joshua insisted on talking to you."

He dropped his head in disgust.

"I'm sorry, Francine. Please put the call through."

After notifying Craig that Venice was okay, Joshua hung up and placed a call to Manley saying, "Katrina Simmons. Find out all the information you can on her and her background. She works for Bennett and Fletcher Design Company. I needed it yesterday."

Manley jotted down the information and said, "I'm on it, Joshua. I'll get back to you ASAP."

"I knew you would. Thanks."

After his conversation with Joshua, Craig felt a little better. Knowing Venice was safe calmed him just a little bit. He was still upset that he didn't know the reason behind her abrupt departure or where she was. After not being able to accomplish any work, he called Lamar and told him he was going home. Craig had confided in Lamar, who was loyal enough to keep his private life out of the office. He offered to help in any way he

could. Craig thanked him but declined at the moment. Later, Craig felt
the need to get away and what better place than where he was headed.
Pulling into the driveway, he realized he would have peace and quiet to
get his thoughts together.

Venice, where are you?

Venice's shower was relaxing and comforting. Her earlier
conversation with Joshua helped ease her pain slightly. She
still missed Craig and wished she could lie in his arms and kiss
his soft lips. She wrapped the towel around her body and stepped into the
bedroom. Her freshly shampooed hair smelled of fragrant flowers. She
reached into the closet in search for something comfortable to wear.
Throwing the sweat pants and oversized shirt on the bed, she proceeded
back into the bathroom to blow-dry her hair.

Craig stepped into the house and immediately turned on the
lights and headed for the kitchen. He searched for something
to eat, then realized he really wasn't hungry. Feeling tired and
emotionally drained, he headed upstairs to bed. He entered the bedroom
at the precise time Venice stepped out of the bathroom.

"Venice!"

Startled, she clutched the towel and screamed, "Craig!"

He crossed the room in two steps and pulled her into his arms. She
braced herself against his chest with the palms of her hands. He was angry
and happy at the same time.

"Venice, what the hell are you doing here? Why did you leave?"

She couldn't swallow, think or breathe.

"How did you find me?"

He stared down at her angrily.

"I came home to try and get my head together. Do you realize you
left me without so much as an explanation? What's going on? And I
want the truth."

Still in his arms she answered, "I can't tell you. Just trust me, Craig,
please!"

"I did trust you and look what happened."

They stared each other down until Venice said, "Let me go, Bennett. I have to get out of here."

He held her tighter.

"You're not going anywhere until you tell me what's going on."

She closed her eyes, dropped her head, and said, "It's impossible, Craig. I can't be with you right now."

Gripping her shoulders, he shook her and yelled, "Tell me! Now!"

Feeling weak and defeated, she screamed, "Katrina is blackmailing me!"

She collapsed against his body, crying, and his blood pressure shot up knowing that someone he thought he knew had betrayed him and hurt the woman he loved. He wanted to punch something, but at the moment, he was concentrating on holding a woman who needed him. His woman. He picked her up into his arms and sat down on the edge of the bed. Venice buried her face into his neck as she continued to cry. He caressed her shoulders in silence, trying to soothe her obvious pain. He was still in the dark but at least he knew who the culprit was.

Softly, Craig said, "Venice, Sweetheart…everything's going to be okay. I'm here and I'll take care of you. I won't let Katrina do anything to hurt you."

Venice eventually calmed herself and Craig told her to get dressed and pack her clothes. She looked at him with glistening eyes and asked, "Pack? Why?"

He pulled her up from the bed. "We're going over to my house so we can talk in private."

His house was the home Craig lived in when they dated in college.

Venice clutched the towel.

"I don't know if that would be a good idea."

He walked over to her and said, "If you need help dressing, I will help you. Now hurry up and meet me downstairs."

When she looked up, he was gone just as quickly as he had appeared. She was stunned and his presence left her breathless, but she was glad he was there. Doing as she was told, she dressed and packed her bags.

When she reached the bottom of the stairs, Craig took the bags from her hand and said, "Let's go."

CHAPTER Twenty One

His house was warm and cozy and not much had changed in the seven years since the last time she was there. Craig built a fire in silence and the warmth of the flames began to knock the chill out of the air. Venice curled up on the sofa and watched. When he bent over, she noticed how his jeans cupped his perfectly-rounded behind. His muscles protruded through the shirt, which caused heat to rise from her feet to her face. The silence was beginning to become unbearable for her. She continued to watch until finally the fire was blazing. He turned toward her, locking gazes. Venice stirred slightly in her seat and dropped her eyes from his gaze. He approached her and sat down, releasing a long sigh. Not knowing what to do, she took a chance and laid her head against his chest. He pulled her close and wrapped his arm around her waist.

"Are you ready to tell me what happened while I was gone?"

She looked up into his eyes, knowing she couldn't keep the information from him any longer. She told him everything. He tensed and clenched his fists together more and more as she revealed Katrina's blackmail plot. Salty tears streamed down her face as she apologized for hurting him.

"Craig, I thought I could handle it myself, but I can't. I'm sorry, but I can't let her hurt my family."

He kissed her lips tenderly. "You should have told me instead of running away. I'll take care of Katrina so you don't have to worry about anything. I won't let anything happen. Okay?"

Closing her eyes and leaning against him, she said, "I'm so glad you found me."

"Me, too, and I hope this is the last time I have to put this ring on your finger."

Venice sat up and held out her hand as Craig pulled her engagement ring from his pocket. He slid it on as Venice looked down at her finger.

"I was scared, Craig, and I didn't know what to do."

He pulled her back into his embrace. "You don't ever have a reason to be afraid. I won't let her hurt you or anyone in our family and just for the record, Venice, I wouldn't have believed the papers. I know you too well, Sweetheart, no matter how long we've been apart. Understand?"

"Yes, I understand and if you still want to marry me, just say the word."

Kissing her, he said, "I've always wanted to marry you, Venice. Nothing has changed. Okay?"

Venice nodded, then cuddled closer and was finally able to relax. She eventually sank into a deep sleep in the arms of her future husband.

Minutes later, as the flames continued to crackle in the fireplace, Craig lifted her and placed her in his bed. He slowly removed her sweatshirt and pants. Leaving her dressed in only her satin undergarments, his body reminded him just how much he had missed her. He gently ran his hand over the soft brown skin of her thigh, then proceeded to the kitchen to call Joshua.

Craig poured himself a cup of coffee as he waited for Joshua to answer the phone.

Relief was in his voice when he said, "Joshua, I found her. She was staying with my sister. They had no idea I was looking for her. Venice told me that one of my employees, Katrina Simmons, was blackmailing her to stay away from me or she was going to print lies in some tabloid. Joshua, I'm so angry, I might really hurt that woman when I see her."

"Chill, Craig, and let me handle it. The woman's your employee, so you don't want to give her any reason to sue you and your company for harassment. That could ruin you personally and financially. What I need you to do is to go on as if everything's okay. Don't give that woman any indication that you know what's up. I'll handle it, okay?"

Rubbing his hand over his head, Craig asked, "What about Venice?"

"Don't tell her I know what's going on. She's been through enough. You concentrate on her and I'll keep you posted on what's going on."

Feeling a slight headache coming on, he said, "Thanks. I'll call you in the morning and Josh?"

"Yeah?"

"Thanks for everything."

"You don't even have to go there, Craig. Just take care of Venice."

"Will do. Goodnight."

Craig returned to his room where Venice slept peacefully. He took a long, hot shower and when he returned, he joined her in bed. It was if she sensed his presence in her sleep. She scooted closer to him, spooning her backside into his front. Craig caressed her back to soothe her and her eyes slowly opened. She turned over to face him with a smile on her face.

"I didn't mean to wake you."

"I'm glad you did."

Pulling her closer against his body, he asked, "Are you cold?"

Searching his eyes, she answered, "No, actually I'm the opposite."

He covered her mouth, devouring the lips he had missed terribly over the last few days. She encircled her arms around his neck, giving him full access to her throat. Pulling him on top of her body, he moaned in satisfaction, but it was not enough. Slowly his lips kissed a trail down from her lips to her hardened nipples. The satin material covering them was no match for him. He quickly unhooked her bra and ran his tongue over her ripe skin. She arched and groaned when his hands inched lower seeking out her heat. He stroked the source of her desire, causing her to tremble and melt before him.

"You're right, Sweetheart. You are on fire."

"Craig?"

"Yes, Babe?"

"I can't take this much longer."

Smiling, he slowly lowered the satin panties over her shapely hips. He followed, discarding his shorts and T-shirt. He came to her allowing her to feel the evidence of his desire against her thigh.

Running his fingers through her hair, he said, "Can't you feel how much I missed you? Love you? Need you?"

She raised to kiss the lips of the man who saved her from despair.

"I love you, too, and I...no, we need you in our lives also."

The sensation to love her had overpowered his will. He couldn't have heard the words any clearer. He protected her, then covered her body with his, entering her body and soul. He pushed his hips deeper, giving in to a rhythm she quickly joined. He lifted her body higher to meet the demand of his loving. Her moans excited him and drove him over the edge. The magic they shared sent their emotions skyrocketing toward the heavens. He still felt like he wasn't close enough to her core. Placing her arms above her head, he interlocked his fingers with hers while nibbling on her neck. This was an erotic zone for her and he knew it. Craig gave his all to his woman and she took and returned the flame he ignited inside her being. The explosion of love and satisfaction sent wave after wave over them. His muscular body seared her soft brown skin until he shuddered and groaned, spilling into her core. Her scream of completion was no different as she trembled and moaned his name repeatedly. Breathless with her legs still wrapped around his body, she kissed him and asked, "Are you sure you're ready to be a dad?"

"Sweetheart, I was ready years ago."

"Congratulations."

Panting, he pressed his lips to her ear.

"Tomorrow, we pick up Brandon and go home. You don't need to be away from him any longer and I will not sleep another night away from you under any circumstance. Got it?"

"But what about Katrina?"

"You let me worry about Katrina."

She smiled, stroking his cheek, and said, "Okay, Babe. I'll let Mom know we're coming for Brandon."

The next morning, after a quick breakfast and family reunion with Craig's family, they headed to the airport. Skeeter stopped by for a visit and to give his congratulations for their reunion. Skeeter had never seen his best friend so happy. He was glad Craig and Venice had finally found each other again. Skeeter had never been one to settle down with one woman. He never allowed anyone to get that close to his heart. Being a lawyer didn't allow him a lot of time to think about settling down and that was fine with him. It was hard for him to even imagine being with one woman for the rest of his life.

Moving to Philadelphia in a few months would hopefully open up some new doors for him. An hour later, it was a tearful and joyous goodbye to their family and friends as Craig and Venice joined hands and entered the plane and their new life together.

Hours Later

Brandon was talking a mile a minute as he climbed from Venice's lap over to Craig's. Mrs. Anderson smiled, seeing her grandson so excited. She was also happy to know Venice and Craig were planning to marry soon. Brandon was a little reluctant when Venice told him they would be leaving for Philadelphia the following day.

"But what about my friends at school? I won't get to tell them goodbye."

"Sweetheart, they'll be here waiting on you when we come back to visit."

He analyzed her answer.

"Mr. Craig, will you bring me back for a visit?"

He ran his hand over Brandon's head and said, "You bet! We'll all come back as much as possible. Okay?"

Brandon grabbed his hand. "Okay! Will you come help me pack my toys?"

He looked over at Mrs. Anderson who nodded with acceptance. "I sure will, Brandon."

They proceeded upstairs to pack Brandon's clothes and some of his toys.

Once they left the room, Venice rose and approached Mrs. Anderson. She hugged her and said, "Venice, it's obvious you're happy."

"I am, Mom. He is a wonderful man and I do love him."

Mrs. Anderson kissed her on the cheek.

"He loves you, too, and Brandon definitely cares about him. So marry him, Venice. What are you waiting on?"

They sat down on the sofa, holding hands in silence. Tears started falling down her cheeks. Mrs. Anderson reached over to wipe them away.

"Now don't go starting that. I thought we already had this talk, Honey. Jarvis would want you to move on, Baby. You have to believe that. You two loved each other very much and Brandon is the product of that love. You have a chance for a new life with Craig. Seize the life you have with him and cherish the love and memories you had with my son. It's time to let it go, Venice."

Venice began to sob as she fully embraced her mother-in-law, who had been gracious in helping her cope with the death of Jarvis.

"Mom, you and Pops will always be welcome in our home."

Brushing Venice's hair away from her eyes, she said, "I know, Sweetheart. Craig is welcome here also. Besides, I have to be able to visit with my grandson."

"Anytime, Mom. Anytime."

Patting her on the thigh, she asked, "Venice, why don't you two let Brandon stay here until Thanksgiving? It's only a couple of weeks away anyway. We can give him a going-away party next week. This will give us time to get his things together and for him to say goodbye to his friends. I'm sure he'll feel so much better leaving his friends if he has a party. You guys can come home for Thanksgiving and it will give you and Craig a little time alone before Brandon joins you."

Venice stared at her for a moment, then said, "What will I ever do without you?"

Hugging her, she answered, "I'm never going to let you find out. Now, let's go tell the guys before they pack up everything."

Upstairs, Venice told Brandon he could stay until Thanksgiving and have a party to tell his friends goodbye. He was so happy, he ran and jumped in his momma's arms.

"Oh, thank you, Momma! I get to play with B.J. longer. Don't worry, after my party I'll be ready to come see my new school. Okay?"

"Okay, Lil' Man. You just make sure your granddaddy and Uncle Bryan take plenty of pictures of you and your friends. We can't wait to come back for Thanksgiving to get you. Brandon, I'm sorry I've been away from you so much lately. Will you forgive me?"

"Ah, Momma, don't cry. Thanksgiving will be here real soon. See here on my calendar? I'll mark off every day until you come get me. Okay?"

The tears fell anyway when she said, "Okay, Brandon. Now it's your bath time so come on and let me help you."

"Momma?"

"Yes?"

"Is it okay if Mr. Craig helps me?"

Venice's and Craig's eyes met for a moment. Craig smiled and said, "I don't mind helping you at all, Brandon. Let's go."

Venice was pleased even though her heart ached knowing Brandon had adjusted better than expected to his dad's death. She watched as they walked hand-in-hand into the bathroom.

Venice wasn't sure if she would be able to handle this visit, but she had to come anyway. It was dusk and the air was crisp and cool. She drove the car through the giant iron gates and parked along the side of the grassy area. It had been a while since she'd been here, but she knew she couldn't leave town without saying goodbye to Jarvis. Exiting the car, she cradled the bouquet of flowers to her chest. She was totally alone as she watched a groundskeeper attend to a nearby gravesite. When she approached the headstone, she saw Jarvis' smiling face on the picture enclosed in a section of the tombstone. Her knees became weak as she stared back at the face of the man she loved dearly. Sinking to her knees, she ran her hand over the picture, touching every detail of his face. Her throat began to ache as the tears pooled in her eyes and all the emotions came flooding back to her. She closed her eyes and the tears ran down her cheeks and onto her jacket. Leaning forward, she kissed his picture.

"Jarvis, I'll forever hold you in my heart. The love we shared will never die and I will make sure Brandon grows up remembering just how much you loved him. Baby, I don't know how or why it happened, but Craig and I have found each other again. I know you had a hard time dealing with my relationship with him, but I do love him and Brandon adores him. We're taking Brandon to Philadelphia to live with us. Babe, please don't be upset with me. I hadn't seen or spoken to Craig in seven years. That was until we ran into each other unexpectedly. I believe in my heart you were sincere on the videotape when you told me not to be afraid to open up my heart and love again. Since I've been with Craig, I have been able to love again. Jarvis, my heart is still broken and I don't know if I'll ever be able to get over losing you. I look at our son and I see you. He reminds me of the wonderful life we had together. I will eternally love you, and Brandon and I will visit you as often as we can. Until we meet again, Babe..."

Venice placed the flowers in the vase and kissed his picture one more time before rising to her feet. She turned to walk away, then looked back and said, "Goodbye, my love."

She needed to drive and drive she did. Saying goodbye to one era before starting another had been both an emotional strain as well as an emotional salvation. Before she knew it, she had driven by all the familiar locations she had frequented with Jarvis. In her own way, she was healing herself of the wounds inflicted by the tragedy.

After about two hours, she returned to her mother-in-law's house where she found Craig sitting on the porch waiting for her. He met her at the car and when he saw her face, he knew where she had been. He helped her out of the car and into his arms.

She hugged him tightly and said, "I'm sorry I was gone so long."

Caressing her back, he answered, "Venice, take all the time you need. Saying goodbye is never easy, especially to someone you love."

She looked up into his eyes feeling his love and compassion.

"Come on inside. Brandon waited up for you to read him a bedtime story."

Smiling, she held his hand as they walked together back into the Anderson home.

Chapter Twenty Two

Manley had done even better than Joshua could imagine gathering information on Katrina. He read over the paperwork as he sat at the table feeding his infant daughter, Sierra. Occasionally, she would stop sucking and look up at him with her big, brown eyes. His heart swelled just from the mere sight of her. Cynthia and his daughter meant everything to him. Seeing that she wanted his undivided attention, he raised her eye level and planted small kisses on her cheeks. She chuckled and grabbed his nose with a death grip.

"Sierra, your mom's going to have to clip those fingernails of yours."

She didn't know what he was saying, but she squealed with laughter anyway. After a few moments of making funny faces, he positioned her in his arms once more to finish off the bottle. He read the last piece of information Manley provided and settled back in his chair, letting out a deep sigh.

"Okay, Ms. Simmons, I think it's about time I paid you a little visit. Isn't that right, Sierra? Nobody messes with your Aunt Niecy. Huh?"

Joshua had made a wonderful living as a federal agent, which allowed him access to private information. Growing up, he and Jarvis said they would one day become FBI agents together. Jarvis' football career altered his plans but he still received his bachelor's and master's degree in criminal justice with honors. Sierra let out a loud belch and fell sound asleep. He quietly rose from his chair and proceeded upstairs to put her to bed.

Venice was nervous, even though Craig told her not to worry. She was afraid that Katrina might be staking out his house or have someone watching it on her behalf. He reassured her that Katrina didn't know he was out of town for personal reasons so there was no need for her to watch his house. Once they exited the cab, she screamed as he scooped her up into his arms.

"What are you doing?"

He kissed her deeply and said, "Claiming my woman."

With all her anxiety about Katrina, she was caught totally by surprise. Before he entered the house, he tipped the cab driver who sat their bags inside the foyer and thanked them. Once safely inside, she was able to somewhat relax, burying her face into his warm neck. She inhaled his manly scent, which was all male.

Softly, she said, "You can put me down now, Bennett."

"I don't think I'll ever let you leave my arms again."

She raised her head to meet his gaze. His gaze lowered to her lips, then kissed her thoroughly.

"Mmmm, Bennett, you do know what I like."

"There's a lot more where that came from."

"Talk is cheap. Show me."

He lowered her feet to the floor and pulled her firmly against his body. She held on for dear life as his lips moved seductively over hers. Small whimpers escaped from her as he ravished her mouth with his tongue. With his arousal pressing against her body, her legs weakened.

Breathless, she moaned, "Bennett?"

"Huh?"

"Upstairs...now."

Not wanting to break the contact, he picked her up and she wrapped her arms and legs around him. His bedroom seemed miles away, but

Craig covered the distance in record speed. They tumbled onto the bed and she immediately pulled his shirt out of his pants. Her hands eagerly sought out his warm flesh as she kneaded the muscles in his back. Venice couldn't unbutton his shirt fast enough so she ripped it open sending buttons to the floor.

"Sorry, Babe, I'll buy you another one tomorrow."

As he planted hot searing kisses on her neck, he said, "Forget the shirt, woman. You have on too many clothes."

Venice wiggled out of the pants and blouse with Craig's assistance. It was then he realized she wasn't wearing any undergarments.

"Venice, Sweetheart, didn't you forget something?"

She cupped his face, pulling him down to kiss her. Between those hot kisses, she said, "I wasn't in the mood today. Aren't you glad?"

His hands trembled as he discarded his jeans and briefs, then stood before her dazed.

Venice rose up on her elbow. "Are you okay?"

He covered her body with his. "Welcome home, Baby."

Manley met Joshua as he exited the airplane in Philly. They shook hands and proceeded through the airport. As they drove off, Joshua asked, "Is everything in place?"

"Just as you requested, Joshua."

"Good. This shouldn't take long at all. Thanks for all your hard work, Manley. I owe you."

"No problem, Josh."

Katrina entered the office with a smile.

Francine asked, "What are you so happy about?"

"Oh, nothing much except for the fact that Craig Bennett will be mine sooner than I anticipated."

Francine gathered some paperwork from her desk.

"You mean you're still at it? I'm beginning to wonder about you. If you put this much energy into your job, you would be part owner by now."

Katrina followed her over to the file cabinet. "What's wrong with you?"

Francine turned obviously annoyed. "I don't like what you're doing, Kat. Craig must love that woman. I don't know what you did, but it has affected him. He's not as happy as he was a few weeks ago."

Katrina scanned the office. "So where is my future baby's daddy?"

Francine slammed the file drawer closed.

"Out of town on business. He should be back in a couple of days. I have work to do, Kat. I'll catch up with you later. Okay?"

"Francine, are you pissed off at me?"

Turning to look her in the eyes, she said, "I just don't agree with what you're doing. It's wrong."

Katrina touched her on the arm. "We'll talk later. I'd better go before Lamar hunts me down. Lunch is on me today."

"Thanks. Catch you later."

Francine sat back in her chair and wondered if she should tell her boss what had been going on behind his back. Craig was a great boss and friend. This was a situation she would have to pray about.

Joshua and Manley watched from the rental car as Katrina retrieved her mail from her mailbox.

"It's a shame that a woman as attractive as her can be so scandalous."

Joshua responded, "You got that right. We'll give her twenty minutes, then we'll ring her doorbell."

Manley nodded and continued to watch Katrina through his binoculars.

Katrina fed her cat and sat down at the kitchen table to go over her mail. Before she started, she prepared herself a small glass of wine to relax. Kicking off her shoes, she noticed a brown manila folder without a return address. She decided to open it first and gasped when the contents were revealed. On the table was a picture of her when she was working in a Chicago strip club. Katrina yelled, "What the...! This can't be happening. I've put that life behind me!"

She started pacing the floor and wondered who would've found out about her past. She moved to Philadelphia three years ago and didn't tell anyone about the job, which put her through college. Also in the envelope was a police mug shot where she had been arrested for prostitution. She only did it a few times to make extra money. One of those times happened to be during a police sting. She stopped pacing, then a thought came to her.

"Venice! So you know how to play dirty, too. We'll just see how far you're willing to go."

Still somewhat nervous, she was chewing on a perfectly-manicured nail when the doorbell chimed. She tried to compose herself before answering the door but only halfway succeeded.

"May I help you?"

Manley flashed a badge and said, "Ms. Simmons?"

"Yes."

"We're detectives from the Chicago Police Department and we want to talk to you regarding the disappearance of Tyrone Waters."

"Who?"

"His street name was Gunner."

Katrina was shaken as her former boss/pimp's name spilled from the detective's lips.

Oh, my God!

Joshua stood quiet, observing the woman's behavior. She finally said, "I'm afraid you have the wrong Katrina Simmons."

Manley then produced paperwork and a photo showing where Gunner bailed her out of jail.

Her knees buckled.

"Detectives, I can't help you and if you don't mind, I'm not feeling well."

Manley said, "Of course, Ms. Simmons. We will call on you tomorrow, but we must discuss this matter. Witnesses put you as one of the last people to see him alive before his body was found in a land fill. May we possibly call upon you at your job?"

"No! Please! You can come by here tomorrow. I should be feeling better by then."

"Very well. We'll see you tomorrow and we hope you feel better."

As she was closing the door, she said, "Thank you. Goodnight."

She watched them retreat to their car and drive off.

Her thoughts were racing through her head. Could it be possible that someone other than Venice was behind this? If not her, then who? Someone could have tracked her to Philly. She would just have remain cool and wait until they contacted her again.

The next day, Katrina called in to use a sick day. She had to get herself together in order to deal with the detectives and the anonymous pictures she received in the mail. She didn't get much sleep, and wouldn't have been any good at work anyway. Around noon, she called Francine to see if anyone had called or been by the office looking for her. Francine confirmed with her that no one had been by to see her, then asked if she needed anything. Katrina told her she was fine, then thanked her for asking.Craig returned to the office after lunch for a meeting. He greeted Francine warm, but not too cheerful. He was trying to follow Joshua's instructions so Katrina wouldn't figure out he knew what she had done to Venice. He just prayed that he would be able to control his temper when he laid eyes on Katrina. He hoped Joshua could get the situation taken care of as soon as possible, especially by Thanksgiving. His plan was to have a Christmas wedding. Sooner, if it could be arranged. The Architects Ball was coming up on December twenty-eighth. By then, he wanted to be able to introduce Venice as his wife. He pushed the intercom on his phone and instructed Francine to order two tickets for the ball. With a smile in her voice, she said, "Will do, boss."

Craig was going to be very busy the next few weeks working on the Garrett design. He hated to leave Venice at the house alone, so he made arrangements to work from home a couple of days. Lamar was the only person who knew what was going on.

One morning when Craig woke up, Venice was not in bed. He turned to look at the clock, which read four a.m. He rose from the bed in search of her. After looking upstairs, he proceeded downstairs. He was starting to get nervous when he heard her enter from the door leading to the garage. Their eyes locked in silence as they stood in the kitchen. Relieved and upset, he asked, "Where have you been?"

"Jogging."

"At four a.m.?"

She walked into the laundry room and proceeded to take off her clothes. As she tossed them in the washer, he followed and watched her intensely.

"What's wrong, Venice? You never jog like this unless something's really bothering you."

Without making eye contact, she took off her sweats

"Nothing, Craig. I should've left you a note. I thought I was going to be back before you woke up."

Standing there with only her sports bra to discard, he scanned her. The thought of her hurt entered his mind. He calmly but firmly said, "I would appreciate it if you wouldn't jog in the middle of the night. Don't do it again."

Pulling the bra over her head, she answered, "I wasn't thinking. Sorry."

She couldn't fool him; he knew something was bothering her and he would eventually get to the bottom of it. She wrapped a towel around her body.

"I'm going to head upstairs for a shower. You can go back to sleep now."

"Since I'm up, I'm going to try to get some work done."

She saw how much her stunt scared him and she needed to put his mind at ease.

"Okay. I'm sorry I interrupted your sleep."

He turned to walk away, then said, "Get some rest, Venice."

She watched him enter his office before heading upstairs.

She just wasn't ready to tell him she was feeling depressed as the first holiday without Jarvis was approaching. She didn't know how Brandon was going to handle it either, which made her uneasy. She tried convincing herself that she should be happy to have Craig in her life, but something was still missing. Their family tradition had ended with

Jarvis' death and she knew this year would feel awkward. Talking about it with Craig didn't seem appropriate so she decided to try and deal with it herself. The last thing she wanted to do was hurt Craig's feelings. He had been so wonderful to her.

The warm water was soothing to her skin. The jog felt good, but didn't remove her anxiety. After her shower, she dressed in her silky red nightgown and went downstairs for a cup of hot cocoa. At the bottom of the stairs, she noticed Craig hard at work at his desk. She decided to make him a cup also, topping it off with some whip cream.

As she entered his office, he glanced up briefly before returning to his paperwork.

Venice cautiously asked, "What are you working on?"

Without looking up, he said, "I'm writing out a proposal to lease a larger building. We need more office space."

"Is everything okay?"

"Nothing I can't handle."

She stood there in silence.

"Craig, I brought you some cocoa and I'm sorry I scared you."

He looked up, searching her eyes without responding. He noticed her wounded look and realized she was presenting him with a peace offering. He stood and took the hot cup from her hands and sat it on the desk.

"Thank you and you're right. You scared the hell out of me. I tremble when I think of what could've happened to you out there. Baby, please don't take chances like that again. It's my job to protect you, but you have to do your part, too. Okay?"

She nodded in acceptance as he embraced her lovingly. She clung to his warm body as tears trickled down her cheek.

"I'm sorry, Craig. I'm on my cycle and when I'm on my cycle, I get a little cuckoo."

He tilted her chin. "Venice, you're always cuckoo."

"Craig!"

Laughing, he said, "I'm just kidding, but seriously, it seems you've been doing a lot of crying lately. I want you to be happy here. Not sad, Sweetheart."

She took a deep breath before confiding in him.

"I wasn't going to burden you, but it's the holidays. It's going to be…"

"Different? Is that what's bothering you?"

She held his gaze, then stuttered with, "Craig, I-I don't mean to-to…"

"Venice, I realize the holidays are going to be rough on you and Brandon this year. I want to help you through it. Let me know what you want to do and we'll do it. If you want to go home, I'll take you home. If you want to stay here, we'll stay here. Just don't shut me out. I'm here for you and I believe you're here for me." He kissed her on the forehead and said, "We have to stick together. Okay?"

She hugged him feeling some anxiety lifted.

"Craig, I don't know what I want to do. I know I don't want you to feel less important in my life, because I still miss Jarvis. I love you so much. But I still love Jarvis, even if all I have are memories. I hope you understand."

He caressed her cheek and answered, "I do. We'll just have to take it one day at a time. Okay? Now, let me sample this cocoa; then we'll talk."

They chatted and cuddled for the next hour as they finished their cocoa. Becoming sleepy again, they returned to their bedroom for some well-needed sleep.

CHAPTER Twenty Three

Brandon was so excited about his party. He was also happy that his mom and new dad would be home in a few days. He finally drifted to sleep. Hours later, he was awakened to find his dad sitting on his bed.

"Daddy?"

"Hello, Son. How are you doing?"

Brandon leapt into his dad's arms and said, "I miss you so much, Daddy."

"I know, Brandon. I miss you, too."

"Daddy, are you really here? I thought you were in heaven."

"Well, Brandon, I'm on my way, but there were some things I had to take care of first."

"Does Mommy know?"

Jarvis smiled and rubbed his head.

"No, Son, she doesn't. I have to hang around and make sure you two are going to be ok after I leave."

Brandon solemnly looked into his dad's eyes and said, "Momma was real sad when you left, Daddy. She cried all the time and would never get out of the bed. Uncle Josh had to make her. I get sad, too, because I miss you so much."

"I know. I love you and your mom and I know she still loves me. I left you guys so fast and it was more than your momma could handle. But I was sick, Brandon. I didn't want to leave you guys, but I had to. You understand don't you, Son?"

"Not really, but I'll try. Daddy, Momma's trying to be happy again. She's going to marry Mr. Craig."

Jarvis smiled and said, "She is? Do you like him?"

"Yes, Daddy. He's fun and nice, just like you, and he makes Momma smile."

"I'm glad you like him. He's cool and I want you to mind him, okay?"

"Okay, Daddy. Are you going to visit Mommy, too?"

Jarvis smiled. "Not right now. Maybe later. Well, I'd better get going."

"Are you going to come back and see me? I'm having my going-away party in a few days, then I'm moving with Momma and Mr. Craig to Piladelkia."

"You mean Philadelphia and yes, I'll visit you before you leave. Tell your mom I love her and to keep the window open for me."

"Huh?"

"Don't worry, Brandon. She'll know what I mean."

Jarvis kissed and hugged Brandon tightly.

"I love you, Son. Don't you ever forget it. Now close your eyes and go to sleep."

"I won't forget, Daddy. I love you, too. Goodnight."

Jarvis stood, tucked his son in bed, and kissed him one last time. When Brandon turned to say goodnight again, he was gone.

Thanksgiving

To help Venice cope with her depression, Thanksgiving dinner was held at her brother Bryan's house. The families knew they had to break tradition this year for her sake. Normally, they alternated the years between the Anderson and Taylor homes. Bryan's wife, Sinclair, invited

Craig's sister and his entire family up for the celebration. The more the merrier was her plan. Venice made sure no one had to stay in a hotel. Her careful planning was able to accommodate everyone. The mood remained festive until it was time to bless the food. Venice had tried to prepare her emotions, but it was to no avail. Things had to be said and she prayed it would be healing for her and it was.

After dinner, she took a walk with her oldest brother, Bryan. They walked for a while in silence, then Bryan said, "Baby girl, I'm real proud of you. You really have grown into a beautiful, strong woman."

Venice smiled. "Thanks, Bryan."

"No, really. You've been through a lot these last few months. Jarvis would be proud of you."

"I don't know about all that. I fell apart and I'm not completely back together either. Bryan, I'll never be the same. Jarvis was my life and I love him so much."

They stopped and sat on a bench under a big oak tree down the block.

"Venice, you guys were young, but you were mature and dealt with your consequences like pros. I always admired ya'll for that."

Venice looped her arm through her big brother's.

"Thanks to you, no doubt. I don't know if I've ever told you, but thanks for being there for me. You have always supported me and answered any questions I asked. I appreciate that, Bryan, even though I made you uneasy with the sex questions."

They laughed together for a moment, then once again it was silent. Venice laid her head on his shoulder and burst into tears. Bryan knew it would eventually come. It was only a matter of when. She had held her emotions throughout dinner, and now she could finally release them. He hugged her tightly and did his best to comfort her. It would take time for her to get past the pain of losing Jarvis. Craig would have a major role in helping, but it would be an uphill journey. Bryan was happy they found each other again and so was the rest of the family.

After finishing off some pie and homemade ice cream, Craig asked Joshua, "Where's Venice?"

"She took a walk with Bryan. They do that every year after dinner."

Craig sat on the sofa. "Did she seem okay to you? I mean, do you think she's okay?"

Joshua's wife, Cynthia, walked over and handed him their baby. Joshua kissed Sierra on the cheek and answered, "Craig, Niecy is going to be messed up for a while. Just bear with her. She's probably going to throw some emotional drama your way, so I hope you're ready. I know for a fact she loves you, but she's still holding onto Jarvis. Since Brandon looks so much like him, she'll have a hard time letting go. Just be patient with her and don't think you're not important in her life. You are her past, present and future. Don't worry, everything will fall into place. Especially after we put Katrina in check."

Craig reached over and tickled Sierra's foot.

"How did it go with Katrina?"

"Chick was shaking in her shoes. I have her right where I want her. When is this banquet of yours?"

"It's a few days after Christmas."

After putting a bottle in Sierra's mouth, Joshua asked, "Have you and Venice set a wedding date yet?"

"I want to do it the Saturday before Christmas. I haven't asked her about it yet. I may talk to her about it tonight."

Sierra stared at Craig, then gave him a big smile, letting the milk run down her chin. This touched his heart so much.

"Can I feed her, Joshua?"

"Sure, man. Take her."

Sierra looked curiously at her daddy, then smiled when Craig cradled her in his arms. Joshua handed him the bottle and he began to feed her.

At that moment, Bryan and Venice entered the room. Seeing Craig with Sierra warmed her heart. Their eyes met and their hearts knew what the other was feeling at that precise moment. After Venice hung up her coat, Cynthia grabbed her arm and whisked her out into the hallway.

"Girl, what are you waiting on? You need to hurry up and marry that man so you can put him out of his misery. All he talks about is you and Brandon, and you see how he's fascinated with Sierra? What's the hold-up?"

Venice took Cynthia by the hand and led her upstairs to Crimson's room.

"To tell you the truth, Cynthia, I'm still a little scared."

Cynthia put her hands on her hips and asked, "Of what? It's obvious you love him and he definitely loves you. Brandon is crazy about him, too. The Andersons act as if they've known him for years. As far as your parents are concerned, he's already family. Look, I know you're still hurting, Girl, but you have to get that pain under control so you can deal with it. Craig is your blessing, Venice, so don't turn your back on it. You've given me some tough love advice over the years. Now I'm returning the favor. Propose to the man!"

Venice sat on the bed. "Maybe you're right, Cynthia. Thank you so much. I'm still full of mixed emotions, but I'll take everything you said into consideration. I love you, Girl."

Cynthia hugged her. "I love you, too. Now let's get back downstairs so I can see if Sierra has spit up on your fiancé."

When they entered the hallway, they met Craig with a sleeping Sierra in his arms. Startled, Cynthia offered to take the sleeping infant.

"Let me put her to bed, Cynthia."

"Okay. Her crib is in here."

The two women watched as Craig placed Sierra in the bed as if she were a porcelain doll. He reached over and turned on the baby monitor, then met them in the hallway. Cynthia said, "Craig, you did that like a pro."

"I've had a little practice. I hope I get a chance to do it with my own soon."

Cynthia observed the two staring at each other.

"I'll see you guys downstairs."

Once Cynthia was gone, Venice said, "Craig, I'm sorry if I've been a little distant with you today."

He pulled her into his arms and said, "No apology required, Baby."

Linking her arms around his neck she looked up into his eyes.

"I love you."

He smiled and pressed his lips to hers tenderly. A soft moan escaped her lips as he pulled her even tighter against his body.

"Will you marry me, Bennett?"

He searched her eyes and asked, "Did you ask what I think you asked?"

She wrapped her arms around him. "Craig Alexander Bennett, will you marry me?"

His eyes glistened and he picked her up into his arms.

"Only if you agree to marry me the Saturday before Christmas."

She kissed him and said, "You've got yourself a date, Mister."

"Thank you, Jesus!"

Katrina flew to Chicago, not only for Thanksgiving with her family, but to gain information. She had to find out who was behind the pictures and putting the police on her tail. She was the oldest of four who grew up in a dysfunctional family. From the time she was ten years old, she became the mother figure to her siblings. Her mom was too busy hanging out in the clubs getting her groove on. Katrina remembered the many men her mom brought home and introduced as her *friends*. Some were nice while others made it clear they weren't going to take care of somebody else's kids. One man in particular watched her too closely when she was fourteen. He made her very uncomfortable and one night she woke to find him standing over her bed exposing himself. She tried to tell her mom but she wouldn't listen to her. That was the beginning of her nightmare. The molestation continued for three years until the man was shot and bled to death in a bar room argument. For some reason, Katrina's mom found a way to blame her. After that, her mom turned to alcohol and drugs.

Katrina was brought back to reality when her sister said, "Trina! Didn't you hear me calling you?"

"I'm sorry, Boogie. I didn't hear you."

"I know you're not going to sit up here in my kitchen and call me by that old name?"

Katrina smiled. "I don't care what you say, Lynette. You'll always be Boogie to me."

"Trina, I'm twenty-four. Don't you think I've outgrown that nickname?"

Katrina picked up a piece of celery, threw it at her, and said, "Never… Boogie!"

They laughed together.

"Where's your knucklehead brothers?"

Lynette stirred the dressing.

"Gone to pick up their trifling, good-for-nothing girlfriends. Trina, wait 'til you see the one Lil' Terry got. She has more gold in her mouth than Fort Knox."

"You have got to be kidding!"

Lynette said, "You'll see. So, what's going on with you? You got a man yet?"

Katrina dipped her finger in the mix.

"Put more sage in the mix, Boogie, and as far as your question, yes I do and I may let you meet him Christmas."

"For real! That's great, Girl. I'm glad you found somebody. I hope he's fine."

"Oh, my sistah, believe me, he's not lacking in any category and the man's got bank."

"What's his name?"

"Craig."

"O-o-o-o, sounds sexy."

"Believe me, Boogie, he is."

Katrina went over, turned off the pot of turnip greens, then asked, "Boogie, have you heard any talk about Gunner lately?"

"Not really. Why?"

Katrina sighed. "Boogie, you're the only one I confided in about what I did to put myself through school and I know you wouldn't tell anybody. But some cops came to my door recently asking questions about Gunner. They said they had information that I may have been the last person who saw him alive."

"Trina, I would never tell a soul. You know that. Maybe some of Gunner's other girls put them on to you."

Katrina put a piece of chicken in her mouth.

"Maybe so. Boogie, I didn't kill him."

"I know, Trina."

They stared at each other for a moment. The front door opened.

"Oh, well, sounds like your brothers are here. We'll talk later, Trina. Let's eat."

CHAPTER **Twenty Four**

Katrina returned to work Monday morning, still wondering who knew about her past.As she walked down the hall, she saw Craig Bennett headed her way. Her spirits immediately perked up on seeing him.

"Good morning, Mr. Bennett. I hope you had a nice Thanksgiving."

He tried his best not to wrinkle his forehead and form fists with his hands.

"Morning, Katrina, and yes, I did. I hope you had a nice one as well."

He knew eventually he would have to face her and it took a lot of effort not to go off.

"Nice of you to ask, and yes, I did. Mr. Bennett, I was wondering if you had anyone to escort you to the ball? If not, I would be honored to be your escort."

Craig's body tensed, then relaxed. He turned and with a smile said, "It's nice of you to offer, Katrina, but I already have an escort."

"Oh, that's nice. Is she anyone we know?"

He chuckled. "No, you don't know her. Well, I'd better get to my office. Have a nice day, Katrina."

"You, too, Mr. Bennett."

He entered his office and let out a sigh. He did it. He'd faced Katrina without wanting to snatch the weave out of her head. Knowing Venice was at his house, in his life, and soon-to-be his wife was his motivation for control. Plus, knowing Joshua was working on a way to intercept Katrina's devious plans allowed him to concentrate on his job. As he went over the stack of paperwork on his desk, his private line buzzed. He answered, "Hello?"

"Hello, yourself."

Smiling, he leaned back in his chair.

"Miss me already?"

"You bet I do. I've finally gained enough strength to get out of this bed. You're sinful, Bennett."

"I'm happy I was able to serve you, Sweetheart."

"I think serving me up is a better statement."

He twirled his chair to face the Philly skyline.

"I saw her a few minutes ago."

"Did she say anything to you?"

"She had the nerve to offer to be my escort at the ball. I told her I already had an escort."

"How did she take it?"

He ran his hand over his head. "She acted as if she were pleased. She did ask if she knew her. I told her 'no' which is true. She has never or will ever know you."

"Craig?"

"Yes?"

"I love you. Now get to work."

"Okay, boss, and I love you, too. Four weeks and counting, Sweetheart."

"I can hardly wait."

He stood up and poured himself a cup of coffee.

"Me either and let Brandon call me when he wakes up. We have some man stuff to discuss."

"Excuse me! He should be up in about an hour."

"Okay. See you guys this evening."

"Goodbye."

As soon as she hung up, she called back and asked for Lamar. There was something she needed him to show her and it had to be today. Lamar agreed and told her he would pick her up in an hour. Venice was glowing when she hung up the phone. She had another important call to make. She wanted to offer Ms. Camille, Brandon's former sitter, a job in Philly. She wasn't sure if Ms. Camille would want to pick up her life in Detroit and move to Philly, but Venice figured she could at least try to make it worth her while. As she dialed the number, she remembered how emotionally distraught Ms. Camille was when Jarvis died. She also remembered how helpful she was in comforting her and Brandon in the midst of the tragedy. Ms. Camille was definitely one-of-a-kind and Brandon absolutely loved her.

"Hello?"

"Hello, Ms. Camille."

"Oh my Lawd! Venice! How in the world are you doing, child?"

"I'm doing okay, Ms. Camille. How are you?"

"Child, I'm hanging in there. How's my baby? The last time we spoke, you mentioned something about moving to Philadelphia."

"Yes, Ma'am, I'm engaged to a wonderful man I knew from college and we're getting married in a month."

"Venice, that's nice. You know, Jarvis loved you and Brandon something awful. I miss his silly little jokes and that beautiful smile of his. He was a good boy and I miss you and my baby, too."

Venice could tell Ms. Camille had teared up and so had she.

"I know, Ms. Camille, and no matter what, I will always be in love with Jarvis."

"I know, child. So when am I going to get to see you, my baby, and this wonderful man of yours?"

"I was hoping you would ask. Ms. Camille, what would you say if I offered you a job here in Philadelphia? Brandon really misses you and so do I. You'll just love Craig and in some ways, he's a lot like Jarvis. I know Detroit has been your home, but hear me out first. We can have the same arrangements we had in Detroit except that I will double what we were paying you. You will have your own home to go to when you're not here with us."

"Baby, I can't afford to buy another house."

Venice smiled. "Ms. Camille, I hope I'm not being too forward, but I found a house similar to yours in Detroit. I didn't want to lose it so I put a deposit on it until I could speak with you. It would mean a lot to us if you would accept the house as a gift of appreciation. You were so wonderful to our family and I hope you will consider my offer to move here. Plus, after we're married, we're planning on adding to our family and I wouldn't want anyone else taking care of our children."

Venice heard sniffling on the other end of the phone.

"Ms. Camille? Are you okay?"

Through tears, she said, "Venice, Baby, this is a generous offer. You don't have to buy me a house, Baby. If I decide to come to Philadelphia, it will be because I love you and that son of yours."

Tears fell from Venice's eyes.

"Thank you, Ms. Camille. My deposit will hold the house for seven days."

"Thank you, Venice. Give me your number and I'll call you in a couple of days. Tell my baby boy that I love him."

"Will do and thank you."

"No, thank you, Venice. God bless you and I'll talk to you soon."

Lamar entered Craig's office and sat down in the leather chair.

"Craig, man, this has got to be over soon. I can't take Katrina much longer. She had the nerve to ask me who you were bringing to the ball."

Craig looked up with an irritated facial expression and asked, "What did you tell her?"

"I told her, first of all, it was none of her business. Secondly, I don't make it my business to inquire about your personal life."

Craig smiled. "You're a good liar, Lamar."

Leaning forward, he grinned. "I know. So, how's that gorgeous fiancée of yours?"

Craig put down his drawing tool. "Venice and Brandon are doing just fine."

"Oh, that's right, her son is here now. How's that working out?"

Craig rolled up the plans he was working on.

"We're doing great. Now, Lamar, when you take these over to Roan's, don't make him angry again. Remember his assistant is his daughter."

Lamar stood and said, "Please! His daughter is a grown woman! I'm not going to give up until I get her to go out with me."

Craig put his hand on his shoulder, laughed, and said, "Don't underestimate that old man. He still looks like he can beat you down. He knows you're a womanizer and he doesn't want you to have any part of his daughter."

"Are you challenging me, Bro?"

Craig took a sip of water. "Lamar, you're full of it. You know yourself you just want that woman for one thing and she's a nice girl. You know you like your women fast and hot."

Lamar suddenly became serious. "It's different with Tressa and I'm going to prove that you and her old man are wrong about me."

Craig raised his eyebrows.

"Lamar, are you saying you're finally ready to settle down?"

Checking his appearance in the mirror, he said, "I wasn't until I saw her. She's so sweet and always nice to me. You can tell she's strong and full of passion. Some of the women I've dated were nothing but gold diggers trying to get their hands in my pocket."

"Lamar, the woman has turned you down every time you've asked her out."

Lamar straightened his tie. "That's because her old man is always hovering over her. I'm just going to have to talk to her when he's not around to intimidate her."

"Good luck. He watches her like a hawk. She's his only child so you know he won't think twice about taking a shot at you."

"We'll see. How do I look?"

"Go get her, tiger."

Katrina sat staring at her computer screen in a daze. The ringing of the phone snapped her back to reality.

"Bennett & Fletcher."

"Katrina, my editor is on my back for that hot story for our newspaper. What's going on? Were you making all of this up?"

"No, Nathan. I just need more time."

"Well, she's not wanting to give us any more time. When I told her it was regarding a well-known NFL player's wife, her head spun around. She said her offer will not stay on the table forever."

"I know, I know. See if you can talk her into a couple of more weeks. Tell her it will be a great story to break just before the holidays. I promise."

"I can't promise you, but I'll see what I can do. Can you at least tell me who it is?"

Katrina smiled. "Not yet but when the time comes, you'll be the first to know."

"Hey, Katrina, why don't we get together tonight for old time's sake? I miss the feel of your smooth brown legs wrapped around my body."

"Focus, Nathan! If you're a good boy, I'll reward you with much more than I used to give you."

"Mercy, woman! You do know how to make a brotha sweat."

"That's my gift, Sweetheart. Later."

After Katrina hung up the phone, she said, "Venice, whether you stay away from Craig or not, your debut in the tabloids will hit the stands right before Christmas. Craig won't be able to deal with your cheating ways and he'll come running into my arms. Katrina Bennett does have a nice ring to it."

Across the street, Manley and Joshua looked up and gave each other a high-five. They finally had the lead they were waiting on. Bugging Katrina's phone had been easy. Finding out who her contact was at the tabloids took some patience. Today, they got the break they had been waiting on.

"Manley, I think we deserve to celebrate. We now know who and when she's planning on breaking the story. We have a couple of weeks before we move to plan B. Let's go home."

The only message Joshua left on Craig's private voicemail was: *Craig, go home and enjoy your family. It's almost over.*

When Craig entered the house that evening, he found Brandon, Venice and his grandmother in the family room snapping green beans. As he leaned down to kiss Venice, he asked, "Nanna! What are you doing here?"

Coming around the sofa for a hug and kiss, she responded, "I'm glad to see you, too."

He kissed her. "You know I didn't mean it that way. When did you get in?"

"This afternoon. Surprise!"

"I'm glad you here."

Brandon ran over and hugged Craig's leg lovingly.

Craig patted him on the back. "How was your day, Brandon?"

He smiled up at Craig. "Good! I have the hiccups."

They laughed and Craig said, "Come, let me give you some soda to make them go away."

He took Brandon by the hand and led him from the room, but not before giving Venice a seductive gaze. She blushed and nearly spilled the bowl of beans.

Nanna said, "I swear, you two act like you did when you first met. I see the winking, blowing kisses and the naughty looks. I think it's sweet. You and Brandon have made my grandson so happy."

"Craig's made us happy and I thought we were being discreet, Nanna."

"Honey! I was young once also, you know. You can't get nothing past an old girl like me."

In the kitchen, Brandon sat at the table while Craig poured him some soda. He asked, "So Brandon, have you thought of anything yet?"

"Not yet. I didn't think it would be this hard. Can't you help me?"

He rubbed Brandon on the head. "No can do. This has to be your decision and your decision only. I want it to be something you're comfortable with. Okay?"

"Okay. Can I go up to my room now?"

"Sure, but dinner will be ready soon."

"Okay, tell Momma and Grandma I'll check on them later."

"I will and don't spill your soda. Your momma will throw a fit."

"I won't. Oh, I forgot. My daddy told me to tell my momma to leave the window open, but I forgot. Can you tell her for me?"

Craig turned and asked, "What did you say?"

"Daddy told me to tell Momma to leave the window open. He said she'll know what it means."

Craig tried not to appear stunned. He calmly asked, "When did you talk to your daddy?"

"He came to see me when I was at my granddaddy's house one night."

Craig leaned down eye-level to him. "Are you sure you weren't dreaming, Brandon?"

Brandon took a sip of his soda. "I'm sure. He tucked me in and everything."

Craig saw the seriousness in Brandon's eyes. "Okay, I'll tell her. Now go on up to your room."

"Thank you."

Brandon hurried upstairs to get on his computer. Craig had bought him a CD showing all types of animals and the countries they lived in. Brandon was fascinated with animals and he thanked Craig over and over for the CD. Craig didn't know how to accept the information Brandon had just given him. He didn't know whether he should tell Venice or not. If he didn't, Brandon might ask her about it. If he did tell her, it might upset her far worse than he'd ever seen. Brandon seemed to accept the possible visit from his dad very well. Could it be that he still didn't fully understand that Jarvis was dead and he shouldn't have been able to see him? Was it a figment of his imagination or did Jarvis really visit him? Craig ran his hand over his head and decided to think about it a little longer before going to Venice.

After dinner, Nanna turned in while Craig, Venice, and Brandon watched a movie. It was about ten o'clock before Brandon fell asleep. He had gotten too heavy for Venice to carry, so Craig made it a point to carry him up to his room. When he returned, Venice snuggled up close in his arms and laid her head on his chest. Still troubled by his conversation with Brandon, Venice noticed he was distracted.

"Are you okay, Bennett?"

He looked down at her and said, "I'm okay. Are you?"

"I'm fine."

She raised up, took him by the hand, and said, "Let's go to bed."

She took the remote and turned off the movie. Smiling with a devilish grin she led him upstairs and into their room. She turned and said, "Take off your clothes and I'll be right back."

He was speechless, but did as he was told. Venice proceeded downstairs and heated up some lotion in the microwave. She returned to find him nude and lying across the bed.

"What is that?"

"Turn over, Bennett. It's only lotion. You look like you could use a massage."

He smiled and turned over as she began massaging him with the hot lotion. His muscles were tense, but she worked the knots out of each one. Craig closed his eyes and seemed to drift into a relaxed state of mind as she massaged his arms and back. It wasn't until she reached his buttock and thighs that his body reminded him of his maleness. Venice heard him suck in a breath.

"Are you okay, Babe?"

"No."

Whispering, she asked, even though she knew the answer, "What's wrong?"

He rolled over to reveal the answer to her question.

"Oh, my."

"Come here, woman."

Venice giggled and went willingly into his arms. His kiss was hot and gentle. Her clothes were discarded and the massage stopped and passion filled the room.

Sometime around midnight, they lay in each other's arms. Neither was asleep, just recuperating.

"Venice?"

Her weak voice responded, "Yes, Bennett."

"We need to decide where we're getting married. I don't care. We can do it right here as far as I'm concerned."

She raised up on one elbow and looked into his beautiful dark eyes.

"Bennett, it doesn't matter to me either."

She ran her hand over his cheek, then down to the silky hair on his chest.

"I don't care about a big wedding, but it's not my first. If it's what you want, I'll do it for you and your family."

Craig played in her hair and said, "If you don't want a big wedding, that's fine with me, but I would like a nice reception. My family will understand."

She smiled. "That's settled. Now where?"

He pulled her atop his chest and asked, "How about Ocho Rios with just our families and close friends? That is where we began."

Venice nibbled at his neck. "That sounds good to me, but what about the reception? I think it would be a good idea to have it in Dawson."

"Are you sure?"

"Yes, I'm sure."

"Then it's settled. We'll tell Nanna and Bernice so they can get to work. In the morning, I'll call the travel agent to make arrangements for Ocho Rios."

Venice smiled. "I'll call Momma tomorrow and tell her to let everyone know. Craig, I want this to be as private as possible. I don't want to look up and have journalists flashing cameras in our faces."

He hugged her tightly. "I'll take care of that, too, Babe."

She nuzzled her face into his neck. "I knew you would. I love you, Craig."

He stroked her back. "I love you, too. Sweet dreams."

Nanna stayed a week, then returned home with ideas for the reception. She had discussed several of them with Bernice over the phone prior to her departure. Venice and Craig let them have full control of the reception plans even though Craig was somewhat worried they would get carried away.

Nanna said, "It's not every day that my favorite grandson gets married."

Twenty Five

Manley and Joshua tracked down Katrina's source at the tabloids. He was Nathan Bowers, an ambitious writer for Philly's most notorious rag magazine. Manley also found out that Nathan was a former lover of Katrina's and in her own way, she still had control over him. He would do almost anything she asked him to.

After asking around, Manley found out that Katrina was notorious for using men to get where and what she wanted. Nathan was no exception. She didn't care who she stepped on to get there either.

Brandon had a huge list of items he wanted Santa Claus to bring him. He also asked Santa to bring gifts for Venice and Craig.

Venice said, "Now Brandon, you know your list is a little longer than it should be. You need to go back over it and only leave the five items you want most."

"Aww, Momma. Santa won't get mad. He knows I've been a good boy all year."

Venice patted him on the bottom. "I know you've been a good boy, but your list is still too long."

"Okay, Momma."

He sat at the kitchen table and began studying his list. He asked, "Can Santa Claus take gifts to heaven?"

Venice was stunned. She calmed herself.

"No, Sweetheart. Once you get to heaven, there's no need for material things. God makes sure you have all you need."

He looked seriously at her. "So I can't get Santa to give my daddy a present?"

Venice hugged him.

"No, Baby, but you can send Daddy a Merry Christmas in your prayers. That will be gift enough for him. Okay?"

"Okay, Momma, but I really miss my daddy."

"I know, Baby. So do I."

Brandon continued to go over his list. Venice walked into the pantry to steady herself. Brandon was still a thoughtful and loving child toward his daddy. She put her hand over her mouth and stifled the tears, which tried to fall.

"Momma! What's taking you so long?"

"I'm coming, Sweetheart!"

She straightened herself and reentered the kitchen to help Brandon with his list.

Back in Venice's hometown, Mrs. Anderson started working on the laundry. When she went into Portia's room to put away some clothes, she noticed a familiar container. Inside her closet was a box containing six packs of birth control. Mrs. Anderson gasped and, for the first time, realized Portia was coming of age. She'd had talks with her regarding sex, diseases, and her body. Her problem right now was wondering whether or now Portia was sexually active. She thought Portia would confide in her about sex, but she had been wrong.

Venice had told Mrs. Anderson about how her brother, Bryan, caught his fifteen-year-old daughter kissing a boy in their recreation room. He was furious and glad he caught them when he did. Had he not, they may have gone further than they did. Portia and Venice's niece, Crimson were best friends. Mrs. Anderson had to know if Portia was having sex. She just couldn't go through a repeat episode like she did with Jarvis, when Venice became pregnant at seventeen. She just couldn't handle it.Craig hung up the phone after making sure the wedding director had all his instructions for the ceremony. He wanted it held in a private ballroom in one of the most exquisite hotels on the island. He knew Venice loved lavender, but that was the color used at her previous wedding. He requested a variety of tropical flowers in an assortment of colors. Venice didn't want to do anything but pick out her dress. She wanted it to be elegant and breathtaking. She wanted Craig to remember their wedding day the moment he laid eyes on her.

Brandon would walk her down the aisle and there would be no bridesmaids or groomsmen. After the ceremony, he planned a small dinner reception for the family at the hotel. Then he and Venice would leave for a private villa on the other side of the island. Here, they would spend the next four days before coming home for Christmas.

Craig was pleased with his organizational skills. Now all he had to do was sit back and wait for their departure day to arrive. He smiled and picked up his phone and invited Lamar to lunch. After Craig left his office, he failed to put the paperwork with the wedding itinerary in his briefcase. When Francine and Katrina came back from lunch, she followed Francine into Craig's office.

"Girl, thanks for lunch. You know next time it's my treat."

"You're welcome. Anyway, it was my turn to buy lunch."

Katrina looked around the office. "My Lawd! I can smell the man and he ain't even in here."

Francine watered the plants. "Katrina, you shouldn't be in here."

"Why not? I work here just like you do."

Francine stopped watering the plants.

"You know why. You've been trippin' lately. I hope you've chilled on trying to get with him."

Katrina went around to Craig's chair, sat down and let out a loud, sexual moan. Francine shook her head at Katrina's antics.

"After I finish pouring this water out, you're out of here, Kat."

"Okay, okay."

Francine went into Craig's private bathroom to dump the water. Katrina was playing with trinkets on his desk when something caught her eye. The word, "ceremony." She glanced up to see if Francine were watching, then hurried out to make a quick copy. By the time Francine exited the bathroom, Katrina was standing at the door. Francine asked, "What's wrong with you?"

"Oh, nothing. I think I'll head on back to my office. I'll talk to you later."

"Okay, I'll see you at four."

Francine had never known Katrina to be in a hurry to leave Craig's office before. She decided to see what Katrina was up to. As she looked over Craig's desk, she also noticed the paper showing the upcoming itinerary.

Francine put it down and said, "So that's it. Katrina, I can't let you go through with whatever you're up to. I just can't."

Katrina's face felt like it was on fire. She hadn't had an opportunity to read the paper, but the nearest ladies room was just around the corner. She checked all the stalls and found the room empty. She then entered the last stall and sat down to read the copy she made.

The Majestic Hotel in Ocho Rios. Saturday, December 17th at 5 p.m. in the Diamond Ballroom, Flowers, Music, Food, and Drinks.

Katrina was stunned. What exactly did she have in her hand? The note was in Craig's handwriting, but what was the occasion? It could be for a friend, associate or family member, but her gut told her something different. It must be wedding plans, especially since it was in Ocho Rios. Her head immediately started throbbing. She put her hands over her eyes and screamed, *"No!"*

Almost as soon as she screamed, she started laughing. "Well, the joke is going to be on you, Venice. I will see how you like getting your private wedding ruined and covered by every newspaper in the country. This would be the perfect place to air Venice's dirty laundry and embarrass her in front of the world." As she left the bathroom, she sang, "It's beginning to look a lot like Christmas…"

A few days later, Lamar stopped in at Roan's to drop off some more plans. His Armani suit fit him to perfection. The ladies always said he was one of the best-dressed men in Philly and he wore his label well. Tressa didn't even have to look up to know who the heavenly scent belonged to.

Slowly she raised her eyes from the paperwork and with a smile said, "Well, how are you, Mr. Fletcher?" His dimples were what captivated her as well as the gleam in his warm, sensual eyes. He returned a smile.

"I'm doing fine, Tressa, but I would be doing so much better if you would have dinner with me tonight."

She stood and glanced over her shoulder to see if her father was in the vicinity. When she saw that he wasn't, she said, "I'm sorry, but I don't date clients. Plus, from what I hear, you have plenty women to keep you company."

His six-foot-four frame leaned forward and whispered, "Don't believe everything you hear, Tressa. Besides, I only want to have dinner with you, so please say yes."

Tressa trembled as the closeness of his body to hers caused her to react. No man had ever challenged her father or been as persistent as Lamar Fletcher. He was definitely a handsome, confident man, but the fact remained, he had a reputation.

"I'm sorry, Mr. Fletcher, but…"

"Lamar…I insist you call me Lamar. Furthermore if are you serious about not dating clients, we at Bennett & Fletcher can take our business elsewhere."

Tressa was startled, especially since Bennett & Fletcher was one of their most prestigious clients. She saw the mischievous grin on his face.

"You're not playing fair, Mr. Fletcher."

He took her hand into his and an instant spark went through both of them. His gaze met her chestnut-colored eyes.

"Who said anything about playing? I'm dead serious, Tressa. I would like to get to know you better and I hope you feel the same way. You must admit that we are attracted to each other."

She was frozen as she enjoyed the warmth of his hand covering hers. He pulled a single yellow rose from behind his back. "Well, if you'll have dinner with me, the other eleven will be waiting on you at our table. If not, please accept this one as a token of my affection. I'll be dining at Salimar's at seven. Goodbye, Tressa."

He turned her hand over and kissed the back of it before turning and exiting the door. Tressa had to admit, the man definitely knew how to seduce a woman. Not that she'd had a lot of firsthand knowledge. Her dad made sure of that, but she was twenty-eight years old and it was time she started living her own life. Maybe tonight would be the night to take that stand. Lamar was a mysterious, sexy man and she was curious to know more about him. Besides, what could having dinner with him hurt?

Back at the office, Lamar couldn't help but burst into Craig's office and bring him up to speed on his progress with Tressa.

"Craig, you should have seen the way her beautiful eyes lit up when I gave her the flower and invited her to dinner."

Craig stuffed his briefcase with paperwork.

"So is she joining you for dinner tonight?"

Lamar jumped up out of the chair. "I don't know, man. She's still hung up on all the rumors about me. I guess I'll know tonight at seven."

"They're not rumors, Lamar. You have too many women."

Lamar flicked lint from his pants leg. "Man, I've cut my list down to two. If I can get Tressa, she'll be the only one."

Craig grinned. "So, you're still going to the restaurant?"

"Hell, yeah! What if she shows up and I'm not there? That'll blow all my progress out the window."

"I guess you're right. Look, if it doesn't work out tonight, I'll talk to Venice about having you guys over for dinner. Maybe she would feel more comfortable on a double date first."

"Maybe so. Well, I'd better get out of here so I can get ready for dinner. What are you guys up to tonight?"

Craig put on his jacket. "We're taking Brandon Christmas shopping.

Hey! If Tressa doesn't show up, give me a call. You can go with us."

Lamar waited as Craig locked up the office.

"I don't want to intrude on you and Venice."

They turned, walked toward the elevator and entered.

"It's no problem, but I hope she shows up, Lamar."

The door opened and they walked to their perspective vehicles.

Lamar said, "So do I. I'll see you in the a.m."

"Later, man, and good luck."

"Thanks and tell the family hello."

"Will do."

When Craig walked into the kitchen, he found Venice hard at work with dinner and the phone cradled under her neck. Brandon was upstairs playing in his room. Craig crossed the room and planted a cheerful kiss on her lips. She smiled as she watched him check the pots, then head upstairs for a shower. Venice continued to talk on the phone.

"Mom, there's no need to panic. I'm sure Portia would come to you for birth control. If not, she would probably ask me and she hasn't."

Venice's former mother-in-law answered worriedly, "I know, Venice, but remember, you went to Sinclair instead of your mom."

Venice sighed remembering the anxiety of talking about birth control with her own mom. That was the main reason she went to Sinclair, her sister-in-law.

"Do you want me to talk to her and see if she mentions it?"

"I don't know. We might be getting ahead of ourselves. I don't even know if they're hers, but they were in her closet."

"She could be hiding them for a friend. God, I hope it's not for Crimson! Got to go, Mom. I'll let you know if I find out anything. I'm glad Brandon was awake so you could talk to him. He misses you guys."

Mrs. Anderson responded, "We miss all of you. Tell Craig hello and we'll see you in a couple of weeks."

"Love you."

"Love you, too, and tell Pops I love him."

Venice became silent.

Mrs. Anderson said, "Venice, please don't…"

Venice sighed. "It's still hard, you know. It hurts. I still miss him so much."

"I know. I miss him, too. Not a day goes by that I don't cry for my son. They're getting less, but the tears still come. You have been blessed with a wonderful man. I love you and we're always here for you if you ever need anything. Now, go take care of your family. We'll talk another day, Baby."

"Thanks, Mom. I love you, too. Goodbye."

After hanging up, Venice ran upstairs to see Craig. Upon entering the bedroom, he was already in the shower. She opened the shower door and said, "Nice!"

He turned, smiled and said, "Come on in. The water's great."

She backed away, just as he reached for her. She approached him again and leaned in for a kiss, being careful not to get her clothes or hair wet. His perfect body, covered in suds, met her at the door. The kiss was wet and warm. He wanted to pull her inside, but knowing Brandon was just down the hall stopped him.

"Woman, you're lucky Brandon's down the hall."

"No, you're lucky. I wouldn't want him to hear you scream."

They stared as if they were challenging each other. Craig finally broke the silence, saying, "We'll see who screams the loudest when I get you on the honeymoon."

"O-o-o, I'm scared!!"

"Funny. Now if you're not coming in, close the door. You're letting all the good steam out."

Venice laughed as she left the bathroom. She checked in on Brandon and made sure he had cleaned up his room. She told him dinner would be ready in fifteen minutes, then it was off to the mall.

CHAPTER Twenty Six

I t was now seven thirty and Lamar had decided to call it a night. She wasn't coming. Just as he motioned for the waiter, she entered the restaurant. Lamar couldn't tear his gaze from her striking beauty.

She had to be at least five feet eight. The thick tresses of hair hung loose tonight, inches below her shoulders. She had not spotted him yet and this gave him more time to admire her physical attributes. The black dress she wore molded to her magnificent curves as if it were custom-made for her. He couldn't take it any longer. He stood and immediately crossed the room to meet her, instantly becoming the envy of every man in the room.

She smiled and said, "Sorry I'm late, Mr. Fletcher."

"Apology accepted and, for the last time, it's Lamar. Otherwise, I will not answer you. Okay?"

She smiled. "I'll try to remember…Lamar."

She took his hand as they followed the waiter over to their table where a vase with eleven yellow roses awaited them.

C raig's truck was stuffed with shopping bags from various stores. They were all tired from walking from one end of the mall to the other on both levels. Before they could exit the parking lot,

Brandon was fast asleep. They had accomplished buying gifts for all the people on his list. Craig looked over at Venice.

"I forgot how much energy he has."

"I know. My feet are killing me."

He patted her on the thigh. "I'll rub them for you when we get home."

"I think I'll take you up on your offer, Bennett."

At that point, she leaned her seat back and closed her eyes. It would take approximately thirty minutes to get home.

Later, with Brandon safely tucked away in his bed, Craig motioned for Venice to join him on the sofa in their room. She had just finished her shower and sat next to him.

He took the lotion from her hand and said, "Let me do that."

She leaned back and allowed him to apply the lotion to her legs. Moving in slow, seductive strokes, he made his way to her sore feet and massaged them thoroughly.

He smiled. "You smell good."

Her eyes were closed as she replied, "Thanks, and that feels wonderful."

"It's my pleasure, Sweetheart."

He finished massaging her feet. "Stay right here. I have something for you."

She opened her eyes. "What is it?"

He didn't answer. He just entered the closet, then came back with one hand behind his back.

"Craig, what do you have behind you?"

He didn't respond. He just had a serious look on his face. It made her curious, so she sat up on the sofa. Staring at her as he approached, he got down on one knee.

"Venice, I just want you to know that having you in my life has made me whole. Until you, there was no me. I have never loved as I love you. There has never been and will never be anyone who could complete me as you have."

Venice was overwhelmed with the words Craig recited. She didn't know where he was going with it, but he did.

He continued by saying, "Sweetheart, what I'm trying to do is properly propose to you. Will you marry me?"

Venice leaned back on the sofa in shock as he produced a small velvet box from behind his back. Inside was a bridal set, which had to be at least three carats. One ring had a huge round diamond in the center with clusters of diamonds encircling the band. The wedding band was a cluster of diamonds also.

Venice stared at the rings. "Bennett! You already gave me a ring!"

"That was from our past. I want you to have something new to represent our new beginning...as a family."

She stared at him, then at the rings.

"You didn't have to do this. I'm perfectly happy with the ring you already gave me." He took her hand into his and slid the old ring off her finger. He looked her in the eye, slid the new ring on her finger and asked again, "Will you marry me?"

"If my memory serves me correctly, I've already proposed to you, Bennett."

"I know, but you know I'm old-fashioned. Traditionally, I feel like I still need to ask you."

She stared down at her finger.

"You already have and you surprise me every day. Yes, I will marry you. I also want to thank you for loving me and my son so much."

He stood up, pulled her up from the sofa, and held her hands. She stared up into his dark eyes.

"You are an amazing man, Bennett, and you make me what I am... complete."

The deal was sealed with a sizzling kiss.

Craig was looking forward to his upcoming wedding and Christmas. They planned a big surprise for Brandon by bringing Ms. Camille to Philadelphia. He had suspended his commutes to Japan until after New Year's Day. Most important was settling the situation involving Katrina. He couldn't understand how she thought he was interested in her in any way except as an employee. Her mental health was in question and he prayed Joshua handled the matter successfully.

School was out for Christmas break so Nanna came and got Brandon to spend a couple of days with her and the rest of Craig's family in Dawson. Craig and Venice met Ms. Camille at the airport to take her to see her new home.

"Craig, it's nice to finally meet you. Venice has told me so many wonderful things about you."

Craig looked at Venice.

"Likewise, Ms. Camille. I feel like I already know you."

Venice spoke up and said, "Turn left here and it's the fourth house down on the left."

Ms. Camille could see the neighborhood was neat and clean and had plenty of shade trees. When Craig pulled up into the driveway, Ms. Camille gasped. It was nothing like her home in Detroit. Craig got out and went around to help Ms. Camille out of the car. She was speechless. Right before her eyes was the house she had dreamed of as a young girl. It was a white, two-story house with a white picket fence surrounding the front yard. Lining the sidewalk were the remnants of colorful flowers and shrubbery. The large house had a wraparound porch with a swing on one end, perfect for relaxing during the summer. The tall trees in the front yard would add plenty of shade on a hot summer day.

"Do you like it, Ms. Camille?"

"How did you know, child?"

Venice confessed that she called Ms. Camille's older brother in Mississippi. He told her of the house she talked about having when they were growing up.

"I had no idea Wilbur would remember talks we had as children."

Craig escorted her up the front steps.

"He remembered perfectly, Ms. Camille. There were some details he gave us and I was able to add them inside. Are you ready to go see?"

"Craig, Darling, I've waited all my life. Let's go."

Inside was the sitting room with a huge fireplace. The kitchen had all the modern appliances as well as a large pantry for storage. Down the main hall was the master bedroom with the window seat Craig built so Ms. Camille would be able to look out over her backyard and into a man-made water garden. The tears flowed down her face as she turned and embraced and kissed both of them.

"How could I ever repay you for your kindness?"

Venice whispered, "You already have, Ms. Camille."

"Children, this is too much."

Craig said, "It was our pleasure, Ms. Camille. There are three more bedrooms upstairs as well as two full baths."

Venice hugged her.

"We can go pick out your furniture and whatever else you need tomorrow. Then, by the time you come back, you'll be all set."

"Where's my baby?"

Craig said, "He's with my grandmother in Dawson. Since you were coming, Nanna told us to let him come visit with her for a couple of days so it wouldn't spoil the surprise. Now, after we finish showing you the house, I'm taking the two most beautiful women out to lunch."

Ms. Camille looped her arm with Craig's.

"You won't hear an argument from me. Lead the way, handsome."

Venice smiled and put her hands on her hips.

"All right, Ms. Camille. Don't forget he belongs to me."

"Hush your fuss, child, and let an old lady enjoy the company of this handsome man."

They laughed and went upstairs to finish the tour.

Brandon was enjoying his visit with Nanna and Craig's niece and nephew. They were helping Nanna decorate her Christmas tree, which was starting to take shape as each child scrambled to put the next ornament up.

Brandon said, "Nanna, this is so much fun!"

"I'm glad you're enjoying it. When we finish, your nanna is going to fix you guys some grilled cheese sandwiches and we're going to watch a movie. How about that?"

All three kids jumped up and down, yelling in appreciation. Nanna went on to say, "Tomorrow, we have to make cookies. Can you guys help with that?"

Craig's niece, Samantha, said, "Oh, yes, Nanna. We can help you. I make the bestest cookies."

Craig's nephew, Thomas James, named after his grandfather, replied, "No, you don't! They taste like mud!"

The arguing started and Nanna said, "Now! Now! I'm not going to have that. Thomas James, quit teasing your sister."

When Nanna turned to open another box, Samantha licked her tongue out at him. He showed her his fist in return. Brandon's eyes widened in amazement, enjoying the exchange between brother and sister. This made him wish even more for a sibling. He would be happy with either a brother or sister and once Santa got his letter, he hoped his wish would be under his tree on Christmas morning.

Katrina was pleased with the fact that Nathan's editor decided to give her the extra time since they now knew where and when the wedding was taking place. Katrina picked out an exquisite dress for the event and she was sure it would knock Craig off his feet when he laid eyes on her. Plus, she wanted to make a grand entrance. After she ran the list of Venice's indiscretions down to Craig, he wouldn't want to be anywhere near her. Even though she was concentrating on ruining their wedding plans, she still had concerns of her own. She was almost sure Venice had found out about her past and was the one trying to torment her. Her final reward would be sending her running back where she came from. The police could question her all they wanted. She knew she didn't kill Gunner even though she wished she had. There had been numerous times he reminded her that she worked for him. She still had the scars as reminders.

Craig and Venice knew they had a lot of business to take care of since they would be marrying soon. Jarvis left Venice very wealthy and Craig's business was worth millions in itself. They had to decide how they were going to handle their finances. Venice was still using the same accountant she used when she was in Detroit. Since she would be living in Philadelphia, she decided to sign on with the same company Craig was using. They met with lawyers to examine their will and testaments, life insurance as well as other personal matters. When Venice mentioned buying Ms. Camille's house, Craig insisted on helping with the expense. He told Venice that Ms. Camille not only helped her and Jarvis with Brandon, but that she would be the one to help look after their children. He felt it was only fair that he be involved in making her move to Philly comfortable and rewarding. Venice was stubborn at first, but finally saw his point. Two days later, they took Ms. Camille back to the airport to fly back to Detroit to finalize her business there. Christmas Day, Brandon would be surprised with Ms. Camille as his caretaker, as well as lots of other goodies.

Craig entered his office and greeted Francine warmly.

"Good morning, Francine."

"Good morning, Craig."

Francine followed Craig into his office and began to read off his appointments for the day.

"Thank you, Francine, and I forgot to tell you how nice you look today."

"Thank you, Craig."

She continued to stand there as Craig shuffled through his mail. He looked up and asked, "Francine, is there something else you want to talk about?"

She fumbled with her notepad and looked down at the floor.

"Francine…is everything okay?"

She looked up at him and clearly looked distressed.

"Have a seat, Francine. Let me get you a glass of water. Whatever it is, I'm sure it'll be okay."

She sat down in the chair opposite his desk and waited as he brought her a glass of water.

After handing it to her, he closed the door and sat in the chair next to her. She took a sip of the water and turned to look at him.

"Now...tell me what's got you all upset this morning. I've never seen you like this before."

"Well...Craig...there's something that has been going on and I think you should know about it. You see, Katrina...she...she has some issues and for some reason she's made it her mission in life to win your affections. I don't know the particulars, but she mentioned something about breaking you and your lady friend up so you can be all hers. She's not a bad person, really. She just don't know when to leave well enough alone. I don't want her to cause you any trouble, but I don't want anything to happen to her either. She just won't listen to me."

"I see, Francine. How long have you known?"

She looked down at her hands in her lap.

"Craig, she hasn't confided in me. I just know she talks about breaking you guys up. I hope she hasn't done any damage to your relationship."

Craig stood up and offered Francine his hand. She took his hand and he gave her a warm hug.

"Thank you, Francine. I don't blame you and I'm glad you told me. I know you two are friends, so I know it was hard for you to come to me. I'll handle Katrina, so just keep this conversation between us. Okay?"

"Okay, and again, I'm so sorry I didn't come to you sooner. I just thought Katrina would drop all that nonsense. She does have some good qualities about her, so please don't be so hard on her."

He walked her to the door. "Forget about it. Now, I guess I'd better get to that meeting. Huh?"

"That's right. Oh, I forgot! I think Katrina saw some paperwork on your desk regarding a ceremony in Ocho Rios."

Craig looked surprised, not realizing he had left the papers visible.

"I see...thanks for letting me know, Francine, and I'll talk with you after I get back from my meeting."

"Okay. If you need anything else, let me know."

"I will. Tell Lamar I'll be back in the office around one o'clock."

"Will do."

Francine closed the door and returned to her desk.

Well, well, well. Miss Katrina is smoother than I thought.

He picked up the telephone and made a very important call. After hanging up he smiled and picked up his briefcase before heading to his meeting.

CHAPTER Twenty Seven

Just as Venice finished wrapping the last present, the doorbell rang. Things had been calm the last few weeks, which allowed her to let her guard down. Right before she got to the door, something stopped her. She wasn't expecting anyone, but a slight chill ran over her body. She decided to play it safe and peeped out the living room curtain. To her amazement, Katrina stood on the porch with a package in hand. Venice held her breath and thought if she let it out, Katrina would hear her. Anger instantly consumed her and made her want to open the door and give her the beat-down she deserved. Katrina rung the bell again, then left the mysterious package on the doorstep. Venice watched her as she walked back to her car and drove away. It was then she was able to relax. Katrina knew Craig was at work and found it the opportune time to stop by his house. Venice opened the door and stared at the package, then left it where it sat.

Will you ever give up, Katrina?

After Craig arrived home that evening, Venice told him about the package on the front step. When he opened it, he found a beautiful gold bracelet with a plain card reading *From a Secret Admirer.* Venice turned away and went upstairs.

"Venice! Wait!"

He caught her halfway up the stairs.

"I'm not going to keep this, if that's what you're worried about."

She looked him square in the eyes. "I am through hiding out from Katrina. I'm sick of her making my life miserable. If she wants to print lies about me, let her. I'll just have to explain it to Brandon the best way I can."

He took her by the hand. "Sweetheart, don't let her win. It's almost over, I promise."

"What are you going to do with the bracelet?"

"I think I will take it to the office and have it as a door prize at our Christmas luncheon. I don't except gifts from strangers."

"Craig, I'm not hungry anymore; I think I'll go to bed." She continued upstairs and when she reached the landing, she turned. "I cooked your favorite. Goodnight."

She disappeared out of his sight. Craig simply stood there staring at the bracelet. He returned it to the velvet case, rewrapping it neatly. He was also tired of Katrina trying to control their lives. He had also lost his appetite. So, he put the food in the refrigerator and turned in for the evening.

That night, Craig stood in the bathroom mirror unable to sleep. The event of the day and previous weeks were starting to take a toll on him. He felt restless, knowing Katrina had turned his world upside-down. His life had become more than he could ever dream. However, sadness filled his heart. He looked over at Venice sleeping peacefully. *How in the world did you end up in my life?*

He was beginning to feel guilty at Jarvis' expense. In a short time he would make her his wife, but would he ever be able to replace the emptiness her heart still carried? He also felt he needed to tell her about his conversation with Brandon. He splashed his face with water and returned to bed. Settling down, she scooted against his body.

"Is everything okay, Babe?"

In a whisper, he said, "Venice, I need to talk to you."

She rose up. "Is something wrong?"

He pulled her into his arms. "Venice, do you remember the week Nanna was here?"

"Yes. What about it?"

"Well, Brandon and I had an unusual conversation regarding Jarvis."

Her eyes widened in curiosity. "What about Jarvis?"

It was obvious that Craig was having trouble getting his thoughts together. He wanted to tell her as gently as possible.

Venice was becoming nervous and asked again, "Craig, what about Jarvis?"

Craig hugged her. "Venice, Brandon said that when he was visiting his grandparents, his dad came to him and told him to tell you to keep the window open."

"What!"

"He said Jarvis told him you would know what it meant."

Venice jumped up out the bed with her hand over her mouth in shock. She backed away from Craig as he tried to console her.

He pleaded, "Venice, what does it mean?"

"No! Wait! Give me a minute! Oh, my God!!"

She was clearly upset and ran into the bathroom where she sank to the floor and threw up in the toilet. Craig followed helplessly as he watched her in agony. The tears streamed down her face as she grabbed her stomach like sharp pains were radiating from the area. Craig felt useless and angry with himself for telling her. He could do nothing to help her. He went to comfort her and this time she did not push him away. She cried openly and held onto him as he lifted her from the floor. He decided not to push for information as he returned her to the bed, then retrieved a cold towel to wipe her face.

Only minutes passed, but to Craig it seemed like hours. He watched as her breathing went from short rapid breaths down to slow deep ones. Her eyes remained closed so he wasn't sure if she had fallen asleep. Removing the towel, he stroked her cheek and whispered, "Everything will be okay, Venice. I love you and I'll do everything in my power to take your pain away."

She slowly opened her eyes after hearing his words. They stared at each other for a moment, then she rose up on her elbows.

"Craig, I need to use the bathroom."

"Are you okay, Venice?"

Between sniffles, she solemnly answered, "I'll be right back."

He stood up, helped her to her feet and watched as she slowly walked into the bathroom. Once inside she looked at her reflection and came to the realization that no one except her and Jarvis knew about their private joke. Knowing that Brandon encountered some type of mystical visit from his dad threw her into a tailspin of emotion. She brushed her teeth and washed her face before returning to the bedroom to explain to Craig what it all meant. She composed herself and opened the door to find an emotionally drained Craig sitting with his head down at the foot of the bed. He stood as she approached, noticing her puffy eyes.

"Sit back down, Bennett. I'm sorry, but I owe you an explanation."

He sat down and she joined him, holding his hand tightly in hers. It still took her a moment, but she found the courage to explain.

"Craig, what Brandon told you only two people on this earth knew about...me and Jarvis. When he said his dad told him to tell me to keep the window open...well..."

Craig hugged her.

"It's okay, Sweetheart. You don't have to explainY"

"Yes, I do. I owe you that. When Jarvis and I were dating, he used to sneak over to my house in the middle of the night and climb up to my bedroom. We spent many nights together this way and I was always afraid my daddy would think he was a burglar and shoot at him. Thank God, it never came to that. Anyway, he would always call when he was on his way. Before hanging up the phone, he would always tell me to keep the window open. I never told anyone, not even Joshua. So you see, Jarvis must have come to Brandon. But why?"

"I don't know."

"This seems like a dream. How did he seem? Should I say something to him?"

"It didn't seem strange to Brandon. He seemed happy to have talked with his dad. It does make me wonder if he really understands what happened to Jarvis."

Venice bit her bottom lip.

"I'm sorry I freaked out on you, Babe. I thought I had gotten a little stronger by now."

He pulled back the covers and motioned for her to get in the bed.

"You are stronger, Venice. You don't have to apologize for freaking out. You should have seen my face when Brandon told me. What happened is eerie and you didn't react any differently than anyone else would have. Try and get some sleep. We'll deal with this day by day. Okay?"

She pulled the comforter over their bodies. "Okay, and thank you."

"No problem."

Craig was spooked by the events that had taken place, but decided there had to be a reason for Jarvis' untimely visit. He just hoped that if he had to encounter a visit, he would handle it in a calm and discreet manner. Before closing his eyes, he whispered a prayer of thanks, peace and tranquility. Venice kissed his neck and buried her face against his chest.

Wedding Week

Venice had found the perfect dress and she couldn't wait for Craig to see her in it. The moment was bittersweet for her. She was about to marry a wonderful man who loved her and yet she couldn't help but think of Jarvis and the life she had with him. Standing in the mirror, holding the dress up to her body, she remembered doing the same ritual when she was about to marry Jarvis. She hung the dress up in the closet and went to the window. Staring out over the yard, she hugged herself and tried to keep the sadness from returning. She never dreamed she would be going through this again.

"Oh, Jarvis. How did I end up here? Why did you have to leave me? I miss you so much."

She closed her eyes and stifled the tears welling in her eyes. She still loved him very much, and yet her love for Craig was so true.

Winter had arrived with a vengeance and she couldn't wait to feel the warm sand at her feet once again. An unusual chill traveled over her body just as someone knocked on her door. She rubbed the goose pimples from her arms and said, "Come in."

Craig entered, carrying a cup. "I thought you might like some hot buttered rum."

She smiled, taking it from him. "I remember the last time I shared this with you. Do you?"

"How could I forget? You were a wild woman."

"Is that what you're trying to turn me into now?"

He embraced her from behind. "I think I've been able to do that without the help of hot buttered rum."

She caressed his arm. "That you have, Bennett."

He sat on the bed, pulling her into his lap.

She sipped the rum in silence.

"What's on your mind? Are you okay with this?"

She lowered the cup and solemnly and truthfully said, "I can't help but think about him, Craig. I'm trying to move on with my life, but it's so hard. I loved him so much. I look at Brandon, who's so much like him and I tremble. The hurt is not going away overnight. You know I love you and I want you to know I'm dealing with this the best way I know how."

He listened, hugging her as he spoke. "Venice, quit worrying about me. I want you to concentrate on you. I don't expect you to get over the pain of losing Jarvis right away. It may take years for it to ease. Either way, I'm here for the duration and I don't want you to feel like you can't talk to me about it. I know it's nothing compared to what you and Brandon went through, but losing you to Jarvis was a pain I can't even describe and something I never got over. But I thank God I found you and love again. I also have to admit, I've been dealing with some guilt myself. It doesn't seem fair for me to be so happy when I think about the circumstances that brought us together. So, you see, we're both dealing with a lot of emotions right now."

She took another sip of her drink.

"You shouldn't feel guilty. I don't know what higher power brought us together, but whatever it was, I'm thankful. I'm also thankful that my son loves you so much."

"I guess that makes two of us."

"No, Bennett, three of us." She hugged his neck and said, "I love you, Craig."

"I love you, too, and I guess you're going to stay here until the wedding, huh?"

She patted him on the thigh. "That's right. I'm also going to remain celibate until our honeymoon."

"That is sheer torture, woman."

"You only have two more days left, then I'm all yours."

She got up from his lap, but he didn't want to break the warm contact. Continuing to hold her around the waist, he took the cup from her hand and asked, "Am I allowed to kiss you?"

She looped her arms around his neck while pressing her body to his and said, "Bring it on, Bennett."

He smiled and lowered his lips to hers, taking his time to savor the sweetness of her mouth. Pulling her closer made her moan as she tried to get nearer. Cupping her hips, he picked her up while she wrapped her legs around his body. He laid her on the bed and covered her body with his just as Nanna knocked on the door.

"Craig! Venice! Dinner's ready!"

They unwillingly pulled apart and smiled into each other's desire-filled eyes. Craig nibbled on her neck.

"I guess you were just saved by the bell."

"You know I'm weak to you, Bennett, and I promise it'll be worth the wait."

He kissed her one last time.

"No, I'm the one weak to you and I'll wait a lifetime for you."

"Thank you, Babe."

He stood up and pulled her to her feet. "We'd better get downstairs before Nanna comes searching for us again."

Chapter Twenty Eight

Katrina called Francine from the airport.

"Hey, Francine! I just wanted to let you know that I'll be out of town for a couple of days."

"Are you going home?"

"No, I'm going to get my man!"

"Katrina, what are you up to? Where are you headed?"

"Don't worry, Francine. I'm going to have me a little fun in the sun."

"Give me a number where I can reach you, Kat."

"I'll call you when I get there. Chow! Got to go."

The phone went dead. Francine had a gut feeling Katrina was headed somewhere to cause Craig a world of trouble. The problem was she wasn't a hundred percent sure. She would just have to wait and pray that she called back. With any luck, she'd tell her where she was and what she was up to. She couldn't allow Katrina to cause harm to herself or anyone else.

Francine's daughter came over and gave her a big hug.

"Momma, I'm hungry."

"I'll fix you something as soon as I make this phone call, okay?"

"Okay, Momma."

Francine pulled out her address book, looked up the particular number, and dialed.

"Hello?"

"Hello, Lynette?"

"Yes."

"This is Francine. I'm a friend of your sister, Katrina."

"Oh, yes. How are you?"

"I'm fine, but I don't know about Kat."

"What's wrong? Is she hurt?"

"No, she's not hurt, but I think she's doing some things that may hurt her in the end. I don't know what else to do, so I called you."

"Francine, please tell me. I don't want my sister hurt."

Francine went on to tell Lynette about Katrina's obsession with Craig and about her suspicion that she had traveled to Ocho Rios to break up his wedding.

When she was finished, Lynette said, "Oh, Francine, I'm so glad you called me. Katrina has been through so much in her life. You see we never had a father in our life and Katrina started reaching out for love from any man she could get. She started confusing kindness for something more. Between you and me, Katrina was molested by one of our mother's boyfriends for years. This man, Craig, is he your boss?"

"Yes and he is one of the owners of the company we work for. He's a nice man but he's already involved with someone else. I think Katrina has been doing things to break them up and now she's going to stop their wedding."

"She didn't mention where she was going?"

"No, just that she would call when she got there."

"The minute you find out, call me. I think my sister needs some help and I love her too much to let her ruin someone's life. Thank you for calling me, Francine, and I hope my sister knows what a good friend you are."

"Thank you, Lynette. I'll call you."

Lynette hung up the phone and said a little prayer of hope that her sister didn't damage herself or anyone else.

Katrina arrived at the Ocho Rios hotel and checked into her room. She picked up the phone and called Francine to tell her where she was, but not why she was there. Nathan and the photo-grapher from the rag magazine would be arriving later. This would give her time to scope out the territory before the ceremony. She called the front desk to see if Craig Bennett had checked in. They confirmed that he was there, which made Katrina very happy. The only thing she had to do now was stay out of sight until the ceremony.

Later that evening, Nathan came to her room to let her know he had arrived. In a few hours, she would break up the wedding for Craig's own good. Venice wasn't right for him and she would prove it.

"Nathan, make sure you get good pictures. We only have one chance at this."

"I know, Kat. I saw the hotel staff setting up the chapel and a small ballroom. I must say, it's beautiful."

"Good, that will make the pictures even better."

"Kat, you want this brotha that bad? I mean, what does he have that I don't?"

Katrina turned and said, "No disrespect, baby. I mean, you're da bomb in bed, but Craig's got bank and he's fine as hell."

Nathan crossed the room and embraced her.

"Look, Nathan, business before pleasure. When this is over, I will have some serious grip and you can help me celebrate. You are going to be the envy of journalists all over the country, so you should be happy. Afterwards, Craig Bennett will be putty in my hand and that conniving heifer will be left out in the cold." Katrina gave Nathan a deep kiss on the lips. "Now leave so I can get ready. The ceremony will be starting soon."

"Whatever you say, Kat. Damn! I'm glad I'm on your side. That brotha ain't gonna know what hit him."

"Yes, he will. Hurricane Katrina is about to sweep him off his feet."

Hours later, Venice eyed herself in the mirror one last time. She was pleased with the dress she'd picked out. It was a beautiful silk, ivory dress, which fit snug to her curves, stopping just above her ankles. It gave the illusion of being strapless, however the dress, as well as her arms, were covered with a thin layer of chiffon. This time she decided to wear her hair down in beautiful, shiny waves and opted to omit a veil. She turned and looked over at the bouquet of tropical flowers, which she put together herself. She wanted this wedding simple, yet elegant. When she walked down the aisle to Craig, she hoped to put the anxieties and fears of moving on with her life aside and just be happy with the man she loved.

Craig waited nervously with Venice's brother, Galen, Joshua and Skeeter. He paced the floor, occasionally stopping to check his watch. He had chosen a tailored tuxedo, which fit his tall, masculine physique to perfection. Any woman in her right mind would have had to be blind not to notice him. He was one gorgeous, sexy man.

Galen had been one of his closest friends at college. He straightened his tie and said, "Dang, Craig, you're about to wear a hole in the carpet. Chill!"

Skeeter agreed. "Yeah, man, you're making me nervous. You don't have anything to worry about. Venice is not going anywhere."

Craig stopped pacing for a moment.

"You guys just don't understand. I've dreamed of this moment more times than I can remember. All those times in the past, I woke up. It's not a dream anymore. I just want everything to go as planned."

Joshua went over and patted him on the shoulder. "Craig, relax. I told you that I would take care of everything and I have. This is *your* day. The day you've been waiting on. Enjoy, man."

A few minutes later, Craig's sister, Bernice, came and informed them it was time.

Craig gave each of them a brotherly hug and they exited the room.

I n the sanctuary, Venice's and Craig's families, as well as her former in-laws, witnessed what they felt was a blessed union. Jarvis' parents were elated that Venice had not given up on love and had found a wonderful man that their grandson adored. Their immediate family and close friends were all in attendance. As the music began, Venice appeared in the doorway on her father's arm. From the moment Craig laid eyes on her, he stopped breathing. She was absolutely stunning. Her slow journey toward him allowed him to have flashbacks from the moment he first met her in college until he last saw her at her wedding to Jarvis seven years ago. Some of the memories were happy and sensuous, while others were sad and depressing. Yet this day had become the happiest day in his life. He thought about his mother and father and how much he wished they were there to share in his joy. Today, the only woman he had ever loved would become his wife and soon the mother of his children.

Venice finally made it to Craig's side with tears streaming down her lovely face. Seeing her so emotional caused his eyes to mist. He reached up and gently wiped away her tears as he whispered, "I love you."

Brandon proudly stood next to his mom, waiting to give her away along with his grandfather. Once the music ended, the minister began, "Dearly beloved. We are gathered here today to join this man and this woman in holy matrimony."

Katrina stood outside the doorway of the chapel. She turned and asked Nathan, "How do I look?"

"Spectacular, Kat. Are you ready?"

"Just as soon as the minister asks, 'If anyone here has any reason this man and woman shouldn't be joined, speak now or forever hold your peace.' Then, Nathan, my darling, this party is on."

Katrina and Nathan listened tentatively as the Reverend recited passages, which the couple repeated. He made it to the section, "If anyone here has any reason this man and woman shouldn't be joined, speak now or forever hold your peace."

Katrina looked at Nathan and said, "Showtime!"

She burst through the door with Nathan in pursuit and shouted, "I do!"

The small audience of guests turned to look at a beautiful, statuesque woman strolling toward the altar. Nathan flashed pictures at Katrina and the stunned guests.

Katrina said, "I object because this woman doesn't deserve this man! She is a backstabbing whore who cheated on her dying husband!"

Katrina put her hands on her hips and smiled.

"I am the only woman who could make Craig Bennett happy. Venice Anderson is not fit for any man!"

At that moment, the minister said, "Miss Simmons! Please, there must be some mistake! This is not the Bennett/Anderson wedding."

Katrina was so into making her speech and facing the camera, she didn't look up at the couple. When she did, it was not Craig and Venice. Her hands covered her mouth in shock.

The Reverend said, "Miss Simmons!"

"How do you know my name?"

The bride, groom and minister all said, "We're Chicago police officers and we have a warrant for your arrest for the murder of Tyrone Waters a.k.a. Gunner."

Katrina froze as a female police officer posing as a guest handcuffed her. She couldn't believe what was happening.

Katrina screamed, "I didn't kill Gunner!"

The officer told her that she had the right to remain silent, etc...

About that time, Lynette and Francine entered the room.

"Boogie! I'm so glad to see you. Tell them I didn't kill Gunner."

Lynette ran up to the officers. "I'm her sister. Please let her go. She didn't kill that awful man."

The officer said, "I'm sorry, Ma'am. If you want to talk to her, you have to come with us."

Francine asked, "Katrina, are you all right?"

Katrina turned and asked, "Where's Craig?"

"I don't know, Kat. Honey, I think you need to see a doctor."

Boogie agreed, saying, "Trina, you're my sister and I love you. I'm going to take you home so you can have the best of care. Okay?"

Katrina looked at her sister, dazed, and calmly said, "Whatever you say, Boogie. I'll do whatever you say."

Manley entered the room.

"Release her, officer."

Lynette, Katrina and Francine all turned and looked at this striking man. He was about six feet four with broad shoulders and handsome features. His dark complexion was smooth and his scent was all male. He moved toward them in a confident stride.

When he stood before them, Lynette asked, "Who are you?"

Katrina said, "He's one of the officers who came to my house."

Manley didn't confirm or deny Katrina's statement. He waited until she was uncuffed and told everyone to exit the room.

Once the room was empty, he sat Katrina, Lynette and Francine down saying, "Have a seat, please."

They sat and waited as he took his jacket off. Francine, in particular, noticed his professionalism and the fact that he was hiding a very fit body under his suit. They continued to wait in silence as he pulled out a small notepad and a tape recorder. He recorded the date and time.

"For the record, I need each one of you to say your name."

Boogie asked, "What is going on here?"

Manley said, "Ma'am, we're trying to wrap up a murder investigation and the only way to do that is to interview the last person he was known to be with. We've tried to interview Miss Simmons in the past but faced difficulty."

The ladies did as they were told.After Manley finished the interview, he said, "Miss Simmons, I found out in our investigation that some crimes were committed against you as a child. It's unfortunate, and I feel because of your experience, you are having some problems in your adult life. We also received a report that you have been black-mailing an individual whom I will not name. This individual does not want to cause you any problems, but I will say if you continue the harassment, I will have you arrested. I don't believe jail is where you belong, but I do recommend you seek some professional help as soon as possible. Lastly, to satisfy all parties involved, you need to consider resigning from your job or changing careers."

Boogie said, "Thank you, Sir. I'll take Katrina home so I can see to her health."

Manley stood. "Good. Katrina, you are not to have any contact, verbal or otherwise with the unnamed parties, *ever*. If you do, you will find me in your face again and you won't like it. Agreed?"

Katrina dropped her head. "Agreed."

"Well, this meeting is over and, ladies, have a safe flight. Miss Lynette, I will be checking in with you from time to time to see how Miss Katrina is doing."

"Thank you."

Manley extended his hand. "Good day, ladies. It's been a pleasure."

He happened to hold Francine's hand a little longer. It wasn't until she blushed that she pulled her hand away. He just smiled and exited the room.

Lynette hugged Katrina. "Let's go home."

Katrina turned and hugged Francine.

"Thanks, Francine. You've been a great friend."

Francine hugged her back. "I'll always be your friend, Kat. I'll come visit you as much as possible. Okay?"

"Okay. Please tell Craig that I'm sorry and that I didn't mean to hurt him. I just love him so much."

Francine said, "I'm sure he knows, Kat. You're a valued employee and just maybe when you get better, you can come back to work."

"I hope so, Francine. I love my job and living in Philly."

Katrina looked at Lynette. "Well, Boogie…I guess we need to be getting back to the Windy City."

"Let's go, Trina. Francine's going to secure your house for you."

Nathan was nowhere to be found. When those officers flashed their badges, he disappeared with the quickness.

Chapter Twenty Nine

B ack in Dawson, Craig and Venice finished reciting their vows and exchanging rings. After Craig found out Katrina saw the itinerary of their Ocho Rios wedding, he changed everything to his hometown.

The ceremony was at the part for Brandon to do his thing. He walked over and lit a candle in remembrance of Jarvis. He then returned and stood beside his mother while smiling up at Craig. Venice had always loved the beautiful sanctuary of Craig's hometown church. She had spent many Sundays there during the time she attended college. Before pronouncing them husband and wife, the minister announced that Craig would be singing a song dedicated to Venice. She looked at him in disbelief as he took her by the hand and led her over to the piano and proceeded to serenade her with a beautiful song he'd written especially for her. Needless to say, when he finished, there was not a dry eye in the room.

Joshua turned to look at his wife, Cynthia, who was clearly overcome with emotion. His pager vibrated and he pulled it from his jacket. The text message read, *All is well in Ocho Rios. The fat lady has sung.*

Joshua smiled, then leaned over and kissed his wife. When he turned back, the minister said, "With the power invested in me, I now pronounce you husband and wife. Craig, you may now salute your bride."

He smiled as he embraced her.

"I love you, Venice."

Their kiss was tender and long. Finally the pastor said, "Son, you have time for more of that later. Amen."

Craig broke the kiss and smiled at his childhood minister.

"Ladies and gentlemen. I present to you Craig and Venice Bennett."

Everyone stood and applauded as Craig took Venice and Brandon by the hand and proceeded down the aisle. Venice stopped when she reached the Andersons and hugged and kissed each one. Mrs. Anderson and Portia were crying tears of joy. Brandon went over and hugged his grandfather, who picked him up into his arms. Craig and Venice continued out into the reception hall where Nanna and Bernice had church friends set up dinner as well as a wedding cake. The rest of the guests followed for what was to be a night to remember.

Joshua walked over to hug and kiss Venice. He embraced Craig, then showed him the text message on his pager.

Craig asked, "Is it really over, Joshua?"

Joshua patted Craig on the shoulder. "It's really over and I'll send you my bill in the mail."

"I owe you, man. I also owe my assistant, Francine. If she hadn't told me Katrina saw the itinerary of the wedding in Ocho Rios, we would have never known to change the plans. "

Joshua laughed. "All you owe me is your commitment to take care of Venice and Brandon and I know you'll do that. As far as your assistant, I'm sure you'll find a way to compensate her."

He answered, "You know I will."

Skeeter came over to embrace Craig. "Man, you did it! I'm so glad I don't have to look at you walking around looking whipped anymore."

Craig smiled. "Go 'head on with that, Skeeter. You'll understand one day."

"You know I'm just playing. Now, let me go kiss your lovely wife."

"Don't make me hurt you, Skeeter."

Skeeter walked off in search of Venice, ignoring Craig. When he found her, she was tying the sash on little Samantha's dress.

Skeeter said, "May I please kiss the most beautiful bride I have ever seen in my life?"

"Of course, you may…Mr. Winston Carter III."

Skeeter gave her a loving kiss.

"You enjoy calling me by my real name, don't you?"

"I think it's nice. It fits you Mr. Big Shot Attorney. When you get to Philly, maybe you can slow down."

Skeeter took her by the hand. "Maybe. Look, Venice, I want to apologize for the way I treated you back in the day. It's just that…Craig's my boy and I didn't want to see him hurt."

Venice hugged him. "I understand and thank you. Craig couldn't ask for a better friend. Now! When are wedding bells going to be ringing for you?"

He took her by the hand. "She has to find me. I'm not going to stand here and lie. I have been thinking about settling down, but you know me, Venice. I haven't been one to be tied down to one woman."

"Skeeter, darling, that will change as soon as you meet her. More than likely, she will slip up on you. You won't even see it coming, then boom! You're in love."

He burst out laughing. "Yeah, right! I have to give it to you, that was pretty good."

"Laugh if you want to, Winston Carter, but I'm going to have the last laugh. You'll see."

Skeeter laughed even harder.

She kissed him on the cheek. "You are so silly. Now stop laughing and escort me to my husband."

Nanna walked up, kissed her grandson, and said, "Craig, go get your wife out of Skeeter's clutches so the minister can bless the food."

"Okay, Nanna, and thank you and Bernice for all you did."

"You're my grandson. I'll do anything for you."

Venice was across the room talking with different family members while holding Brandon's hand. Craig walked up and said, "There you are, Mrs. Bennett. The Reverend is getting ready to bless the food so Nanna sent me to get you."

"I'm all yours, Bennett."

Craig took her hand and they walked over to their seats.

Venice's brother, Galen, was one of Craig's best friends in college. He was in attendance with his wife, Sidney, and daughter. He hadn't seen Craig in years and was glad this particular occasion brought them all together again. Craig's aunts and cousins, as well as some of his closest friends, helped make up the guests. They ate dinner and prepared to enjoy the rest of the evening with music and dance. During their first dance, Craig informed Venice that Katrina would no longer be an issue in their lives. He also decided he would never reveal to her that Joshua made it all possible. Halfway through their dance, Brandon tapped Craig on the arm and asked if he could dance with his mom. Craig smiled and stepped away so Venice could dance with her son. "Ooohs" and "aaaahs" could be heard from the guests.

Venice said, "Brandon, I am so proud of you. You stood by me like the little man I know. Your daddy would be proud of you, too."

He smiled and looked up at his mom. "I know, Momma. I'm glad you married Pops."

"Pops? Where did that come from?"

"He told me he didn't want me calling him Mr. Craig anymore, so he told me to think of something else."

They continued to dance.

"I see, so that's the man stuff you guys have been discussing. Do you like calling him Pops?"

"Yes, he likes it, too. I used to hear my daddy call my granddaddy Pops, and I like it."

Venice bent down, kissed him, and said, "I love you, Brandon. I always have and I always will. I want you to remember that your daddy loved you so much. Don't you ever forget that. Okay?"

"I won't, Momma."

"Good, now go ask your grandmothers to dance."

Without an answer, he went and asked Mrs. Anderson to dance first, then Mrs. Taylor. He was his father's child.

As Venice stood and watched him, Craig embraced her from behind. "Can I have another dance with my beautiful wife?"

She turned into his embrace, kissed him, and said, "Lead the way, handsome."

Hours later, after tears had been shed, cake had been cut, and pictures taken, the evening came to a close. Craig and Venice sat and talked with Bryan and Craig's Uncle Victor.

Bryan said, "If I wasn't here, I wouldn't have believed it. It's a miracle you two are together."

"You got that right. This boy lost weight, and looked like hell when ya'll broke up," Victor said.

"If you two don't mind, I'd rather not talk about that. What's important is now," Craig said.

Venice agreed, saying, "You're right, Babe, and I'm a little tired."

It was going on eleven o'clock and they knew they were going to be leaving the following day for their honeymoon. That night they were staying at Craig's house. Venice's family and the Andersons stayed between Nanna's and Bernice's homes.

They said goodnight and headed to the house while the rest stayed back to help clean up. On the drive there, Venice asked, "Are you going to tell me what went down with Katrina?"

"I don't want to talk about her, especially tonight. My main concern is getting you out of that dress. I remember you challenging me. Something about who was going to have whom screaming on our honeymoon."

Venice couldn't believe he remembered their playful conversation, but he had. He also seemed anxious to hold her to the challenge. She laid her head against his shoulder and asked, "Are we there yet?"

When they entered the foyer, a trail of red, white and pink rose petals greeted them. They followed the trail that led into Craig's bedroom where the room was glowing with an assortment of candles. The bed was also covered in rose petals and the trail continued into the bathroom. The garden tub had floating candles and sprinkles of rose petals in the water.

"Bennett, did you do all of this?"

He embraced her. "No, I think Bernice had a hand in this, but before we go any further, I have something for you."

He picked up a beautifully wrapped box from the bed.

"When I saw it, I thought of you. I hope you like it."

Venice took the gift from his hand. "You didn't have to get me a gift, Bennett."

"I know, but I wanted you to have it."

She proceeded to open it, removed a velvet box and just stared. He removed the expensive gold charm bracelet from the box.

"It only has two charms on it right now: the dolphin, which represents Ocho Rios; and a bell, which represents our wedding."

"It's beautiful, Craig. Just as beautiful as the first one you gave me in college. Remember?"

He smiled. "How could I forget?"

She held out her arm so he could place it on her wrist. She looked into his handsome eyes and said, "I still have the other bracelet."

He took her hands into his and kissed them. "I knew you would always keep it, Sweetheart, and I'll add to this one as we go through our life together. Okay?"

"Okay and thank you so much. I'll never part with it." She kissed him and said, "Oh, well, I might as well give you my gift while we're at it."

His eyes widened. "You got me something?"

"Of course, Bennett. Now close your eyes."

Venice got up and pulled a white envelope from her purse. She sat down next to him. "Okay, you can open your eyes now."

Venice handed him the envelope.

"I hope you accept this with all my love. I had to be a little devious behind your back, but I hope you're pleased. Lamar helped."

Craig looked at her in confusion and opened the envelope. Inside was the deed to the office complex he'd wanted to lease.

"Is this what I think it is?"

"It's yours, Bennett. You're my husband and I wanted you to have it. Besides, there's some nice office space there and I thought about opening up a sports medicine clinic on the second floor. I don't want to go back out on the road as a team doctor, especially since we're planning on having more children. I think the building has plenty of room for the both of us. It even has room for a sandwich or coffee shop. That is, if you don't mind sharing it with me."

He grabbed her and kissed her deeply on the lips, hugging her closely to his body. Once he released her, he said, "Venice, you are unbelievable. But I can't accept this from you, Babe. It doesn't feel right. I mean, being Jarvis' money and all."

She grabbed his chin and, with fire in her eyes, she stared at him.

"Craig Bennett! Jarvis wasn't the only one who had a job. No, I didn't make the amount of money he did, but I held my own. Jarvis left this money to me to use as I see fit! If I want to buy you something, there's nothing you or anyone can say to make me feel guilty about doing it! I would never do anything to disrespect Jarvis or the money he left me!"

She angrily got up from his lap and went into the bathroom, slamming the door behind her. Craig dropped his head.

"Damn! I just messed that up."

He rose slowly from the bed and tapped on the bathroom door.

"Venice…Babe, I'm sorry. I didn't mean to upset you. May I come in?"

There was silence for a few seconds, then she said, "Come on in, Bennett."

He opened the door and saw her standing by the sink, but she didn't face him.

He approached her and rested his chin on top of her head while hugging her from behind.

"I'm sorry, Venice. I didn't mean to upset you and I do appreciate your gift."

She didn't respond to him. Instead, she said, "Bernice left us a tray of chocolates, fruit, cheese, and champagne. Isn't it beautiful?"

"I think you're beautiful."

Venice turned and ran her hands up his chest and began to unbutton his shirt. Her hands trembled, not from nervousness, but from sheer emotion. She unbuttoned the last one and pushed his shirt off his shoulders.

He looked down at her. "Are you still mad at me?"

She finally looked him in the eyes. "I'm not mad at you. I'm mad at myself. I guess I overstepped my boundaries. I just wanted to surprise you."

He played in her hair. "And you did. It's a wonderful gift. I would have to be a fool not to accept it."

"Are you sure, Craig, because I can…"

Placing his finger to her lips, he said, "I'm sure, Venice. I was just surprised, that's all. Now come back into the bedroom so I can figure out how to get you out of that dress. I've never seen so many buttons before."

Craig worked anxiously to unbutton it. Venice smiled and closed her eyes as he succeeded, slowly peeling the dress from her body. All that was left was a beautiful ivory bustier, lace panties, garter and stockings, all of which matched perfectly to the pumps she wore.

"Mercy, woman!"

Venice sat on the edge of the bed and placed her foot in his lap so he could remove her shoes.

"Craig, do you think you could help me with my garter, too?"

He swallowed hard and pulled her to her feet as he slid to his knees to unhook the garter. He slowly ran his hands up her inner thigh, causing her to sway. Once they were unhooked he slid her stockings down her legs, kissing her thighs, inch by inch. Venice pulled him to his feet and unhooked his pants, pushing them down over his perfectly round rear. The evidence of his love showed as she placed her hands in the waistband and freed him from the last piece of clothing separating them. The warmth of his body caused the hardening of her nipples and moistness in her lower body.

"Bennett, you are beautiful."

He couldn't answer. "ll he could do was free her of the bustier and panties and lower her to the bed.

"Venice, I love you."

Before another breath was taken, he parted her thighs and slid into her. His thrusts were necessary to fulfill all his dreams and desires of the past, present and future. She was finally his…*all his*.

Wanting to get deeper, he raised her hips to meet his demand. She was only able to moan his name as he claimed her body. Their lovemaking was different, yet familiar. She held on as long as she could, not wanting this ecstasy to end. Wrapping her legs around his body gave him complete access to the core of her being. He devoured her lips as he quickened his pace. His groans were steady and loud as he filled her body to the hilt. Venice was the only woman he would ever make love to without any barriers between them.

As he neared completion, he heard her scream his name like she never screamed it before. Moments later, he released his seed of love and passion into her heated desire.

"Sweet Jesus! Venice!"

Out of control and wet with perspiration, their bodies shook harder than they ever had before as they trembled in each other's arms. Exhausted he kissed her, mating his tongue with hers in a ritual designed only for lovers. The sweetness of her mouth and body kept him wanting more.

"Are you okay?"

"No, because you've stopped kissing me."

He smiled, kissed her on the neck and said, "You know I'm addicted to you so you don't have to worry about me not kissing you or making love to you. If it was up to me, I would stay inside you forever, Sweetheart."

Grabbing him by the hips, she said, "Then don't move, Babe. I can't think of a better place I'd want you to be."

He kissed her harder, then inched lower to sample her ripe breasts.

She closed her eyes and moaned, "Oh, Bennett."

His body quickly responded again as he took her on another journey of heated passion. Rolling over onto his back, he held her firmly as she moved her hips against his body vigorously. He covered her breasts with his palms stroking her nipples as she rode his body hard. He rolled over, placing her underneath him. He drove his hips into her moistness, causing her body to go up in flames. His release was longer and harder than before as he moaned, "I love you, Venice." She was no different as she screamed out her love for him. Tears flowed out of her eyes as he kissed each one away. Brushing tendrils of her hair from her face, he said, "I hope those are happy tears."

She kissed him. "They are."

"I hope so, 'cause we're probably going to make a baby tonight."

She snuggled her face into his neck. "I can't wait to have your baby, Bennett."

He kissed her on the forehead and said, "Our wait shouldn't be long."

"Just in case, we might need to make love a few more hours. Our plane doesn't leave until noon."

He looked at her in amazement and said, "Don't start nothing you're not going to finish."

"Oh, I plan to finish all right."

Chapter Thirty

Spending a few days in Hawaii was going to be ideal before returning home for Christmas. Venice and Craig were looking forward to surprising Brandon with Ms. Camille and starting a new life together. Craig was going to be very busy once he returned. Venice hired his firm to design the new Jarvis Tyler Anderson Youth & Educational Center. She wanted the project done right so she couldn't think of a better person than her new husband to design it. She also wanted to break ground on it as soon as possible. This would allow them to spend some time at home, which was very important for Brandon and his grandparents. While Craig and Venice were on their honeymoon, Ms. Camille stayed at their house. Her new home was getting the finishing touches Craig had ordered. When they returned for Christmas, she would be all set-up and ready to surprise Brandon. Her furniture would be arriving in a few days and she couldn't wait to get settled in.

Their honeymoon in Hawaii was nothing short of breathtaking. One day, Venice decided to play a little joke on her new husband. After spending most of the morning in each other's arms, they figured it was time to hit the white sands for a little fun in the sun. While Craig was in the shower, Venice hurriedly put on one of the tiniest thong bikinis she could find. It was fire-engine red with bright yellow flowers. She had no intentions of wearing it in public, but Craig didn't know that. She was eager to see his reaction.

When she heard him cut off the shower, she went over to the patio doors and pretended to be looking out over the beach. Craig opened the bathroom door to release the steam, but had yet to come out.

He stood in the mirror and asked, "So what do you want to do tonight? Do you want to try and find a jazz club or just chill at the lounge here?"

She turned, realizing he hadn't looked her way. "It doesn't matter as long as I'm with you."

As he continued to towel off, she decided to walk over to the bathroom door to ask him for the lotion. "Bennett, could you hand me the lotion, please."

He turned to her and said, "You bet, Sweethea....Venice, what the hell do you have on? No, what is that you *don't* have on?"

Smiling, she twirled. "You like? I bought it yesterday. I just knew you would like it."

He scanned her from head to toe, then turned to brush his hair while staring into the mirror in silence. Stopping, he turned to her and said, "Woman! You have lost your mind if you think I'm going to let you leave this room naked!"

"Naked! I have on a bathing suit."

"No! You have two strings wrapped around your body!"

Venice hugged him. "Don't you just love the bright colors?"

He froze, looked down at her, and said, "You're trippin'."

Pulling him by the hand into the bedroom, she twirled again for him. "Come on, Bennett. Why are you so old-fashioned? This is the style!"

He stared her down calmly. "We're not going anywhere until you change swimsuits."

She folded her arms. "Well, if you want me to take it off, you have to take it off for me."

There was silence as they stared each other down, something they did quite often.

Venice then burst out laughing. "Gotcha! Baby, I wasn't going to wear this piece of nothing out on the beach. It was a joke!"

Still laughing, she hugged him and said, "I couldn't resist, Bennett. You should have seen your face."

He managed a small chuckle. "Oh, you want to play. Huh?"

He tackled her, landing on the tangled sheets they had just gotten out of. She let out a playful scream as he covered her body with his. Slowly, he untied the small strings giving her a kiss here and a kiss there.

"Bennett?"

"Huh?"

"Order room service. We can go to the beach tomorrow."

That was all he needed to hear as he managed to maneuver the garment away from her body. He quickly discarded his towel and began to sear her skin with the touch of his lips. The love showing in his eyes was undeniable as she arched to fit her body to his. Words were not needed as the passion consuming their souls touched. His kisses were like magic and his touch was pure ecstasy. She threw her head back to give him full access to her most erotic zone. Craig met her halfway as he covered her breasts with his hand.

"I love you, Venice. Even though you take pleasure in making me the butt of your jokes."

"I'm happy to oblige my man in any and every way I can."

His kissed her fully on the lips. "Do you mean that?"

She moaned provocatively as she felt his erection pressing against her thigh. "Most definitely."

He buried his face into the curve of her neck causing soft moans to escape her throat. He moved lower to sample the beautiful lips he loved so much, linking his tongue with hers. They both moaned in unison as they savored the taste of each other. Going even lower, he toyed with the hardened, caramel nipples, which teased him so often. He covered one, then the other, making her tremble with anticipation. His hands sought out her heated core and he inched even lower and tasted the very essence of her. She arched and jerked as he took pleasure in her immediate response to his assault on her womanhood. Gripping the sheets, she mumbled incoherent words of fiery desire as her body went through a series of spasms.

Craig was skilled in this area and wanted to make it clear that he would forever fill her life with explosive passion. Leaving her paralyzed with desire, he parted her thighs and slowly entered her trembling body. He raised her hips, filling her body as he moved in and out of her fire-engulfed body.

Venice shuddered and screamed, "Bennett! My God! I love you!"

His body stiffened, then shuddered hard, filling her with his seed. With his face pressed firmly into the pillow, Venice could still hear him profess his love for her. Holding his glistening body tightly to hers, she breathed heavily.

"Baby number one, coming right up."

"That was number six. Remember? We started this two days ago. Ready to start work on number seven?"

Venice smiled as she kissed him. "Be careful what you wish for, Babe."

"I wish you would shut up and kiss me, woman!"

And that she did…and then some.

Arriving back from Hawaii was welcomed, but the change in weather was a shock. Christmas Eve was only one day away so Venice's family still had their traditional party. It was going to be hard this year just like Thanksgiving, but she felt like she would be able to handle it. The Taylors' home was filled with friends and family like every year. Craig's presence and Jarvis' absence were the only differences to the ritual. As guests continued to arrive, Craig volunteered to answer the door.

Joshua and his family appeared and as soon as he walked through the door, he said, "Dang, Craig, you've got the serious tan! I can't imagine what Niecy looks like."

"Joshua, she has me beat. Wait until you see her."

Venice walked into the foyer and Joshua burst out laughing.

"Venice, what did you do, lay out? And what's this? War wounds?"

Joshua pointed to an obvious passion mark between Venice's neck and shoulder.

"Forget you, Joshua. At least we did spend some time outside the bedroom on our honeymoon, unlike you and Cynthia."

The smile left Joshua's face. "Oh, Niecy, that was cold."

She kissed him on the cheek. "Oh, but it's the truth, my brotha. Sorry, Cynthia. Now hand me my goddaughter."

Joshua pushed his hands in his pockets. "Whatever."

Craig asked, "Ya'll are not going to go at it all night, are you?"

Cynthia handed Sierra to Venice. "Get used to it, Craig. They've been doing it all their lives and there's nothing anybody can do to stop it."

They laughed and walked into the den together.

The night was filled with love, laughter, and the sharing of presents. The next morning, Craig, Venice, and Brandon would depart for Philly, and it was going to be bittersweet for the rest of the family. They always spent Christmas as one big family when Jarvis was alive. This year was going to be the start of a new era.

Their plane was leaving in ninety minutes. Craig was taking Brandon on his rounds to say goodbye to different family members. At the Anderson home, Venice asked Mrs. Anderson if a particular box of personal items were still stored in Jarvis' old room downstairs. She acknowledged that they were and told her that she was going to run over to the Taylors to pick up Craig and Brandon and would be right back.

Downstairs, Venice entered the room where she spent many hours. It was weird to be there alone. She hadn't been there since coming home after Jarvis passed away. She looked at her watch and realized she didn't have much time left. She opened the closet and pulled over a chair so she could see the top shelf. As she shuffled the boxes around, she heard a noise.

She froze. "Mom, did you forget something?"

There was no answer so she returned to her search.

"Where are you? Found it! No, that's not the box."

She came across a box marked *"Brandon's baby clothes"* and couldn't help but smile. She opened the box and pulled out a bib that read *"Daddy's Running Back."* She ran her hand over it for a moment, then sat down and really stared at it. She remembered the day Jarvis bought it. Looking at her watch again, she climbed back up on the chair and placed the bib back in the box.

"Going down memory lane?"

Venice turned and when she laid eyes upon him, her legs gave completely out. She slumped down in the chair and started hyperventilating. Her body trembled and her throat tightened up on her as she came face-to-face with…Jarvis.

The air was thick, but he could see that she was in distress. He came to her, taking her hand into his. "It's okay, Niecy. Calm down. It's only me."

She closed her eyes, knowing she couldn't be feeling his touch. But, she was. Her breathing was still erratic as he said again, "Calm down, Baby. It's just me. It's okay." Dazed and confused, she reached up, cupped his face in her hands and hugged him tightly. Hugging her back, he said, "You look beautiful, Niecy." His scent was the same it had always been, but how could it be? She ran her hands over his face in amazement and cried hysterically.

"Niecy, please don't cry. I came to say goodbye. I never got a chance to tell you goodbye. But, I couldn't leave without knowing you and my son were in good hands. Now that you are, there's no reason for me to hang around."

Still cupping his face, she kissed him tenderly. "Brandon was telling the truth. You did come to him. Jarvis, why did you leave me? You weren't supposed to leave me."

He hugged her. "Baby, I didn't want to. You know that. You were my life and I will always love you. I can leave now, knowing you and Brandon are happy and will be taken care of well. Craig is a decent guy. I trust him with the two of you."

He wiped away her tears as she asked, "You're not mad?"

"He's the only one I trusted to take care of you and Brandon and no, I'm not mad." He held her in his arms. "Niecy, I have to go now but I just had to hold you one more time to let you know I'll love you forever. I believe Craig will do a great job helping you raise Brandon."

Venice held on tightly, pleading, "Please don't leave. I need *you*!"

He placed his lips to hers and gave her a kiss.

"Not anymore, Sweetheart. I've loved you all my life, now it's Craig's turn. You'll be all right; trust me. We'll see each other again one day. Goodbye, Niecy. I love you."

She screamed, "Jarvis! No!"

When Venice opened her eyes, she was lying across the bed. Her face was wet with tears, but she didn't know why. She sat up on the bed and, for some strange reason, felt calm.

"I must have fallen asleep."

Upstairs she heard a door slam shut and small footsteps running across the floor.

"Momma! Where are you?"

She got up from the bed and yelled, "I'm downstairs!"

Brandon and Craig joined her, and Craig noticed her confused state of mind.

"Are you okay? You don't look well."

She looked around the room. "I think I'm okay. I must have fallen asleep. I guess I was more exhausted than I thought."

"Are you sure that's all? I mean are you cool being down here?"

She held his hand. "I'm fine. We'd better get a move on it if we're going to catch that plane."

Craig looked at his watch. "You're right. Venice, go on up. We'll bring the boxes."

"Okay, but hurry up."

"We will."

Venice disappeared upstairs and Craig proceeded to shut the closet. Brandon was running around the room his dad grew up in, playing with different items.

"Pops, look what I found."

Craig turned to see Brandon holding up a gold chain. He walked over to him and asked, "Where did you find it?"

Pointing, he said, "Right there on the bed."

"Your momma must have dropped it. I'll give it to her later. Ready to go get ready for Santa?"

"I'm ready!"

Craig picked up one box, then told Brandon to get the other. As they proceeded up the steps, Craig turned one last time to make sure everything was left in place.

Chapter Thirty One

Back in Philly the threesome was met with six inches of snow and more on the way. After a delicious dinner, Craig threw more wood on the fire, went through mail and called to check on Ms. Camille. Venice was upstairs helping Brandon get ready for bed. As usual, he was hyped knowing in the morning, Santa Claus would have come and gone.

"Come on, Brandon. I've already let you stay up longer than I should. You know Santa is not going to stop by if you're awake."

Climbing under the covers, he said, "I know, Momma. It's just…I'm just so…"

"I know, Sweetie. I was the same way when I was your age."

"Really?"

"Really. Now did you say your prayers?"

"Yes, Ma'am."

"That's my lil' man."

Venice went over to the window and said, "We might have about ten inches of snow before it stops."

Brandon rose up. "Can I go out tomorrow and build a snowman?"

She turned and said, "We'll see, but you have to go to sleep first."

Tucking him in, she leaned down and kissed him goodnight. Before getting up from the bed, she turned on the monitor so they could hear him if he called for them in the middle of the night.

As she walked toward the door, she said, "Sweet dreams, my baby, and before you ask, Craig will be up to say goodnight after he finishes with the fireplace."

"Okay. Goodnight, Momma. I love you."

She said, "I love you, too, Brandon Tyler Anderson. Goodnight, and I'll see you in the morning."

"Okay."

Venice turned off the light and closed his door.

When Venice returned to the den, Craig was still on the telephone with Ms. Camille. She gave him *that look*.

"Ms. Camille, I'd better turn in if I'm going to pick you up early in the morning. Oh, Venice? She's still upstairs tucking Brandon in. I'll tell her you asked about her. Goodnight."

Venice hugged his waist. "I should spank you for telling Ms. Camille a lie."

He lowered his lips to hers. "Spank away, Baby."

Kissing her had always been his favorite pastime. A strange sound escaped her throat as he pulled her tighter against his body. She broke the kiss and said, "That was sweet, Bennett."

He kissed the curve of her neck. "I have more where that came from."

"I know you do, but first, we have cookies to bake and things to put together before morning. Are you going to be able to hang?"

He started unbuttoning her blouse. "I might, but first I need a little something to get me through the evening."

"And what might that be?"

He smiled and slid his hand inside the waistband of her shorts. She sucked in a sharp breath and moaned, "Ben-n-n-ett."

He kissed her on the lips, smiled and asked, "So what do you want to do first? Bake cookies or put the things together?"

She looked up into his eyes, amazed at his calmness.

"Right now I can't move. You are so sinful, Bennett."

He smiled. "Come over by the fire so I can warm you up."

"Craig, heat is not what I need right now."

He laughed, then took her hand into his and led her over to the fire. They sat by the fire, sipped wine and shared wonderful conversation while putting the unassembled items together.

It was now eleven o'clock. The cookies had been baked and all the unassembled items had been assembled. Venice lay sound asleep on the pillows in front of the fire. Craig covered her with a blanket, sat beside her and started opening Christmas cards. He came across one from Francine. He opened it and found a short letter inside. He figured now was a better time than any to read it.

Merry Christmas, Craig,

I hope all is well with you. I thought I would let you know that you shouldn't be bothered with Katrina anymore. She made a spectacle of herself in Ocho Rios thinking she was breaking up your wedding and was almost arrested for something that happened a few years ago in her hometown. Luckily for her, things worked out. I had contacted her sister and she's taking Kat back to Chicago to get some well-deserved rest. Like I said before, Katrina is not a bad person. I may be out of order for telling you this, but Katrina was sexually-abused when she was younger and I believe it's the reason she acts the way she does. Anyway, she's getting help and I was just wondering if there was any way you would consider rehiring her? She voluntarily resigned and her papers were sent by courier to your house. I know she caused you a lot of undeserved stress, but I know Katrina is one of the smartest designers in the office. Just think about it. I can accept whatever you decide. Have a Merry Christmas and I'll see you at the banquet.

Sincerely,

Francine

P.S. I also hope congratulations are in order!

Craig covered his face with his hands for a moment, then returned the letter back inside the envelope. He stood and placed all the Christmas cards received on the mantle. Turning, he stared at Venice, still sleeping peacefully in front of the fireplace. After reading about Katrina's awful childhood, Craig now understood her unstable behavior. Only moments passed before he leaned down and picked Venice up to take her upstairs to bed. After looking in on Brandon, he returned to the den and his thoughts. It was there he would wait until the fire died down before going to bed.

Christmas Morning

It didn't take long for Brandon to come screaming into their bedroom at precisely five. Little did he know, Craig had just laid down and gotten into a well-deserved sleep. Venice, however, got a head start on sleep.

"Momma! Pops! Santa's been here! Hurry up! Come see!"

Brandon was obviously excited as he pulled at his mom's arm.

"Hold on, Brandon. Give us a minute, Sweetie."

Brandon ran around to Craig's side of the bed and yelled, "Pops! You ought to see it!"

Barely able to open his eyes, Craig somehow found the strength to pull himself up into a sitting position. Venice looked over at him and said, "Babe, you don't have to get up right now. Lie back down. Brandon, Craig is very sleepy. He'll see what Santa brought in a couple of hours, okay?"

Brandon stopped in his tracks. "Aw, Man! Momma!"

Craig said, "It's okay. I can go look now. I want to see what Santa left for me, too."

Brandon jumped up and down on the bed. "Yeah!"

Pulling on their robes, Brandon yanked them by the arm out the door and down the stairs.

Entering the living room was like going into a child's wonderland. Everything looked different than it did last night. Venice remembered that she crashed on Craig early and was surprised to see what he had done with the room. Everything seemed to glitter and sparkle.

As Brandon and Venice looked at toys galore, Craig built a fire. When he was finished, he walked over to the window.

"Looks like it finally stopped snowing."

Brandon ran over to Craig. "Look, Pops! This is the same computer game I showed you in the store."

Craig took it and asked, "Did you put it on your list to Santa?"

"I sure did. Santa also got me a new bike. It's bigger than the one I have at Grandmomma's house."

Venice sat quietly and watched the exchange between Brandon and Craig. The scene was so similar to the ones she had with Jarvis. Craig found a box labeled "To Brandon, From Nanna." Brandon tore open the box to find the skates and hockey stick he wanted.

"Wow! Look what Nanna got me, Momma!"

Smiling, she said, "I see, Lil' Man. That's real nice. You're going to have to call Nanna and thank her."

The telephone rang. Venice answered, "Merry Christmas."

"Good Morning, Venice. Where are my two favorite men?"

"Hello, Nanna. They're under the tree tearing open boxes. Hold on."

"Wait, Venice! I just wanted to let you know that I've been dreaming about fish. Is there anything you and Craig want to tell me?"

Venice smiled, remembering the old wives' tale that when someone dreamed of fish, it meant someone in the family was pregnant.

"I don't mean to burst your bubble, Nanna, but as far as I know, your dream is not about me."

"Well, time will tell, my dear. Now let me speak to Brandon. I love you, honey."

"I love you, too, Nanna. Here's Brandon."

After Brandon and Craig had their chance to talk to Nanna, Brandon continued tearing through the many boxes sent to him from various family members. Once all of his presents were opened, he called each family member to thank them.

"Pops! Here's your present from me."

"You got me a present? You didn't have to do that."

"Yes, I did, and you're really going to like it."

Craig sat down next to Venice and said, "I know I will."

Brandon sat in his mom's lap as they watched as Craig opened his gift.

"Hurry up, Pops!"

"Okay! Okay!"

When the wrapping paper was torn away, Craig saw a beautiful leather coat. One he had admired while they were Christmas shopping weeks earlier. He smiled at Venice and said, "Brandon, this is da bomb! Thank you so much."

"Momma said you would like it."

"Your Momma was right, Brandon. I love it."

Craig stood and tried the jacket on which fit him to perfection. He then picked Brandon up and hugged him affectionately.

"Your turn, Momma!" Brandon ran around the Christmas tree and grabbed another box. He sat back down in her lap and said, "Open it, Momma!"

Venice slowly opened the beautifully wrapped box and pulled the tissue paper aside. She pulled out a new pair of Nikes as well as a new jogging suit.

"Thank you, Lil' Man! You knew your momma needed some new ones, huh?"

Smiling proudly, he answered, "Yes, Ma'am. Pops helped me pick them out."

She blew him a kiss across the room.

After about thirty minutes of opening gifts, Brandon asked, "Pops, what did you get Momma?"

Craig grinned. "Thanks for reminding me, Brandon. Craig pulled a box from under the tree and handed it to her.

Venice eyed him seductively. "Well, Bennett, what have we here?"

Leaning back on his elbows, he said, "Open it and see."

Venice put it up to her ears and shook it, but heard nothing. Slowly she started peeling the wrapping paper away from the box. Opening the lid, she found a pair of ruby earrings and a necklace to match. She was stunned at the exquisite jewelry before her.

"Bennett, they're beautiful."

Brandon said, "I helped pick them out, Momma."

She leaned over and kissed Brandon, then Craig. "Thank you so much. I can't wait to wear them."

Craig pulled her down to him and began kissing her softly. "They'll never be as beautiful as you are."

Her response was to wrap her arms around his neck and plant butterfly kisses on his neck and lips.

Brandon said, "Aw, man! Yuck!"

Craig pulled away and said, "We'll see how you feel about kissing in a few years, my man."

Brandon said, "You'll never catch me kissing on no stinking girl."

Craig and Venice laughed at his response.

Craig said, "Brandon, give me the video camera so I can get that statement on tape." Brandon handed him the camera and said, "Pops, Mom, you'll never, ever, ever see me kissing on no stinking girl."

Craig turned the camera to Venice and she said, "You heard it first here on Christmas morning, year 2000. Brandon Tyler Anderson says we will never, ever catch him kissing on no stinking girl."

They laughed and Brandon asked, "Momma, what did you get Pops?"

She sighed. "Well, after a deep consultation with a dear friend of yours, I came up with this."

She handed him a small white box with a big red bow. Craig looked at her in amazement. "What could you possibly have in this little box?"

"Open it, Pops!"

Craig slowly opened it and pulled out a large key. He looked at the insignia on it.

"You didn't?"

Venice smiled. "I did, but we have to set some ground rules, Bennett." Before another word was spoken, he dived on top of her, pushing her to the floor while giving her seductive kisses. Brandon was too preoccupied with his electronic games to care that they were making out on the floor.

"Mmmm. I take it you like your gift?"

He kissed her neck. "A Ninja motorcycle? Let me take you upstairs and show you just how much."

Giggling, she said, "In a little while, Babe. But seriously, Craig, Skeeter promised me you already knew how to ride it and you will be careful!"

He pushed strands of hair from her eyes and noticed the anxiety.

"Sweetheart, I'm not going to take any chances and hurt myself. I've known how to ride a motorcycle like this for years. I just never made the effort to get my own. I usually wait and ride Skeeter's when I visit him. Now I have you to ride on back with me."

Laughing, she said, "I don't know. I'm kind of scared of them."

He gave her a peck on the lips. "Don't worry. I'll be gentle. You're going to love it. So, where is it?"

Picking up wrapping paper, she whispered, "It'll be delivered tomorrow. Now, I know you're tired, but don't we have another surprise for you-know-who?"

He pulled her to her feet and whispered back, "I'm already ahead of you."

Venice was unsure what he meant by this, but she watched as Craig exited the room cheerfully.

As she continued to pick up wrapping paper, Brandon said, "Look, Momma!"

"I see; it's snowing again."

As they looked out the window, they heard, "Merry Christmas!"

Brandon's head spun around after hearing a familiar voice.

"Ms. Camille!"

He ran across the room and practically knocked her over as he jumped into her arms. Craig had to steady her. Venice was surprised, not knowing Ms. Camille was already in the house. Brandon sounded like he was talking in a foreign language.

"Where did you come from, Ms. Camille? When did you get to my house? Are you gonna stay with me? I really, really missed you!"

Ms. Camille was overcome with emotions as she stared into the loving eyes of a little boy who had somehow managed to win her heart.

Craig laughed. "Brandon, let Ms. Camille sit down."

Brandon grabbed her by the hand and dragged her over to the sofa.

Laughing, she said, "Child, you're going to have to slow down. And, to answer your questions, yes, I'm going to stay with you. I missed my baby."

Brandon hugged her. "I'm so glad you're going to be with me. I love you so-o-o much. Can we have some blueberry pancakes for breakfast?"

Venice said, "Brandon! Ms. Camille just got here. She's not working today."

Ms. Camille stood up and said, "If my baby wants blueberry pancakes, he gets blueberry pancakes."

Brandon jumped up and down and screamed, "Yeah!" They disappeared into the kitchen.

Venice put her hands on her hips, looked at Craig and said, "See? I told you, spoiled rotten!"

Craig hugged Venice and said, "This is what you wanted. Remember?"

She put her arms around his neck. "Didn't you say something about taking me upstairs to thank me properly?"

A wide grin stretched across his face as he took her hand and led her to the stairs. Venice shouted toward the kitchen, "Ms. Camille, we're going back to bed for a while!."

She shouted back, "Okay! We'll be fine!" She smiled and shook her head as she heard the playful sounds of Venice giggling as they ascended the stairs. She mumbled, "Just like old times."

Brandon handed her a bowl and asked, "What did you say, Ms. Camille?"

"Just saying how happy and I am to be here with you."

"Me, too!"

Chapter Thirty Two

A Week Later

The Architects Ball was being held in one of Philadelphia's most prestigious hotels. The lobby was still vividly decorated with Christmas designs, giving it a warm feel. Venice wore a red velvet dress with matching pumps. Tonight gave her the perfect opportunity to wear the ruby earrings and necklace Craig had given her for Christmas. Craig looked unbelievably handsome in his black tuxedo as he held Venice's hand.

While mingling with co-workers and associates, he looked over his shoulder to see Lamar and Tressa enter the room. Smiling, he motioned for him to join them. Tressa seemed to glow as the black satin and velvet dress she wore complemented her figure. Lamar turned many female heads as he crossed the room. He took special pride in his appearance. The customized tuxedo had a lot of women fanning themselves and whispering. Unfortunately for them, he only had eyes for Tressa.

When they finally made their way over, Lamar said, "Happy Holidays!" He kissed Venice on the cheek and shook Craig's hand.

Tressa and Craig exchanged greetings, then Venice and Tressa got involved in a deep conversation. It wasn't long afterwards that Francine and her date joined them in conversation. Francine's royal-blue silk pantsuit gave her a sensual sexiness that Lamar and Craig didn't get to see often. She was radiant.

Tressa whispered, "Venice, I love that dress and those shoesY"

"Thank you, Tressa. You look stunning yourself and if I'm not mistaken, Lamar is glowing. How are things with you two?"

Blushing, Tressa said, "He's so sweet and we're doing just fine. I told my dad that he can't pick and choose the men I date. I told him that he did a wonderful job raising me and it's time that he started trusting my decisions. He's still having a hard time dealing with me dating Lamar, but he'll get over it in time."

Francine said, "Well, I don't know what you did to him, but whatever it is, keep it up."

The three women laughed, then Venice hugged her again. "I'm happy for you."

"Thanks, and I believe congratulations are in order for the two of you. Wow! What a ring!"

Tressa and Francine held Venice's hand, admiring her wedding ring. Venice smiled and said, "Thank you, guys. I love him so much. I've been through hell and high water, but life goes on."

Francine sighed. "Yes, it does."

Craig and Lamar were talking briefly about business when Lamar said, "Don't look now, but I believe a friend of yours is headed this way." When Craig turned, he came face-to-face with Melanie.

"Hello, Craig, Darling, Lamar."

Lamar answered, "Hello, Melanie. It's been a while."

Melanie spared no expense when it came to her wardrobe. Her white silk gown didn't leave much to the male imagination.

"Hello, Melanie. What brings you here?"

Hearing a female voice, Francine, Venice, and Tressa turned to see a woman with the physique of a model.

Francine said, "Oh, brother."

Tressa asked, "Who is she?"

Venice said, "Craig used to date her. Her name is Melanie."

Francine added, "She's an attorney. I don't know what he ever saw in her. She's nothing but a socialite who wants to be seen. I was so happy when Craig broke up with her. She wasn't his type."

Venice and Tressa didn't respond. They just scanned the woman, eyeing her carefully.

Giggling, Melanie said, "Oh, Craig, I didn't stop living when you broke up with me. I'm dating Zachery Mathews."

Zachery was one of Bennett & Fletcher's strongest competitors. He certainly played hardball and was very good at what he did. Craig looked into Melanie's light brown eyes and said, "I'm happy for you, Melanie. I'm sure Zachery can give you what I couldn't."

Melanie linked her arm with Craig's and said, "We'll see. So who's your flavor of the month?"

Craig reached for Venice's hand, pulling her into his embrace. After kissing her on the lips he said, "Melanie, you remember Venice?"

"Oh, yes! Hello, Venice. How are you?"

Shaking hands, she responded, "Fine, thank you."

Craig smiled at Venice. "Melanie, Venice is my wife."

Melanie froze in shock as she looked down at the wedding rings they both wore.

"You're married?"

Hugging Venice tighter, he said, "Yes, and I couldn't be happier."

After clearing her throat, Melanie said, "This is funny. That last time I saw you two together, I thought you were going to start throwing punches at each other."

Venice explained, "Well, it was all my fault and I'm so glad we were able to work out our differences."

Melanie said, "Well, I guess congratulations are in order."

Craig and Venice smiled and in unison said, "Thank you, Melanie."

Melanie took a step back and looked at them.

"Well, you didn't waste any time did you, Darling?"

Staring into Venice's beautiful eyes, he confessed, "Actually, we dated in college. After running into each again, I guess we couldn't deny what was still there in our hearts. I guess the rest is history."

Still somewhat stunned, Melanie said, "How sweet. Well, congratulations again!"

Melanie stared over their shoulder and said, "Well, I'd better go. Zachery's probably looking for me. I guess I'll be seeing you two around. I hope you have a nice evening."

Craig responded, "Likewise, Melanie. Goodbye."

Craig looked down at Venice and smiled.

Venice pinched his finger. "Flavor of the month, huh? I didn't know you had it like that, Bennett."

Laughing, he said, "She's exaggerating, Sweetheart. Your taste is the only one I crave."

"I know, Babe. I'm starving so let's eat."

Craig turned to Lamar. "We'd better be making it over to our table. They'll be serving dinner shortly."

Lamar and Craig escorted their ladies to their table to enjoy a splendid dinner and night of dancing.

Thirty Three

New Year's Eve came and went. Craig and Venice spent theirs alone at home. They watched the ball drop in Times Square as they toasted their new life together. Brandon was enjoying New Year's with his grandparents. It had been a few weeks since they'd seen Brandon, so having him for a few days was going to be very exciting. Plus, this allowed Brandon to have a belated Christmas celebration with them. Crimson and Portia would be flying back with Brandon for a short visit before they started school.

It had been a cold winter, so Craig made it a point to build a fire in their bedroom's fireplace almost every night. Venice had been busy over the past few days trying to get her clinic stocked and staffed while Craig had spent time drawing up a design for the Jarvis "nderson Youth & Educational Center. Being who he was, he requested input from Jarvis' parents whom admired and adored how he had helped Venice and Brandon cope with the death of their son.

One night, the telephone rang around midnight while Craig was working in his office. Venice had been sound asleep for hours. Since she had been exhausting herself with the clinic, she had been going to bed a lot earlier than usual.

"Hello?" There was silence on the line. Craig asked again, "Hello?" He could hear someone breathing, so he knew someone was there. Leaning back in his chair, he asked, "Katrina?"

"I'm so sorry, Craig. Please forgive me."

Then the telephone line went dead. It was her. The situation with Katrina was trying to haunt him again. His parents had always taught him to have a forgiving heart, but he just wasn't sure if he could handle this. Tomorrow he would talk to Francine to check up on Katrina's progress.

Craig and Lamar traveled to the prospective site for the youth center days later and were welcomed by his in-laws and extended family. Lamar saw first-hand the friendliness of Venice's friends and family, and he understood why Craig felt the way he did about them. His in-laws insisted they stay with them instead of a hotel. This way, Venice's mom could spoil them with her soul food, which included world-famous peach cobbler. Joshua came by and like old times, had dinner at the Taylor home. Bryan and Venice's parents all sat down to a table full of home-cooked food.

Over dinner, Bryan asked, "So Craig, are you ready to send Venice back home yet?"

Craig laughed. "Not on your life. I'm keeping her and Brandon."

Lamar stuffed his last fork full of macaroni in his mouth. "Man, you couldn't pry Venice from Craig's grip if you wanted to."

Bryan took a sip of tea. "Give him a few more months. Once he sees just how stubborn she really is, he might reconsider."

Mr. Taylor put another piece of fried chicken on his plate. "Ya'll better quit talking about my baby girl. Don't make me put a cap in ya'll."

Joshua said, "Pops, that's old and don't forget, I'm packing, too."

A round of laughter filled the room.

After dinner, the guys settled in the den while the Taylors went to the Andersons' house to see Brandon. Craig had spent the earlier part of the day with Brandon before working on the building site.

Joshua asked, "Hey, Craig. Do you have an assistant named Francine?"

"Yes, why?"

Joshua extended his legs in Mr. Taylor's recliner and said, "My partner asked about her. I think they met a few weeks back when he was helping with that Katrina Simmons case. Is she married?"

Craig smiled and said, "No, she's divorced, but she has a seven-year-old daughter. She's a very intelligent, strong, and attractive woman. What's your partner's name?"

Working the remote control, he answered, "Jonathan Manley. He's good people and he has never acted interested in a woman since I've been partners with him, until now. He dates occasionally, but it never seems to get serious. He's also divorced, but they had no children together."

Craig took a sip of coffee as he looked over and saw that Lamar was sleep on the sofa, snoring.

Joshua stared at the TV screen. "Craig?"

"Yeah."

"I think Manley wants to see her again, but on a personal basis."

Craig looked at him and asked, "How do you know?"

"Because he can't stop talking about her."

"I don't know, Joshua. She brought a date to our ball a few days ago."

Joshua asked, "Could you talk to her and see if she's interested?"

Craig grinned. "I'll talk to her, but I'm not promising anything."

"Cool and thanks, Craig."

CHAPTER Thirty Four

Venice greeted her family at the airport upon their return. Crimson and Portia returned for a visit and held Brandon's hand as they exited the plane. Craig immediately embraced and kissed his wife, telling her how much he missed her.

She nuzzled her face into his neck. "I missed you, too, Bennett. Did everything go ok?"

"Everything went just fine."

Venice giggled. "So, how's my lil' man?"

"I'm fine, Momma. Just a little sleepy."

Venice hugged and kissed him. "Well, I plan to hold you in my arms all the way home and when we get to the house, you can take a nap."

"Okay, Momma."

Venice turned, hugging and kissing both teenage girls, telling them how much they had grown. Both were teary-eyed as they hugged Venice back. Tressa was there to pick up Lamar so they said their goodbyes after claiming their luggage. Brandon reached up and held Craig's hand as they waited for their luggage. Venice couldn't help but notice how Crimson and Portia had developed into two beautiful young women. The talk she would be having with the both of them later was going to be bittersweet. Somehow, she wanted them to stay little girls a little longer so she could dress them up like baby dolls as she used to.

Back at the house after dinner, Brandon took his bath and went to bed. The girls stayed up to watch videos while Craig worked in his office. It was only nine o'clock, but Venice was exhausted. After putting the leftovers in the refrigerator, she walked into Craig's office to tell him goodnight. Hugging his neck from behind, she said, "I'm getting ready to turn in. I'm a little tired." He pulled her into his lap and felt her forehead.

"You're not coming down with anything, are you?"

Smiling, she answered, "No, I guess I need to start taking my vitamins again. I haven't had the energy to work out lately and I've been spending a lot of time trying to get the clinic opened."

"Well, try not to work so hard, woman. I can't have you getting sick on me."

Rising from his lap, she gave him a kiss saying, "Goodnight, Babe."

"Goodnight, Sweetheart."

"The girls are in the den watching TV. Keep an eye on them and don't let them stay up too late."

Craig said, "I'll take care of them. Go on and get some rest."

She blew him one last kiss before she walked out. Before going upstairs, she stuck her head into the den.

"Goodnight, girls. Don't stay up too late and if you need anything, Craig's in his office next door."

In unison, they answered, "Okay, goodnight."

It was almost eleven o'clock and Craig was still working on his computer. The telephone rang and he answered, "Hello?"

"Sorry to call so late, boss, but I'm just getting in and I saw you left me a message."

Craig turned away from the computer screen. "Hello, Francine. It's really nothing. It can wait until tomorrow."

Francine chuckled. "It must be something. What is it?"

There was a moment of silence, then Craig said, "Katrina called me the other night."

"Katrina? What did she say?"

Craig sighed.

"Nothing at first, then she told me she was sorry. After that, she hung up. Do you know how she's doing?"

Francine took her earrings off. "Her sister said she's doing okay, but goes into a state of depression at times. I believe in time, she'll be fine. She has to deal with the sexual abuse trauma before she can begin to heal from the present."

"Well, keep me posted. I don't think it would be fair to Venice to rehire her. The only thing I can possibly offer her might be a recommendation elsewhere."

"I understand, Craig. Well, if there's nothing else, I'm going to turn in."

Craig hesitated, then asked, "Francine, do you remember meeting an officer by the name of Manley recently?"

Francine's heart skipped a beat, hearing the name of the only man who had affected her soul the way Manley did simply by the touch of his hand. Not even her former husband stirred the kind of raw emotions Manley did, even after being married to him for five years.

"Francine?"

"I'm here, Craig. Yes, I remember him. Why?"

"He wants to see you on a personal level."

A lump was forming in Francine's throat. She started remembering the many nights since meeting Manley that she woke up in a sweat. The erotic dreams she had been having were starting to get the best of her.

"Francine, he would like to call you and possibly take you out to dinner or something."

Still somewhat speechless, she asked, "How did you find out this information?"

"I have my ways. So, can I give him your number? I met him and he seems to be a nice guy. You're a great judge of character so I don't think it would hurt to go out with him. Who knows, if you don't make a love connection, you might gain a good friend. So, what's your answer?"

Francine played with her telephone cord, then answered, "I'm taking a real chance here, but I guess it wouldn't hurt to have dinner with him."

"Good! And Francine?"

"Yes?"

"I'll keep my fingers crossed for you."

"Thanks, Craig, and tell Venice and Brandon hello."

"I will. Let me know how it goes. Goodnight."

Craig decided to take a break and joined the girls in the den to watch videos. When he entered, a video was playing that was really demeaning to women. He watched as Portia and Crimson bobbed their heads to the beat.

"Do you two like that video?"

Crimson spoke up saying, "Yeah! It's da bomb!"

"Crimson and I can't wait until we're twenty-one. We're going to go to California and be in videos."

Craig watched the video to the end, then leaned forward and asked, "Do you really want to be in videos with guys putting their hands all over your body like that?"

Crimson grabbed a handful of popcorn and said, "It's just a video, Craig. I didn't say I wanted to marry them."

Portia nodded her head in agreement.

"You do know that's demeaning to women. Right?"

They burst into laughter and Portia said, "Craig, that's no different than what goes on in the hallway at school."

Surprised, he asked, "For real? I hope you two are not letting guys do that to you."

There was silence as Portia and Crimson looked at each other. Portia turned and said, "Craig, it's different than when you went to school. There's nothing wrong with hanging out with the cool guys."

Craig stood and made fists with his hands as he watched them talk about it so casually. He walked over to the window and looked out in silence. He finally turned and calmly said, "Girls, there is something wrong if you let a man disrespect you like that. Are you saying you like it when they do that to you?"

Crimson took a sip of her soda and answered, "Well, it depends on who it is."

Craig couldn't take it anymore. He had to know. He just had to.

"I want to ask you something and I promise, it won't leave this room. Okay?"

In unison, they said, "Okay, what is it?"

He took a deep breath and asked, "Are you two having sex with any of these guys?"

Portia looked at Crimson and said, "Well, I have with a couple of them."

The air left Craig's lungs. He knew it; he could just tell. He sat down in the chair opposite them and asked, "What about you, Crimson?"

Stuttering, she asked, "Are you going to tell Venice or my dad?"

"I said what we talk about stays in this room. I want you two to be able to talk to both me and Venice. You're going to have to trust us because we're only trying to look out for your well-being."

Crimson said, "Well, I have been with this one guy. Daddy doesn't like him, but I do."

Craig flinched because he knew Bryan very well and he would throw a fit if he knew his daughter was getting busy. He regained his composure and said, "Please tell me you ladies are using protection."

Portia spoke up first. "I take birth control pills."

Craig took a handful of popcorn and asked, "What are you doing to protect yourself from getting a disease like HIV?"

Portia didn't answer. Crimson folded her arms and said, "I'm not on birth control, but we use condoms."

Portia said, "I do, sometimes, but my friend says it's uncomfortable."

Craig firmly said, "Portia, if you're gonna do it, you have to use condoms. You can't play Russian roulette with your life. Sex can get you killed these days and I'm sure you don't want to get HIV. I believe you're both too young to be having sex anyway, but if you're going to do it, have common sense enough to take care of your body. If you don't, nobody else will. Remember, you're responsible for your own actions, so you can't blame anyone but yourself if something happens."

Portia said, "Craig, I don't want to get HIV."

Craig turned the TV on another channel and said, "I know and if that knucklehead tells you that again, tell him you're not about to risk getting it for anybody. If he has a problem with it, call and let me know. I'll pay him a little visit if I have to."

The girls laughed and Portia said, "Thanks, hit man Craig."

"You're welcome. Just remember what I said. Nobody can protect you better than you can."

Crimson stood and said, "Portia, help me clean up. I'm sleepy."

Craig grabbed their soda cans and said, "It is late. I'm going to turn in myself. Sleep well, girls."

Before he could turn, they both hugged and gave him a tender kiss on the cheek. He smiled and said, "Now you want to get all mushy. Grab those bowls. We'll get the rest in the morning."

When Craig left for the kitchen, Portia hurried and finished cleaning the den. Crimson washed up the dishes they used, even though he tried to get her to leave them. It only took about ten minutes for them to complete their task.

Together, all three climbed the stairs to turn in for the night. Craig had no idea that the reason Venice wanted the two girls to come up for a few days was to talk to them about sex. Her former mother-in-law's suspicions were on target, but Craig had single-handedly taken care of the situation. Venice was in for a big surprise.

After a few days and nights of fun, Venice figured it was time to have her talk with the girls. The night before they were to leave, she told Craig what she was planning to do. He was in the bed reading and she was brushing her teeth. She came out of the bathroom with toothpaste on her face and asked, "What do you mean, you've already talked to them?" She was obviously surprised. Not that he had talked to them, but the fact that he didn't tell her he had talked to them.

"Venice, it just came up one night while we were watching videos."

She rinsed her mouth and joined him on the bed. She made him put his book down and asked, "Why didn't you tell me?"

"I really didn't see the need. Sweetheart, I didn't know you were planning on talking to them. God knows if I had, I wouldn't have done it."

Sliding under the comforter, she asked, "So tell me."

He leaned over and kissed her on the cheek. "I'm sorry, Venice. I told
the girls what we talked about would stay between us. I want them to
trust me. Everything's okay, so don't worry."

He started reading again, then she put her hand across the pages and
asked, "You're really not going to tell me, Bennett?"

He closed the book and said, "I love you, woman, but no, I'm not
going to tell you. If you still want to talk to them about sex, go right
ahead. Now, goodnight."

"Traitor."

"I love you, too."

He smiled and started reading again, then heard her say, "Thank you,
Craig."

Chapter Thirty Five

It had been a harsh winter in Philly and February fourteenth, the day for lovers, was no different. The thermometer read thirty-three degrees, but it felt more like twenty-three. Venice usually arrived at her clinic an hour earlier than Craig did at his office, which resided on the floor below her. Since they started sharing the same office building, it made it convenient for them to meet for romantic lunches. Lamar and Tressa were still dating hot and heavy, and Francine and Jonathan Manley seemed to have hit it off perfectly. Who knew what Valentine's Day had in store for the happy couples?

Since it was Valentine's Day, Craig made it a point to beat Venice to work. He wanted her three dozen white and red roses to greet her when she entered her office. It would be later when he surprised her with the real gift: a four-day getaway to Ocho Rios. Little did Craig know, Venice was working on her own little surprise. Being sneaky, she slipped it in his briefcase in the middle of the night.

He did beat her to the office and smiled, knowing that she would love the flowers. The receptionist called to let him know that Venice had arrived in her office. It would only be a matter of time before she called. As he twirled in his chair, Lamar burst into his office.

"Lamar! Will you ever learn how to knock?"

Grinning, he said, "Sorry, Bro. Check this out."

Lamar handed Craig a velvet box and when he opened it, he laid eyes upon a beautiful sapphire and diamond ring.

Craig smiled. "What's this?"

Lamar unbuttoned his jacket, sat down, and said, "I'm going to do it, Man. I'm going to pop the question."

Craig looked up from the ring.

"Are you serious? You're taking yourself off the market?"

Lamar crossed his leg. "She means everything to me, Craig. I love her."

Craig handed the box back to him. "I'm happy for you, Lamar. Congratulations!"

He gave him a brotherly hug. "I must say, Lamar, I didn't think you would be able to pull it off. She must be the one. Tressa is good for you. I know you two will be happy together. How's her old man doing?"

Lamar chuckled. "He's come to accept Tressa's wishes. He finally realized I'm for real with her."

"Good for you!"

"Thanks, Man. So, how's Venice and Brandon?"

"Both are fine. Now, are you ready for our meeting? We only have a couple of hours before Jenkins and Maston arrive."

Lamar tucked the ring safely back into his jacket. "Did you finish the drafts?"

"I have them right here."

Craig opened his briefcase and froze. He just stared down at it.

Lamar stood and asked, "What's wrong? Did you forget the drafts?"

Craig wasn't able to form words. His mouth suddenly became dry. When Lamar rounded the desk, he also was startled. Inside Craig's briefcase were a pair of white baby booties and a baby bottle with red and white ribbons tied to it. There was a card that read: *Happy Valentine's Day, My Love! I hope you like your gift. I love you! Venice*

Lamar laughed. "Well, damn! I guess congratulations are in order."

Craig still couldn't talk because he was so full of emotion. He grabbed the booties and the bottle and headed out the door to Venice's office. When he entered, her partner, Arnelle, said, "Happy Valentine's Day, Craig."

"Happy Valentine's Day to you, Arnelle. Where's Venice? Is she with a patient?"

Arnelle stood about five feet nine and was considered tall for a woman. She was an attractive twenty-eight-year-old with dark brown eyes and thick lashes. She had recently relocated to Philadelphia and had been a lifesaver helping Venice with the clinic. Craig often teased her about the long wavy hair; referring to it as a weave. However, her thick mane hung midway down her back and was definitely all natural. When working, she always placed it in a long braid so it wouldn't interfere with her responsibilities.

Arnelle answered, "No, but I think she's on the phone."

Arnelle was originally from Texas and her Navajo and African-American heritage showed in her physical appearance.

"Thanks, Arnelle."

When he entered her office, Venice had the telephone up to her ear. She smiled and said, "I was just calling you to thank you for my beautiful roses."

In two steps, he had her in his arms. With his eyes full of tears, he held up the items and asked, "Does this mean what I think it means?"

She put her arms around his neck and said, "Yes, it does "Daddy.""

Tears fell as he lowered his head, kissing her with all the love in his heart and soul. When he finally was able to speak again, he asked, "How long have you known?"

She kissed his neck and said, "It was officially confirmed about twenty-four hours ago. I've suspected for a few weeks, but I wanted to be sure before I told you."

"I love you, Venice."

"I love you, too, Bennett, but there's more."

He leaned his head to the side in confusion and wondered how there could possibly be more to their blessed news.

"What do you mean more?"

She smiled, opened her desk and pulled out another pair of booties, then handed them to him.

In total confusion he held both pair of booties and asked, "What's this for?"

She put her hands on her hips and said, "Dang, Bennett! We're having twins!"

Craig yelled, "Twins!"

At that point, the room went dark and Craig fainted.

C raig woke up and found himself lying on the sofa in Venice's office. Lamar, Arnelle, and Venice were all staring down at him. He felt his head and asked, "What happened?"

Lamar started laughing hysterically.

"Man, you passed the hell out!"

Knowing Craig's ego was bruised, Venice said, "Leave him alone, Lamar! Sweetheart, are you okay?"

Craig rose up into a sitting position.

"You're going to pay for laughing at me, Lamar."

Arnelle handed Venice an ice pack and asked, "Craig, are you sure you're okay?"

"I'm fine, Arnelle. Thanks."

She hugged both of them as she congratulated them on the news.

"Venice, you and Craig take all the time you need. I can hold down the office for a few."

Venice smiled and thanked Arnelle before she left the room to attend to a patient.

Lamar continued to laugh and said, "I'm out of here, too. I'll leave you two lovebirds alone. You don't know how bad I wish I had got that on video, Craig. Congratulations, guys."

Craig said, "Thanks, Lamar. Now get out of here."

Venice gave Craig a glass of water and as Lamar exited the room, she said, "Thanks for helping, Lamar."

He smiled. "Anytime, Venice."

He closed the door and left them alone. They could still hear Lamar laughing as he left the office.

Venice sat down next to Craig and asked, "Does your head hurt? You hit the floor pretty hard, Babe. I didn't know it was going to shock you that much."

He took her hands into his and said, "Don't mind me. Are we really having twins?"

She kissed him and said, "You bet. In about seven months, so you'd better let Lamar know that you'll have to scale back your trips to Japan."

Craig slowly stood and repeated in disbelief, "Twins."

CHAPTER Thirty Six

Epilogue (Seven Months Later)

T he beeping noise on the monitor was irritating Venice. As a matter of fact, everything was irritating Venice. Craig was still in shock to know they were having twins. They did agree to keep the sex of the babies a mystery, but Brandon told them he already knew what the babies were going to be. He wrote down his guess and gave it to Ms. Camille for safekeeping. Venice was still trembling from the ride to the hospital. Craig had violated every traffic rule in the book to get her there in record time as Skeeter rode on the back seat with her, looking like he was about to cry. Venice remembered the fear on Skeeter's face as they sped to the hospital. If she didn't know better, he was probably afraid he might have to deliver the babies if Craig didn't get them to the hospital in time. Men!

In the waiting room, Skeeter called both family members when Lamar, Tressa, Francine and Arnelle arrived. He had met everyone except the beautiful woman with long wavy hair spilling over her shoulders. He stood in awe as Craig's sister, Bernice, yelled at him on the other end of the phone.

"Yeah, Bernice, I'm still here and yes, I'll keep you posted."

He hung up the telephone and, for the first time in his life, a woman had him feeling nervous and out of control.

Lamar walked over, shook his hand, and asked, "How's Venice?"

Skeeter shook his head back to reality. "They just got started. So far, so good."

They all sat down, but he was unable to keep from looking over at the brown-skinned beauty. He didn't get to move to Philly in February like he had planned. His mother had taken ill so he had to postpone his move until she recovered. He'd only been in Philly for about two weeks and hadn't had a chance to relax. His law firm put him directly to work on some of their biggest cases.

Lamar walked over to the coffee machine to buy a cup. Skeeter joined him and asked, "Lamar, who is that woman in the blue sweats that came in with you?"

Lamar smiled. "That's Arnelle. She's Venice's partner at the clinic. You've never met her?"

Skeeter shoved his hands in his pocket and said, "Nah, Man, I've been busy."

Lamar grinned and asked, "You like?"

Skeeter tried to appear uninterested and said, "She's aight. Just wondering who she was. She looks familiar."

Moments later, Lamar caught Skeeter off guard and formally introduced him to Arnelle. He already knew Tressa and Francine from previous visits to Philly. Oddly, he never got a chance to meet Venice's partner. Every time he popped in at the clinic, Arnelle was either out of the office or with a patient. When he shook Arnelle's hand, his voice cracked as he said hello. Her soft hand inside his larger one felt unbelievable. Arnelle greeted him nicely, but didn't appear to show any type of interest. This was new to Skeeter, because most women couldn't help but fall all over themselves when they were in his presence. Arnelle, however, seemed uninterested. Skeeter was now wondering why he was unable to charm Arnelle. Was he losing his touch? He wasn't used to putting a lot of effort into winning a woman's interest. He ran his hand over his neatly groomed goatee and realized he was about to walk on unfamiliar territory.

Arnelle put the magazine she was reading down and walked out of the room and into the ladies restroom. Once there, she leaned her head against the stall door and willed herself not to faint. She couldn't believe he stood there like he didn't know her. Bastard! All this time, Venice talked about Craig's friend Skeeter. She had no idea Skeeter was the man she knew in the past as Winston. All kinds of thoughts were running through her head.

How could he look me in the eyes and act like we've never even met? I know he's angry at me and what I did is unforgivable, but if this is the way he wants to play...Fine!

Damn it! I finally stopped crying over him and now he's back.

Craig noticed Venice was about to have another sharp contraction, but he didn't want to warn her; just help her through it.

"Craig!"

Holding her hand, he said, "It's almost over, Sweetheart. Hang in there."

"Easy for you to say! You did this to me!"

He smiled and said, "I know, Sweetheart, but wasn't it fun?"

Pushing his hand away, she snapped, "Don't touch me, Bennett!"

Knowing she was irritated, he leaned down and kissed her on the lips. "I love you anyway."

At that time, Dr. Miller entered asking, "How's my patient?"

"Mean as a rattlesnake."

The doctor said, "Okay, Venice, are you ready to meet your babies?"

Since she was having another contraction, she could only nod her head. The doctor checked and found that Venice was ready to push.

He asked, "Craig, are you ready?"

"I'm as ready as I'm going to be."

Venice said, "Let's do this, Doc, and get your nurses ready to pick him off the floor. Punk! I can't believe you did this to me."

Craig laughed. "I see you're still able to be a comedian, Sweetheart."

Dr. Miller then said, "Okay, let's do this. Get ready, Craig, because you're cutting the cords."

Twenty-five minutes later, Craig and Venice met the first baby. Dr. Miller yelled, "It's a boy!!"

As he handed the baby boy to his nurses, Venice asked, "Is he okay?"

Craig kissed her on the forehead. "He's perfect."

The name they decided on was Craig Alexander Bennett, Jr. He weighed in at five pounds, two ounces and came out screaming. Craig cut the cord proudly.

Dr. Miller said, "Okay, Venice, one down, one to go. Are you ready?"

Still in pain, she responded, "I'm ready."

Exhausted, he asked, "Craig, you still with me?"

Still in awe from seeing his son born, Craig humbly said, "I'm here, Doc."

As the doctor prepared to deliver the other baby, his nurse looked at the monitor and said, "Doctor Miller." He didn't respond. He just looked at the monitor and in a calm but concerned voice, he whispered, "Craig, I don't want to alarm you, but your other baby is having some trouble."

Venice yelled, "What is it!"

Craig went to her side and said, "It's okay, Sweetheart, but the other baby is being stubborn like someone else I know."

Venice could see it in his face even though he tried to conceal it. Something was wrong. The way the nurses were hurrying around the room confirmed it. In a calm, but serious tone, Dr. Miller said, "Venice, we have to get your other baby out right away. I'm going to have to do a C-Section so we're going to numb you from the waist down."

Venice started crying and screamed, "I can't lose my baby!"

Dr. Miller said, "Venice, calm down. I need you to relax for me. Can you do that?"

She looked into Craig's eyes and saw the same fear ripping through his heart. Craig leaned down to her ear and whispered, "We're going to get through this, Sweetheart. Everything's going to be all right. You'll see. I love you."

Tears were still streaming down her face when she said, "I love you, too.

It only took a few minutes for Dr. Miller to numb her. During that time, Venice noticed their voices became faint and the room became dim. Venice couldn't understand what was happening.

She closed her eyes and prayed; then she heard a voice call out to her. "Niecy!"

Opening her eyes, she realized she couldn't move. Everything seemed to be moving in slow motion. She heard the voice again, "Niecy!"

Out of the corner of her eyes, she watched as Jarvis approached seemingly from nowhere. Unable to move, she looked into his smiling face as he leaned down and planted a kiss on her lips. He placed his hand on her stomach and closed his eyes. She looked around the room, then realized she was the only one who could see him. Craig was holding her hand with a bowed head and closed eyes, obviously praying. Only moments passed, then Jarvis opened his eyes and smiled.

"Niecy, don't worry, your baby is just fine. I had to make sure there was no more sadness in your life. You've suffered enough sorrow for this lifetime. I love you and tell my son I love him also. I'm so proud that he keeps me in his prayers every night."

Tears spilled out of her eyes.

"Jarvis, it's really you. Oh, my God! You've come back to me!"

"No, Sweetheart. I'm only back to help you and to say goodbye. You were and will always be the love of my life. Be happy and know that I'll always be with you. You and Craig have some beautiful children. I'm glad you two are together. I have to go now. Kiss Brandon and remember I'll always love you."

"Jarvis, whatever you did just now, thank you. I'll always love you, too, Babe. Thank you so much for making me happy and for giving me Brandon."

He kissed her one last time, looked up at Craig and said, "He's a good man, Niecy. I'm happy for you. Goodbye, Babe."

Before she could answer, he was gone. Seconds later the room became bright again and she heard Dr. Miller yell, "It's a girl!!"

Even though she was stubborn and had already caused her parents to worry, Clarissa Alexandria Bennett had arrived. She weighed in at five pounds, six ounces.

Craig let out a sigh and asked, "Is she okay?"

Dr. Miller said, "She seems to be fine but we'll check her out to be on the safe side. It was the damnest thing. One minute, the cord was around her neck; the next minute, it wasn't. I'm glad I didn't have to do the C-section after all. Congratulations!" Venice was overwhelmed as she heard their two babies fill the room with noise.

Craig said, "You did it, Venice."

Solemnly, she answered, "No, I didn't...it was Jarvis. I saw him, Craig. I was praying and he touched my stomach and told me everything was going to be all right. He said you were a good man."

Craig was speechless upon hearing about Venice's vision. All that mattered was that they had two healthy babies.

He kissed her and said, "All I have to say is, I'm glad I brought this necklace with me."

"Where did you get that?"

"Brandon found it at Jarvis' house. I'd been meaning to ask you about it but I forgot."

Venice took the necklace from his hand and clutched it to her heart.

He asked, "Whose is it?"

"I gave it to Jarvis as a gift a year before he died."

Venice swallowed hard and said, "Craig, he was buried with it around his neck."

Silence engulfed them. For at that moment, Craig knew Jarvis had been their divine intervention who had saved their daughter. They never spoke about it again.

Six weeks later, on an October night, Craig was awakened by his hungry son. It seemed like only moments earlier that he had read Brandon a bedtime story and turned in for the night. Venice was exhausted from an earlier feeding with little Clarissa. Since deciding to breast-feed, there had been little time for sleep. He picked him up and stared into the tiny face, which looked like Venice. He was proud to say that Clarissa looked more like him. "fter staring each other down, he let out a loud squeal. Not wanting to wake up Venice and his daughter, they went downstairs to warm a bottle of recently-pumped breast milk.

The house was quiet and the moment was tender. Craig changed his son's diaper, then let him finish off the bottle. In little or no time, he was sound asleep. Reminiscing over the past year, Craig couldn't believe the wonderful things that had happened to him. He married his true love and she had an outstanding medical practice. They shared three beautiful children and he owned his own company. Needless to say, he couldn't forget the tragedy that brought them back together. Looking to the heavens, he closed his eyes and said, "God bless you, Jarvis."

After putting his sleeping son back into his crib, he climbed back into bed and held Venice securely in his arms.

ABOUT THE AUTHOR

Darrien Lee, a native of Columbia, Tennessee, resides in LaVergne, Tennessee with her husband of twelve years and two young daughters. She is excited about the release of her sequel, *Been There, Done That*. Darrien picked up her love for writing while attending college at Tennessee State University, and it was that experience which inspired her debut novel, *All That and A Bag of Chips*.

She is a member of A Place of Our Own Bookclub, Women of Color Bookclub and Authors Supporting Authors Positively. Darrien also writes for the hot e-zine, *The Nubian Chronicles*, an online magazine where she shares her opinion on controversial issues on her page titled, "From The Desk of Darrien Lee." You can view her work monthly at www.NubianChronicles.net

Please visit her website www.DarrienLee.com for upcoming appearances and events.

What Goes Around, Comes Around

BY DARRIEN LEE

Arnelle sat in her office, twirling an ink pen on her fingers. She was feeling homesick for the first time since coming to Philly. She missed the warm Texas evenings. Especially sitting out watching the sun set on her parents' porch. She also missed her daughter, MaLeah, the source of all her determination to succeed. She was two years old now and right in the middle of that terrible-two stage. Leaving her was difficult, but necessary. She was very reluctant about relocating, leaving her parents in Texas to watch over MaLeah. Especially since her father had announced his candidacy to run for Mayor. She had to remind herself to be strong because she had a long road ahead of her. At that time the telephone rang.

"Bennett Sports Clinic. How may I help you?"

A deep baritone voice from the past answered.

"Hello, Arnelle, remember me?"

Arnelle froze and asked, "What's up, Cyrus?"

He laughed.

"You know exactly what I want."

Arnelle held her ground, but was becoming agitated.

"Forget it, Cyrus!"

With firmness in his voice, he answered, "You owe me and you know it!"

She stood and yelled, "Why can't you just leave it alone and face it?"

"Come on, Arnelle. I'm sure your daddy wouldn't be too pleased with what I could tell him about you; especially since he's running for Mayor. The media would love to get a hold of this kind of information."

"Are you trying to blackmail me?"

"I'll do whatever it takes. You're supposed to be my friend. You owe me!"

"Go to hell, Cyrus!"

Arnelle slammed the phone down and practically ran from her office. When she turned the corner, she ran right into a tall, hard body. Strong, firm hands kept her from falling to the floor.

"Excuse me! I'm so sorry!"

Arnelle lowered her head and tried to hold in the tears but was unsuccessful. She looked up into Winston's eyes and broke down crying in his arms.

Startled by her response, he embraced her. "What's wrong, Arnelle? Did somebody hurt you?"

She shook her head as he led her back into her office and sat her on the sofa. He retrieved some bottled water from her small refrigerator and handed it to her.

He sat next to her and asked, "Arnelle, why are you crying? Where's Venice?"

She took a sip of water and wiped her tears away with her hand. "I'm fine, Winston."

"If you insist."

"Thanks for being here for me though."

"You're welcome," he said softly.

"Venice went out to lunch with Craig. They should be back shortly," she said as she wiped her nose with a tissue.

She still wouldn't make eye contact with him. She just stared at the bottle she held in her hands.

Winston was mesmerized because she was absolutely gorgeous. He was also angry that someone had caused her pain.

"Who upset you, Arnelle?"

She finally looked at him.

"You're getting a little personal, Winston. I'm allowed to cry sometimes."

Reaching over, he wiped a lone tear from her cheek. "I'm not trying to get in your business, Arnelle. I'm just concerned and wanted to make sure no one had hurt you. You're a friend of my best friend. I just wanted to make sure no one messed with you."

She stood and so did he. He was dressed in a dark, gray suit looking every bit the great attorney he was. His neatly-trimmed goatee outlined a pair of luscious lips and, for a moment, she couldn't take her eyes off them. The slight contact she was having with him caused chills to run over her body.

I can't believe he's still pretending he doesn't know me. Now here he sits trying to be compassionate and concerned. I'll play along, but not for long.

Clearing her throat, she asked, "Was Venice expecting you?"

"Not really. I just dropped by to see if I could take Brandon to the ball game Saturday."

"Brandon will love that."

"We've been before. It's really cool. We always have a good time."

She folded her arms. "I'm sure you do. Thanks again for being concerned. I'll be fine…really."

He shoved his hands in his pockets. "Well, I guess I'd better go. I'll just leave Venice a note on her desk."

His eyes were doing a number on her and she tried her best not to let it affect her.

"Why are you doing this, Winston? What's with the act?"

"What do you mean? I'm concerned about you and it bothers me to see you cry. Wait, what are you talking about, Arnelle?"

Something's wrong here. I'm not sure if this is an act anymore.

Waving him off nervously, she said, "Never mind. Forget I asked. I'm sure Venice will call you as soon as she gets back. I'll walk you out."

What is it about this woman? What did she mean by that statement?

Winston left Venice a note on her desk as Arnelle waited for him in the front lobby. When he walked toward her, she felt his awesome magnetism. He stood over her and without any warning he picked her up and hugged her. Arnelle hugged him back and tried to recover from his sudden action. He released her, reached into his jacket pocket, and pulled out a small card.

"Arnelle, if you ever need anything or you just want to talk, call me. This card has my home, cell and private office numbers on it. OK?"

Arnelle took the card from his hand and smiled. "Thank you, Winston. Goodbye."

She watched through the window as he walked in long strides out to his truck, climbed in, and drove away.

"Winston Carter III, I will find out why you're acting like you don't know me if it's the last thing I do. If Cyrus is involved, I'll never forgive him."